Taken from reviews

Mossy Creek Home

"Delightful." — *Marie Barnes, former First Lady of Georgia*

"Mitford meets Mayberry in the first book of this innovative and warmhearted new series from BelleBooks."
— Cleveland Daily Banner, *Cleveland, Tennessee*

"MOSSY CREEK is as much fun as a cousin reunion; like sipping ice cold lemonade on a hot summer's afternoon. Hire me a moving van, it's the kind of town where everyone wishes they could live."
— *Debbie Macomber,* NYT *bestselling author*

"A fast, funny, and folksy read. Enjoy!"
— *Lois Battle, acclaimed author of S*toryville, Bed & Breakfast, *and* The Florabama Ladies' Auxiliary & Sewing Circle

"SUMMER IN MOSSY CREEK takes you to a land that time has not forgotten, but has embraced."
— *Jackie K. Cooper, WMAC-AM, Macon, GA*

"Colorfully and cleverly portrayed. A wholesome story."
— *Harriet Klausner, Amazon.com's top reviewer*

"The characters and kinships of MOSSY CREEK are quirky, hilarious and all too human. This story reads like a delicious, meringue-covered slice of home. I couldn't get enough."
— *Pamela Morsi,* USA Today *bestselling author*

"[MOSSY CREEK] is a book you will not lend for fear you won't get it back."
— *Chloe LeMay,* The Herald, *Rock Hill, SC*

"These southern belle authors have done it again, even better this time."
— *Bob Spear, Heartland Reviews*

"In the best tradition of women's fiction, MOSSY CREEK points to a genuine spirit of love and community that is our best hope for the future."
— *Betina Krahn,* NYT *bestselling author of* The Last Bachelor

The Mossy Creek Hometown Series

Mossy Creek

Reunion at Mossy Creek

Summer in Mossy Creek

Blessings of Mossy Creek

A Day in Mossy Creek

At Home in Mossy Creek

At Home in Mossy Creek

At Home in Mossy Creek

A collective novel featuring the voices of

Debra Leigh Smith, Sandra Chastain
Debra Dixon and Martha Crockett

with

Susan Goggins, Maureen Hardegree,
Carolyn McSparren, Carmen Green,
Wayne Dixon and Sabrina Jeffries

Smyrna, Georgia

BelleBooks, Inc.

ISBN 978-0-9768760-8-3

At Home in Mossy Creek

Published by:
BelleBooks, Inc. · P.O. Box 67 · Smyrna, GA 30081
We at BelleBooks enjoy hearing from readers. You can contact us at the address above or at BelleBooks@BelleBooks.com

Visit our website— **www.BelleBooks.com**

First Edition July 2007

10 9 8 7 6 5 4 3 2 1

Front cover photo: Deborah Smith
                   with permission from Bill and Mary Scott
Back cover photo: Jeff Kinsey
Cover design: Martha Crockett
Mossy Creek map: Dino Fritz
Printed in Canada

Many thanks to all our friends, loved ones and wonderful readers. We couldn't do it without you.

Acknowledgements

Many thanks to Bill and Mary Scott of
Dahlonega, Georgia, for allowing us
to photograph their historic home for the cover.

You'll know when you reach the Mossy Creek town limits — just look for the charming, whitewashed grain silo by the road at Mayor Walker's farm. Painted with the town's pioneer motto — *Ain't goin' nowhere, and don't want to* — the silo makes a great photo opportunity. The motto perfectly sums up the stubborn (but not unfriendly) free spirits you'll find everywhere in what the chamber of commerce calls "Greater Mossy Creek," which includes the outlying mountain communities of Bailey Mill, Over, Yonder, and Chinaberry.

Lodging, Dining, and Attractions: Shop and eat to your heart's delight around the town's shady square. Don't miss *Mama's All You Can Eat Café*, *Beechum's Bakery* (be sure to say hello to Bob, the "flying" Chihuahua), *The Naked Bean* coffee shop, *O'Day's Pub*, the *Bubba Rice Diner*, *Hamilton's Department Store* (featuring the origami napkin work of local beauty queen Josie McClure), *Hamilton House Inn*, the *I Probably Got It* store, *Moonheart's Natural Living*, and *Mossy Creek Books and What-Nots*. Drop by town hall for a look at the notorious Ten-Cent Gypsy (a carnival booth at the heart of a dramatic Creekite mystery). Stop by the town jail for an update on local shenanigans courtesy of Officer Sandy Crane, who calls herself "the gal in front of the man behind the badge," Mossy Creek Police Chief Amos Royden (recently featured in *Georgia Today Magazine* as the sexiest bachelor police chief in the state). And don't forget to pop into the newspaper offices of the *Mossy Creek Gazette*, where you can get the latest event news from Katie Bell, local gossip columnist *extraordinaire*.

As Katie Bell likes to say, "In Mossy Creek, I can't make up better stories than the truth."

At Home in Mossy Creek

Odd Places & Beautiful Spaces
*A Guide to the Towns & Attractions
of the South*

Mossy Creek, Georgia

Don't miss this quirky, historic Southern village on your drive through the Appalachian mountains! Located in a breathtaking valley two hours north of Atlanta, the town (1,700 residents, established 1839) is completely encircled by its lovely namesake creek. Picturesque bridges span the creek around the turn-of-the-century town square like charms on a bracelet. Be sure to arrive via the scenic route along South Bigelow Road, the main two-lane from Bigelow, Mossy Creek's big-sister city, hometown of Georgia governor Ham Bigelow. (Don't be surprised if you overhear "Creekites" in heated debate about Ham, who's the nephew of longtime Mossy Creek mayor, Ida Walker.)

A Who's Who of Mossy Creek

Ida Hamilton Walker — Mayor. Devoted to her town. Menopausal. Gorgeous. Trouble.

Amos Royden — Ida's much-younger police chief. Trying hard not to be irresistible.

Katie Bell — Gossip columnist and town sleuth. Watch out!

Sue Ora Salter Bigelow — Newspaper publisher. Fighting the Salter romance curse.

Jasmine Beleau — Fashion consultant. Her secret past is a shocker.

Josie McClure — Failed beauty queen. Budding interior designer. Talent: origami napkin folding.

Harry Rutherford — Josie's mountain man and fiance. PhD and local version of Bigfoot.

Hamilton Bigelow — Governor of Georgia. Ida's nephew. A typical politician. 'Nuff said?

Win Allen — *aka* Chef Bubba Rice — the *Emeril* of Mossy Creek.

Ingrid Beechum — Baker. Doting surrogate grandma. Owns Bob, the famous "flying" Chihuahua.

Hank and Casey Blackshear — Run the veterinary clinic. Most inspirational local love story.

Sandy Crane — Amos's scrappy dispatcher. If Dolly Parton and Barney Fife had a daughter. . .

Ed Brady — Farmer. Santa. The toughest, sweetest old man in town.

Rainey Cecil — Owns Goldilocks Hair, Nail and Tanning Salon. Bringing big hair to a whole new generation.

Michael Conners — Sexy Chicago Yankee whose Irish pub lures dart-tourney sharks.

Tag Garner — Ex pro-footballer turned sculptor. Good natured when bitten by old ladies.

Maggie Hart — Herbalist. Tag's main squeeze. Daughter of old lady who bit him.

Millicent Hart — See above. Town kleptomaniac. Sorry she bit Tag. Sort of.

Del Jackson — Hunky retired lieutenant colonel. Owns Ida's heart. For now. See Amos.

Bert Lyman — The voice of Mossy Creek. Owner, manager, DJ of WMOS Radio.

Opal Suggs — Retired teacher who adopts needy kids. Talks to her sisters' ghosts who foretell NASCAR winners.

Dwight Truman — Chamber president. Insurance tycoon. Ida's nemesis, along with Ham Bigelow. Weasel.

Swee Purla — Evil interior design maven. Makes even Martha Stewart look wimpy.

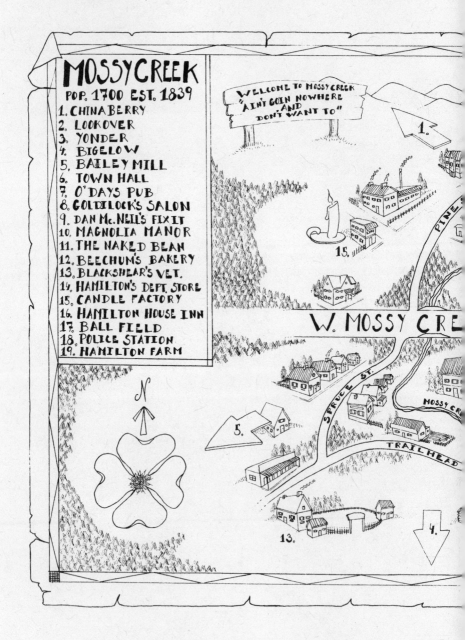

MOSSY CREEK

POP. 1700 EST. 1839

1. CHINABERRY
2. LOOKOVER
3. YONDER
4. BIGELOW
5. BAILEY MILL
6. TOWN HALL
7. O'DAYS PUB
8. GOLDILOCK'S SALON
9. DAN Mc.NEIL'S FIXIT
10. MAGNOLIA MANOR
11. THE NAKED BEAN
12. BEECHUM'S BAKERY
13. BLACKSHEAR'S VET.
14. HAMILTON'S DEPT. STORE
15. CANDLE FACTORY
16. HAMILTON HOUSE INN
17. BALL FIELD
18. POLICE STATION
19. HAMILTON FARM

WELCOME TO MOSSY CREEK
"AIN'T GOIN NOWHERE
AND
DON'T WANT TO"

1.

15.

PINE

W. MOSSY CRE

SPRUCE ST.

MOSSY CR

TRAILHEAD

N

5.

13.

4.

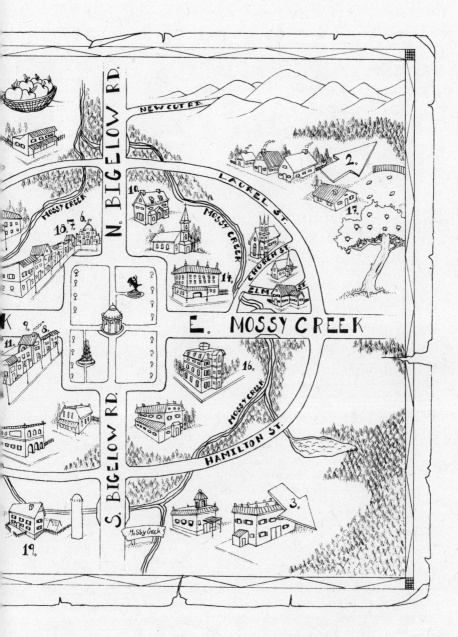

Mossy Creek Gazette
106 Main Street • Mossy Creek, GA 30000

From the desk of Katie Bell

Lady Victoria Salter Stanhope
The Cliffs
Seaward Road
St. Ives, Cornwall, TR3 7PJ
United Kingdom

Dear Vick:

Remember how I told you I sensed
trouble in the air last month,
on that whacky winter Saturday
when common sense left town on
a cold January breeze and all
heck broke loose? Miss Irene
led the elderly Creekites in a
handicapped scooter protest, and
Honey and Bert Lymon escaped from
their gas-filled house thanks to a
miracle, and Amos hauled Ida home
from another of her escapades
only to have Ida's boyfriend,
Del Jackson, catch the two of
them kissing in Ida's yard at
Hamilton Farm like a pair of
lovestruck teenagers? Ida backed
away from the romance faster than
a cat in a room full of rocking
chairs, and she hoped no one

in town would find out. But you and
I both know how gossip travels in
Mossy Creek, so now everyone knows
our police chief and our mayor are an
item. Only they aren't. Or are they?

Well, my dear English girl, you ain't
heard nothing yet.

We have just survived the weirdest
Valentine's Day weekend in the
history of Mossy Creek. Let me just
tell you this much up front: People
aren't kidding when they say romance
is like a circus.

Your clown-faced gossip columnist,

Katie

FRIDAY AFTERNOON

The Circus Arrives in Mossy Creek

Chapter 1

Ida

All right, here's the short and sweet of it: Last month, Amos Royden and I had a Las Vegas moment. That's all. End of gossip. Nothing to see here, folks. Move along. What happened in January *stays* in January.

Why? Because I won't risk having Amos look at me one day as I'm scrubbing my dentures or adjusting my support hose and wish he'd fallen in love with someone closer to his own age. I have my pride. Even when I no longer have teeth or vivacious leg veins, I'll *still* have my pride.

He won't be honest with me about the brutal facts of life. Maybe he wants children. Maybe he doesn't. He refuses to say. Men have the luxury of postponing fatherhood until they're old enough to shop for their own diapers as well as their baby's. Women don't have that choice. Oh, sure, aging celebrities and the occasional Romanian grandmother make headlines with miracle births, but not without medical assistance. Besides, any woman over forty-five who tries to get pregnant needs to have her menopausal head examined. Just my opinion. I'm not sending a team of doctors on an Easter egg hunt through my ovaries.

I don't deserve this romantic dilemma. My life is just fine the way it is, thank you very much. I'm fifty years old, have been respectably widowed for twenty of those years, and have served five sterling terms as mayor of Mossy Creek; I have a wonderful son, daughter-in-law, and grand-daughter. I'm wealthy, an accomplished businesswoman, and last but not least, I'm a good-looking redhead who can still wear skinny jeans and pass for thirty-five in the right indoor light.

Listen, I have my choice of lusty, fine-looking men my *own* age, and no one accuses me of being prim about enjoy-ing their, ahem, *attention*. I'm a passionate woman. I wear heirloom pearls with my Lynard Skynnard t-shirts, I listen to Fleetwood Mac, drink bourbon, drive my late husband's red Corvette well over the speed limit, and recently sang a fabulous, jazzy rendition of *The Lighthouse* at a gospel music competition up in Nashville, Tennessee. I lost in the finals to a young Aretha Franklin clone who said I was the loudest white woman she'd ever heard.

I took it as a compliment. I'm proud of who and what I am. I like being unpredictable. People know that about me. "That Ida Hamilton Walker, you can't pin the same notion on her twice," Eula Mae Whit likes to say. At 101 Miz Eula Mae is the oldest and wisest person in town, and I like how she puts things.

So, given all of the above credentials, I should have been able to kiss Amos, our police chief, last month without everyone in Mossy Creek rushing down to Bigelow Mall to buy us "His and Her" monogrammed towels at Bed, Bath & Beyond. My fellow Creekites ought to *know* I have no intention of making an honest man out of Amos. For one thing, there was nothing dishonest about *his* part in the dastardly kiss. I'm the one with a significant other to consider. I'm the one who betrayed retired Lt. Colonel Del Jackson, a man I adore.

Okay, I admit it. I've dreamed of kissing Amos at times. A lot of times. Twenty years of times. Again. The first time I kissed my future police chief he was a tall, awkward, consoling teenager struggling to elude the shadow of his legendary lawman father, Battle Royden. I was a grieving young widow whose beloved husband had died up on Colchik Mountain while trying to rescue two stranded deputy sheriffs.

It was one of those cinematic, *Summer of '42* incidents, completely spontaneous and unplanned and relatively innocent. In my misery I wanted to slash my breasts, saw off my hair, wail to the moon. I had my son, Rob, to raise and an important Hamilton family legacy to manage, but during those dark weeks after Jeb was killed I could barely *think* of moving forward. I couldn't even breathe. The slightest brush of a butterfly's wings would have stopped the air in my lungs for good.

With that one kiss, Amos saved my life. He forced me to gasp in shock, to inhale the sweet, startling sensation of need, of want, of life. Amos will never know how close I came to pulling him down on the soft mountain grass that day at The Sitting Tree. Only an immediate tidal wave of shame—*How can I betray Jeb's memory this way? How can I take advantage of Amos, he's only sixteen!*—made me push myself away. And has made me keep my distance ever since.

The kiss has remained our secret. We never mention it, even to each other. But neither of us has ever forgotten it, either, and now, yes, twenty years later, we've gone and done it again. Maybe just to see if it was as good as the first time.

It was.

This time the kiss happened in my own wintry front yard at Hamilton Farm. Right in front of the naked branches of the butterfly bushes and the pink Rose of Sharon. Absurdly, I kept thinking of a Lewis Grizzard book title: *Don't Bend Over In The Garden, Granny, 'Cause Them Taters Got Eyes.*

Del never expected to see Amos drive up the farm lane with me locked in the back of a Mossy Creek patrol car. And he certainly never expected to watch us argue outside the patrol car then throw ourselves at each other in a kiss hot enough to make my red nandina hedges blush scarlet. Actually, it wasn't just one kiss. It was a *series* of them, delivered with swaying, back-bending, on-our-tiptoes urgency.

I turned and there was Del, on my veranda. I'll never forget the pain in his eyes, the disappointment, the anger. My heart hurt for him. He's gorgeous, funny, sexy, smart, and a decorated hero of the first Gulf War. He's become my best friend, not just my bed partner.

Del took the betrayal as well as he could. He pretended to blame Amos for provoking me and he said he forgave me. He can't deny our relationship has been under some strain lately, since his adorably needy ex-wife arrived in Bigelow to buy a condo near their grown son and grandson.

By "adorably needy" I mean a cute blonde with Botox, implants and an eyelift, who's three years younger than me and looks thirty-five even in strong *sunlight*. Every time

I'm forced into her presence I try not to stand beside her near a window.

People think I'm a bastion of middle-aged confidence. Yes, I am an upbeat person at heart. But anyone who's honest at mid-life will tell you that they now see a horizon in the distance. Like a haunting panorama of our farthest Appalachians, misty and lavender-blue, that border between earth and Heaven is faint but discernible now, something I take a step closer to everyday. You have to be a lot younger than fifty to believe you'll live forever. I won't call the distant horizon *Death* because I believe it's a crossing point, not a final destination. But it's there.

Some day that smoky-blue mountain horizon will loom up before me, and I'll smile and climb the rounded, ancient peaks as easily as a child, and when I get to the top Jeb will be waiting with open arms, along with my parents and Big Ida, my favorite grandmother, and every other person and every pet animal I've loved, and maybe even my favorite camellia shrubs and rose bushes. And in the background, Stevie Nicks will be singing *Crystal*.

How the faces of love have changed turning the pages, and I have changed oh, but you … you remain ageless …

I don't know if Heaven's a golden kingdom or an astral plane, a stopover between reincarnated lives or, as my cousin Ingrid Beechum envisions, a celestial bakery where no one gets fat eating cheesecake. All I know for certain is that anywhere Jeb is will be Heaven to me.

That's my dream. I'm not anxious to reach its horizon for a long, long time—Big Ida lived to over ninety, and I think I have a good chance of pulling off the same feat—but I know my life's at least half over.

And I know that Amos's life, at the tender young age of thirty-six, is not.

There will be no more kisses between us. No more

swaying, hugging, deep, soulful kisses. No dating. No engagement. No marriage. No dentures. No support hose. No regrets. No more of the town twittering over us.

Enough said.

Amos

Bubba Rice's place had earned a spot on my restaurant rotation. Good food served with a minimum of fanfare. Until today. Bubba was certainly serving it up with gusto today, piling it on thick. Everyone in town had taken a whack at me since the infamous kiss.

"Listen, you're gonna love this meatloaf." He sat down one of those oval platters. Bubba's didn't serve skimpy portions. "I've added cayenne pepper for an extra kick. You know, just to shake things up. Some people—not everyone—experience *hot lips*. So I brought you some iced tea to cool you down."

I did my best not to snatch the napkin off the table but I did snap it to shake it out. "Thank you."

"Ah, think nothing of it. We'll just . . . pretend it didn't happen." And there it was. A little side dish of subtext to go along with the meatloaf. Half of Mossy Creek, the male half, were incredulous that I hadn't sealed the deal. The other half giggled and sighed and expected an engagement ring to be produced any moment.

"Win, I don't forget a friend who's looking out for me." I tried for a reassuring smile as I attempted to calculate how many line drives I could send right at Win Allen's head during spring ball practice. I was willing to bet that if I put in some hours at the batting cages over in Chinaberry that I'd hit my target as often as not. For now I raised an eyebrow and tried to look pleasant. "Anything else?"

"No. That about wraps it up."

I tapped the platter with my folk. "Good. This is about all I can stomach right now."

"I wasn't certain. You seem to be able to stomach a lot before pushing back from the table and saying, 'Enough.'"

Someone two tables away made one of those honking *ha's* that you make when you nervously cut off a laugh.

My silverware clattered a little louder than I actually intended. "What is it with you people? I have my love life under control, thankyouverymuch for the concern." I scanned the restaurant. Most had the decency to pretend they hadn't noticed anything. Katie Bell was scribbling furiously, one hand held up as a stop sign so we wouldn't continue until she was ready. Unbelievable.

"Excuse me." I reached over to the bread basket on Dan McNeil's table and helped myself to two slices of some thick, whole-grain bread. I slapped a wedge of meatloaf between them and told Bubba to bill me.

"Right, then!" he shouted after me. "I'll put you down for a table for two Saturday night."

❦ ❦ ❦

Patrolling is good for the soul. And the temper. I eased off the gas pedal before I had to give myself a ticket for speeding. *Shake it off,* I told myself. I'd asked for this the moment I decided to cross that line with Ida. I knew this wasn't the easy road.

Every angler in America will tell you that the best fish don't jump into the boat. Nope. You have to wait it out, use every trick in your book of tricks and hope to God that when you get them close to the boat—close enough to accepting they can't break free—that they don't freak out, find superhuman strength (more ridiculous objections) and slip away again.

If you weren't committed to your plan, then you'd spend the next who-knows-how-many years talking about the one that got away. I had no intention of letting Ida get away, but some of the guys in town were beginning to make me second-guess myself, my plan. I thought I had her hooked. Maybe running out the line for all she was worth, but hooked all the same. Not that she'd appreciate the fishing analogy. And I sure didn't appreciate the speculation and ribbing coming my way. I didn't like seeing her on Del's arm.

Maybe Win had a point. Maybe it was time to change strategy.

And lanes!

On the northbound lane of Bigelow a long tour bus that looked as if Walt Disney World's magic had exploded all over it was pouring smoke and slowing down. I slowed and hit the light to warn any traffic behind me. The bus lurched to the side of the road and settled with a nasty clanking sound punctuated with a backfire. They weren't quite on the shoulder so I angled the Jeep and left the light going.

As I got out I had to wonder. If you could get seven clowns in a tiny circus car, how many could you get in this monster of a bus? *Cirque d'Europa.* Oh, boy, this was gonna be good. Or really, really bad.

The door whooshed open but I waved them back in and followed. "We'll get this sorted out but stay in here where it's warm as long as you can. Who's in charge?"

I lost count of the languages as people on both sides translated for their neighbors. One woman had a white knuckled grip on the panel separating the driver from the rest of the bus. "Me. Quinn James. I think we've broken down. The bus has been making noises for miles." She cut her eyes toward where her hands were clenched. "Sorry. I have a touch of vertigo."

Several questions and several grinding attempts to restart the engine later, it was clear that this bus wasn't going anywhere without the help of a very large tow truck.

"Don't worry about a thing. Let me get some help. You just stay where you are." I radioed Mutt and told him to rally the troops. By the time he arrived, I was all but certain Mossy Creek would have to pull together. The performers were getting restless and beginning to leave the bus as Mutt arrived. There were a lot of them.

"Listen, Ms. Quinn. Our mayor will be here soon to help you with the logistics of your people, and I know we're going to need to put some of your folks up in town. See, I have a friend and it would just thrill him to host one of your clowns."

"We don't have clowns, not like American circus clowns. We've got a couple of mimes."

"Perfect. If he could host one of the mimes, it'd just make his year. Win Allen—you might want to write that down—Win used to work with a clown down at the radio station. There was a fire and well, the clown had to move on. Win was really sad about that." I glanced up, checking for lightning, ready to push Ms. Quinn out of harm's way. Apparently the Powers-That-Be thought Win deserved a little mime punishment as well.

"Of course, Chief. I'll make a note about Mr. Allen liking mimes. But call me Quinn."

I'd been watching what appeared to be a family of jugglers. The patriarch looked like the kind of worldly charming guy that could give Del a run for his money. If I were Del, I certainly wouldn't want this guy hanging around screwing up my Valentine's plan with Ida. "One more thing, Quinn. Our mayor would be the perfect home for them."

I pointed. "If anybody knows how to juggle life, it's our mayor. She's got a nice-sized home place and could host a family easily. You wouldn't have to split them up."

"Thank you."

Suddenly a teenage girl in the patriarch's clan turned and saw me. She was jail bait, and I wasn't interested. But she was. And not shy, either. "Rhett Butler!" she squealed in a French accent. "Monsieur Butler! Be still my heart!"

The patriarch glanced my way with a dismissive smile, then said something quiet to the teenager. She scowled and turned away after batting her eyes at me one more time.

I wasn't having a good time, here. "Mutt!" I yelled. I turned to see if he'd heard.

"Yeah, Chief?"

"Tell Peavey's to haul the bus to Mount Gilead Methodist first. They have the biggest parking lot and it's on the way to their garage. It's too dangerous to unload luggage here. And it's time to call the mayor."

Ida

"There's a *what* broken down on the side of Bigelow Road?" I said into the portable headpiece of my phone. Bigelow Road is a fast two-lane—a beautiful but isolated mountain route framed by vistas, fields and deep woods—and it serves as our main artery south to the county seat, Bigelow. In Mossy Creek we tend to name roads according to where they go. Which is why we have several obscure little lanes named Ruin, The Dogs, and No Good.

"Bus fulla circ . . ." Mutt's voice disappeared. Cell phone reception in the mountains can be iffy.

"Bus full of what?" I asked loudly as I paced my office

at town hall. I glanced at a clock that said most of Friday afternoon was gone and I still had a dozen phone calls to make. Sheaves of computer print-outs from the water department filled my mud-crusted left hand and a pad of mud-stained notes for the next council meeting filled the other. Being mayor of a small town isn't glamorous. I'd just spent the cold February afternoon with a crew crawling around a giant, leaky pipe at the town water plant, aka the *Upper Mossy Creek Reservoir, Water Treatment Facility, and Bass Pond.*

That last part is unofficial.

My jeans and sweatshirt were splattered with mud, my feet were freezing inside wet socks and hiking boots, and I smelled like fish. Cats and sushi chefs would have craned their heads when I walked by.

"A bus of circus people, Mayor," officer Mutt Bottoms yelled clearly, this time. I heard the strangled rumble of a large diesel engine in the background. Then an ominous clanking sound. Then silence. Mutt sighed loudly. "Well, that settles that. Broke down for good. Yes, ma'am. The Chief's here but he said you'd want to be involved. Peavey's Garage is already here peering under the hood, but in the meantime, we got us a busload of . . . of, well, people with funny accents who can hook their legs behind their heads. They're all out here on the side of the road, stretchin' and shivering and . . .oh, man. There goes another one. That looks painful, y'all. Y'all are all gonna need new hips one day."

"What kind of circus people?"

"I'm readin' the name painted on the bus. 'Circ-Q D Europe A.'"

"Spell it."

He did. I bit back a smile. *"Cirque d'Europa."* I'd heard of it. One of the small, elegantly surreal European troops, a baby cousin to the famous *Cirque du Soleil*.

Mutt slowly repeated the name. "Mayor, I just sprang a muscle in my tongue."

"Peavey's thinks their bus is a lost cause?"

"Yep. Figures it'll take 'til Sunday to get it running. They got no other bus. Just a tractor-trailer hauling their tents and some equipment trucks. No elephants or nothing. Not even a trained monkey or two. As far as I can tell."

"They don't use animal acts. It's not like American circuses. More theatrical."

"Oh, I can sure see *that*." Mutt's voice dropped to a stunned whisper. "Mayor, there are foreigners out here doing handsprings. In the road. I don't know what languages they speak, so I can't even yell at 'em to get off the pavement."

"Try this. *Arrete*! That's French for 'Stop!' I expect most of them will understand."

Mutt bellowed, "*Air rat tay! Air rat tay, y'all*!" Long pause. Then, "Okay, Mayor, they're kinda snickerin' at me, but they're off the road. Thanks."

"How many people are we talking about? Total."

"About three dozen."

I groaned. It was the start of Valentine's Day weekend, with Sunday being the holiday. Hamilton Inn, our only hotel, was booked solid. So were all the romantic rental cabins in the mountains around Mossy Creek, including the cabins at my late husband's namesake, Jeb Walker State Park, up on Colchik Mountain.

"Mutt, I'll put my staff on phone duty, and we'll rustle up some rooms at local homes. Just tell the circus people to hang in there."

"Yeah, the Chief's already pickin' out homes for some of 'em. He's got you set up for a bunch of jugglers."

I arched a brow. "Oh, is that right?"

"Yeah, he told 'em you'd be perfect 'cause you like to keep a lot of stuff hangin' in mid-air."

"I'll have to thank him for that . . . compliment." I sighed. "Just tell the visitors that here in Mossy Creek we never let strangers go cold and hungry."

"How do I say all that in French?" Mutt moaned.

"*L'aide vient.* 'Help is coming.' *L'aide vient.*"

"Got it, Mayor. LAID VENT!" he yelled. "LAID VENT!"

It was going to be a long and decidedly *unromantic* Valentine's Day weekend.

Sandy

My baby brother Mutt's voice crackled over the radio of my brand-spanking new blue-and-white cruiser. I slapped the dashboard of the 1998 Crown Vic Mayor Ida Hamilton Walker had just donated to the Mossy Creek PD—the paint job was brand-spanking new, anyway—and Mutt's voice cleared up a little.

"Say again, Dogface," I instructed. I assure you, people don't call him "Mutt" for nothing.

"I need you to come to where a circus bus has broke down right outside of town on the road to Bigelow."

"A circus bus? You mean with clowns and trapeze artists and lion tamers and such?"

"Yeah. Only there's no animals here. Well, only Bob. He's running around sniffing people's pants legs and peeing on everything. There's a tattooed trapeze woman with a big eagle on her back, and when Bob saw it he started howling like a banshee with a toothache, not to mention peeing like a racehorse. I reckon it reminded him of the hawk."

Bob the Chihuahua had famously survived being

kidnapped by a hungry hawk which flew Bob around the town square before being coaxed to let go. I take credit for shooting at the hawk and making it put Bob down. Don't worry, the hawk escaped without even losing a feather. But Bob has never been quite the same since. I had to ask my brother what in the world Bob the incontinent flying Chihuahua was doing on the scene. "Ingrid heard about the breakdown and came to see the spectacle," Mutt said. "Along with about half of Mossy Creek."

I grimaced. Ingrid Beechum, Bob's over-protective owner and a first cousin of Mayor Ida's, was on my "list." And you know what list I mean. The catty heifer had told me just that morning that she'd seen my husband, Jess, sitting with that cute Julie Honeycutt at The Naked Bean coffee shop not once but twice in the last week. "Yes indeed, they had their heads together, talking about something very serious," she said.

Everybody knows Julie is sweethearts with that nice sheep farmer, Russ Green, which I pointed out to Ingrid. She hooted and said the last time Julie was in her bakery she asked her when Russ was going to make an honest woman of her after all these years. She said Julie squinched up her face like she was fixing to cry and ran out of the shop like the devil was after her. "There's something wrong with that relationship," Ingrid said and clucked her tongue, nodding to me and shop owner Jayne Reynolds. "You mark my words."

Jayne, whose little boy, Matthew, is Ingrid's godchild, just nodded back respectful-like. But I informed Ingrid that there is nothing wrong in *my* marriage. *Nothing that she needs to worry about, anyway*, I thought to myself. "I'm sure that's true," Ingrid said, but not in a convinced way. Her son had been ruined by a wild wife. Ingrid had a short fuse for philanderers. "I expect Jess was just giving Julie that broad shoulder of his to cry on," Ingrid went on. "I just never knew that Jess and Julie were friends."

The truth of the matter is, neither did I. But I am not worried about my husband's friendship with another woman. He's not the cheating kind. But then, what woman thinks her husband *is* the cheating kind?

My brother's words snapped me back to reality. "Everybody's running around here like a bunch of chickens with their heads cut off," Mutt said. "The people from the bus are squawking in a dozen different languages."

"That's not illegal, bro." I swear, sometimes that boy doesn't have the judgment God gave a Billy goat. "Why do you need me?"

"Tempers are running short," he said. "I need you to help me calm everybody down. It's Valentine's Day weekend. These circus people don't look too happy to be stuck in Mossy Creek on a romantic holiday, and our folks don't look to happy to be stuck in charge of 'em. I've got a bad feeling."

Calming people down, eh? Now he was talking. That sounded to me like a job for Officer Sandy Bottoms Crane. "Looks like you could use my conflict resolution skills," I said.

"Uh, yeah," Mutt said. "Whatever. Just get here as soon as you can. Over and out."

I turned on the siren with the flick of a switch. If I do say so myself, conflict resolution is my specialty. Why, only a month ago, in January, I defused a delicate domestic situation between Miss Ada Lou Womack and her big sister Inez over an heirloom quilt.

If anybody is ever kidnapped and held for ransom in Mossy Creek, I feel sure that my skills will qualify me as the chief hostage negotiator. Not that anybody has ever been kidnapped and held for ransom in Mossy Creek, you understand, but there's a first time for everything. And besides, it's better to be safe than sorry.

Like I said, a domestic conflict situation can be tricky and dangerous. I've even started reading books about relationships to help me figure people out. For research, you might say. The most interesting one is called, *Men Are from Mars, Women Are from Venus*, and boy howdy, did it ever open my eyes.

I spent all last weekend reading it. And eating Bubba Rice's newest creation at his restaurant here in town—"Bubba's Bodacious Burrito." Bubba cooks a lot of fancy dishes—his restaurant uses tablecloths and real silverware and he lights candles on the tables at night—but he does regular food, too.

Anyhow, it all started last weekend. I was planning a romantic pre-Valentine's weekend dinner with Jess, to get him primed for Valentine's Day this weekend, so I got a double takeout order. Then, just after I'd finished setting the table with my best wedding china, Jess called to say he was spending the weekend in the woods. Can you imagine? And he didn't even ask me to go camping with him. He said he had to get off by himself.

I found myself wondering if Julie Honeycutt was the outdoorsy type, but I slammed the door of my mind shut on that thought. I was not going to go there.

So I ate those burritos all by my lonesome and read that *Mars and Venus* book. The most interesting thing I learned is that men, bless their sports-obsessed little hearts, are all about keeping score. That means that if they take out the garbage without being asked, they feel like they have scored a point, and you owe them. And if you fix their favorite meal, it means you just evened the score. In their warped minds, if they run up the score on you, they feel like they have a right to get all mopey and resentful.

Now, my Jess is just a big sweet teddy bear. Thirty-something years old and dependable as grits. He's never had a mopey and resentful day in his life. *Me*, on the other hand, now that's another story. I've been out of sorts for a while now, not to mention hungry. I've been craving those new burritos like nobody's business, and I don't have the frame to carry around the extra pounds. I'm no bigger than a washing of soap, as my granny used to say. My khaki uniform pants are getting tight. I figure by giving my husband all the space he needs, I'm running up the score on him, at least. And he owes me, big time.

My cell phone rang and I flipped it open. "Babe," Jess began. I must say his voice still put a little thrill through me even though I had been peeved with him lately. "I got tomorrow off, so I'm going to go camping again tonight and tomorrow night, but I'll be back for Valentine's Day on Sunday. I haven't forgotten our special date." I took a deep breath. "Sandy, are you there?" he asked.

"Yeah," I said. "Look, I gotta go."

"Duty calls, eh? I hope you're not having to respond to a dangerous situation."

I thought about the volatile mixture of a bus breakdown in the middle of rush hour on a cold mountain night—not that we had much of a rush hour in Mossy Creek, where we can paint a clean white stripe down the center of a busy road and it'll dry before the next car comes along—though this breakdown included not just circus people but *foreign* circus people, and a neurotic, peeing Chihuahua. Okay, no, it was not exactly big city crime fare. Amos, who had worked the mean streets of Atlanta as a detective before moving back home to be Mossy Creek's police chief, was probably bored by the whole thing. "Not really dangerous, no," I said shortly.

"Okay then, you go get 'em, girl," Jess said, ignoring my peevish tone. I flipped the phone closed. My Jess is a reporter at the *Mossy Creek Gazette* and writes scary novels on the side. He hasn't sold one yet, but he's got loads of talent, and he works hard. As soon as he gets home from work he sits down at the computer in the living room and writes until midnight. Lately I've started to get lonesome even though he's sitting right there.

It's not like me to be needy, honest. I just don't know what's gotten into me lately. Besides five pounds of Bubba Rice burritos, that is.

❧ ❧ ❧

I was on the scene of the bus breakdown within minutes. Mutt had summed up the situation right well. Chaos. Various Creekites had parked their cars and pick-ups along the road and stood gawking. A big tractor-trailer was parked forlornly behind the busted bus. *CIRQUE D'EUROPA* was scrolled in large, florid lettering across the side of the trailer and the bus, too. There were more circus performers wandering around the wintry brown roadside than Carter had liver pills. A few of the acrobats were practicing their back flips to stay warm against the afternoon chill, I guess, and I'll be a suck-egg mule if they weren't locomoting *exactly* like chickens with their heads cut off.

I should know, since the earliest chore of my recollection involved helping my grandma with the chicken dinner. She would wring the chicken's neck, chop off its head and go back in the kitchen to get on with the rest of the cooking. My job was to stand by the chopping block to keep the barn cats off the chickens until the carcasses stopped flopping. A grisly chore for a five-year-old, I know, but you have to start earning your dumplings sooner or later. When you are raised up in the countryside around Mossy Creek, you are not coddled for long.

I approached the circus bus from the back end of the broad side, and I saw a swarthy man draw back with a knife big enough to skin a mule. A woman screamed to my left and when I turned I saw a petite but buxom brunette standing in front of a six-foot-tall board with a huge bull's-eye. Several knives protruded from the board in the vicinity of her head.

Boy, Mutt wasn't kidding; tempers *were* getting short. In an instant I drew my service revolver drawn and pointed at his head. "Put down the knife, sir. *Now*," I hissed. He dropped the knife out to his side and raised his hands in the air.

"Do not make shooting of my husband!" squealed the target in an accent that reminded me of *Natasha Fatale* on the *Bullwinkle* cartoons. "He ees but practicing throwing of knives!"

"*Oui, oui*," said another woman, clutching her heart. Her sweatshirt was embroidered with her name with a dagger through it. *Monique*. She must be a knife thrower, too. *Oui?* Even I know what *that* means in French. But it was also what Bob the Chihuahua did as I glanced over at the acrobats. Bob went *oui-oui* on an acrobat's foot.

"Sorry," I said, lowering my weapon. "I didn't see the target for the bus." A little embarrassed, I pointed to the direction from where I had come. "But that's kinda worrisome." Laying on the frostbitten winter grass was a flat, open case jam-packed with wicked-sharp blades.

The man put his hands down but didn't seem much relieved. "Mariska, are you goink to stand in front of board or are you not?"

"And wind up a kebab?" She gestured at the pattern of

knives where her head had been. "No, tank you!"

"You coward!"

"You amateur!"

"Whoa, whoa," I yelled, waving my gun. "No name callin'!"

Mutt appeared by my side. "I called you here to calm 'em down, not shoot 'em."

I ignored him and holstered my weapon. "What's with these two?"

"As near as I can figure, these here have a knife throwing act. He's the throw-*er* and she's the throw-*ee*." He pointed at the other woman. "And she's an assistant."

"I picked up on that much." I muttered.

"Only the main throw-ee don't want to stand in front of the knives no more. I don't know what the problem is, but the woman, Quinn James, who runs the circus said if they don't straighten out their act by the time the bus gets fixed, he's going to leave them on the side of the road."

I tried to imagine the two knife-wielding foreigners trying to hitch-hike out of town. My other brother Boo, who's a paramedic, would have to save some poor old farmer from cardiac arrest. "We can't have that," I said.

"Dang tootin'. Why don't you see what you can do? And while you're at it, find them a place to spend the night. The Hamilton Inn is full up 'cause of a Valentine weekend promotion. So me and the chief are lining up volunteers with spare bedrooms."

Mutt walked away and Bob the Chihuahua skittered up to sniff at the swarthy knife-thrower's feet.

"Giant, urinating rat has returned!" the woman yelled. "Keel eet!"

Her husband obediently went for his knife again, so I scooped up the trembling rat—I mean, uh, Bob—and scratched him between the ears. The look of revulsion on the faces of the two Europeans nearly made me laugh. "This is not a rat. This is an expensive Mexican house dog."

"You are keeding me," the man said.

"Nope," I said.

"Thees rat-dog is most unpleasant," the woman said.

"Oui," Monique added.

"You're telling that right," I agreed. Bob wouldn't be so bad if it wasn't for his nerves, but as it was, he could be the poster dog for doggie Prozac.

"In my country, dogs are large and powerful beasts good for tracking and hunting."

"Well, this one here is good for nothing except yipping and peeing."

"Bob, there you are!" Mayor Ida's Scottish housekeeper, June, ran up and grabbed the dog from me. "The mayor is babysitting him for Ingrid. I turned my back and he was out the veranda door. I don't know how he got this far. *Ock*."

Me neither. Hamilton Farm, Mayor Ida's place, was a good mile off the main road. I eyed the knife throwers darkly. "Bob must've smelled blood."

June cuddled Bob to her thick winter coat and scurried away.

I turned back to the knife act. "I'm Officer Sandy Crane of the Mossy Creek Police Department. What's the trouble here? Anything I can help with?"

"My name is Sergei and this ees my wife, Mariska," the man said. He handed me a business card with a picture of the two of them standing in front of the bull's eye. Their last name was totally unpronounceable, made up as it was of all consonants. *Vanna, buy me a vowel.*

"Our problems are not a matter for the constabulary," he said.

Mariska glared at him as she crossed her arms over her ample chest. "At least not unteel you pierce my flesh with one of those blades," she said, inclining her head toward the knife collection. "When I am dead, you vill have no shortage of weemen lined up to take my place."

"Mais non," Monique said urgently, pointing at herself and shaking her head. "Non!"

French for, *Not me, not in this lifetime, buddy*.

Sergei turned to me, looking pained. "I gave up career as lion tamer, just so we could start act together," he said. He was a tall man, handsome in the way of old-time movie stars. His hair and mustache were inky black, his eyes dark and deep with emotion. Somebody needed to tell him to go easy on the hair product, though.

"He got shut down by animal rights activeests," Mariska said. "I was hees assistant in dat act as well. It was I who gave up stardom as aerialist to go with heem so we could make new act and new life together. He promised me moon and stars! But instead we wind up in tiny troupe traveling United of States in bus. And now we are stuck een middle of nowhere beset by giant peeing dog-rats!" Mariska let loose with a sob and hid her face with the backs of her hands. Monique patted her shoulder sympathetically.

What a couple of drama queens. I thought about the prospect of letting two knife-fighting foreigners share my guest bedroom while Jess snoozed by a cozy campfire somewhere in the woods.

"Get your things and come with me," I told them. "I'm taking you to jail. Monique, I'll find you someplace else to stay."

"What? But we haf done nutting!" Sergei cried.

"Simmer down. I'm just taking you there so there'll be a roof over your head tonight."

"Eet has come to dis," Mariska grumbled. "I should have listened to my old babushka. She always said to me,

Mariska, these one weel come to no good. And now he has gotten me into American chain gang run by American KGB!"

I chewed my tongue. These two were more melodramatic than a Mexican soap opera. I waited while they scrambled around getting their stuff together, jabbering at each other in whatever their native language was. I couldn't tell what they were saying, of course, but I was pretty sure they were accusing each other of everything but killing Cock Robin.

I thanked my lucky stars I didn't have to keep score for *them*.

Quinn James

The ground tilted as I stepped down from the broken tour bus in the crisp February air, the lingering scent of leaking diesel making my nausea worse. I grabbed on to the folding door to steady the motion only I could see. It figured that the vertigo would return when I least needed it. I had to corral the stranded *Cirque d'Europa* performers into some semblance of order and give them their room assignments. The generous people of Mossy Creek and its outskirts were offering rooms in their mountain homes.

Like Blanche Du Bois, I was grateful for the kindness of strangers, but that's where the likeness between me and Blanche ended. Raised in the Virginia tidewater, I was Southern by birth, but had no belle-like qualities. A tomboy at heart, I'd excelled at gymnastics and disappointed my parents by joining the circus after college. They could at least brag it was a European circus. "Like *Cirque du Soleil*, only smaller," Mom liked to say.

I had been the only American acrobat in the troupe.

Now, after being sidelined with recurring vertigo, I was the owner's executive assistant and chief babysitter to thirty-five adults who were more demanding than a preschool full of whining three-year-olds. I might be sidelined by my illness, but I wasn't giving up the big top. That disappointed my father, who'd hoped I'd return home to find a "decent job that utilized my degree." For some reason, using my B.A. in Romance Languages in the circus didn't count.

"Miss James, you are all right?" Otto, the German bus driver, who was shaped like a tank, expanded my one-syllable last name into two. *Jay-mess*. It was bad enough that I had an odd first name for a woman—Quinn—without Otto turning my surname into, well, a mess. A Jay-mess.

"Fine, thanks," I said, tucking my clipboard under my arm. "I just need to get my bearings."

Only four steps separated me from the luggage bay, where Otto was unloading the performers' suitcases and duffel bags. Like a ship with a broken rudder, I listed over to the bay and steadied myself on the lip of the door.

The phone in my pocket buzzed. Even from halfway around the world, Mr. Polaski, owner of *Cirque d'Europa*, had the uncanny ability to call me at the worst possible moments. I knew it was him as certainly as I knew that it wasn't a good idea to tell the Bulgarian jugglers that the town of Mossy Creek had a pub. Our worried owner had called once already, not fifteen minutes ago. Leaning against the bus for support, I let go of the door, quickly reaching up to turn on my cell phone's earpiece.

"Hello." I spoke loudly to compensate for the conversations in at least three different languages going on within my earshot. I heard yelling and darted a gaze toward the sound. A local Chihuahua, shivering in the winter chill, lifted his tiny, shivering but determined tan leg on a mime's make-up kit. Tartuffe, the mime, feigned a shriek. It takes a lot to get a mime to mime a noise like that.

Mr. Polaski fired off his questions in a barrage not unlike gunfire. Why hadn't I called him back with the estimate on the cost of the bus repair? Had I gotten all the performers accommodations in Mossy Creek? Had I canceled our reservations for the night at the Dollywood theme park, up in Tennessee? As enamored as he was of Dolly Parton's assets and hometown, he didn't want the Best Western where we'd planned on staying to charge us for rooms we weren't using.

He stopped to take a breath, so I seized the opportunity to reassure him before he could reload. "Relax. I've got everything under control. I called the hotel and cancelled. A young man from a place called 'Peavey's' is waiting to tow the bus to his garage."

I didn't tell him the young man, Jason Cecil, was still in high school and only worked part-time as a mechanic. "We're unloading the luggage in the Mossy Creek Mount Gilead Methodist Church parking lot, thanks to Reverend Phillips. I was getting ready to read off the room assignments when you called."

Crossing my fingers would have been a good idea for luck that everything would go smoothly, but I was using them to keep the rest of me from falling to the hard blacktop shifting in front of me. Long shadows fingered the ground. It would be dark in an hour or so. I gazed upward at a horizon of darkening blue mountains. Were there wolves around here? Hillbillies? Albino banjo pickers with no teeth?

"Okay. Okay," Mr. Polaski said. "I call you back in a few minutes."

"I need more than a few minutes!" I shouted. The people standing around me grew quiet. The Chihuahua lowered its leg. "How about if I call you once I have every-one situated and the estimate for the bus repair?"

"Okay. Okay," Mr. Polaski said. "You know me, I worry so very much. You call as soon as you get estimate. Yes?"

"Yes." I glanced out at the performers who'd formed small countries on the sea of dark pavement. Spain, France, Germany, and Belgium clung together loosely, their breath vaporizing in the cold evening air. Luxembourg and Monaco hung off to the side of France. The Eastern Europeans puffed away on their unfiltered cigarettes and kept their distance almost as if we had our own cold war going on.

My former partner, Erik Aelbrecht, was standing with the rest of the Belgian acrobats. The street lights gilded his short brown hair and the shoulders of his dark wool pea coat. He smiled at me, and I felt a different sort of dizziness. His gaze moved to my gloved hand gripping the door of the luggage bay for support, and he frowned.

My 'little problem,' as I called it, bothered him. That fact made him less than perfect in my eyes. I couldn't help that I'd gotten vertigo. I didn't want it, the doctors said they couldn't help me, and there wasn't much I could do to relieve it other than some nearly useless exercises I'd found on the Internet.

Erik took a step in my direction only to have his path blocked by his new partner, the dramatic Magdalene Schelde, who wore more make-up off stage than on and went exceptionally heavy on the eye and lip liner. She tossed her long red mane, pouted, and stomped her booted foot.

Magdalene had been working with Erik for almost a year now, ever since my third bout of vertigo. The first bout we'd called a fluke. The second, a coincidence. By the third, I admitted my acrobatic days were over. I missed working with Erik, and I wondered if he missed working with me, too. Maybe that was why my vertigo upset him. We'd been closer friends than most non-romantically involved acrobatic partners.

Now he had Magdalene, with whom he partnered outside the ring, too. Theirs seemed to be one of those tumultuous relationships. One day, I'd hear rumors of a break up and the next she'd be climbing all over him. He wasn't big on public displays of romance, so I could understand why he always had an irritated look on his face when she felt the need to kiss him with abandon in front of everyone.

I'd tried to tell myself I was satisfied with what was left of our friendship, which had cooled since Magdalene took up so much of his time. I even tried to convince myself that I was the lucky one. Friendships last longer than romantic flings, right?

Sometimes, though, I let myself wonder what it would be like to kiss Erik, to see if our lips fit together like our bodies had on stage. Erik was broader, but he and I shared the same height and proportions, which made our former act unique. Our torsos, our hands, our arms and legs, even our fingers were the same length. We had been incredibly synchronized.

I released my hold on the bus, took the whistle hanging from my necklace, and blew a long *beep*, wobbling like a Weeble but gaining the attention of Creekites and performers alike. "Thanks to the assistance of the mayor's office and several local civic groups, I'm happy to report that the nice people of Mossy Creek are opening their homes to us for the next two days. Listen carefully as I tell each of you where you'll be staying."

The circus performers craned their heads and waited.

Erik pushed his way through the crowd, pried my fingers from the luggage bay door, and linked my arm through his so I could use him as a support. He smelled good, like spearmint gum and cedar. He kept cedar sachets in his coat pockets to keep moths away.

"Thanks," I whispered.

"No problem," he said, rolling his "r" slightly, his accent somewhere between French and German, like the country he came from.

"Could you do me one more favor?" I asked, as the rest of the circus performers crowded closer to hear their assignments. "I have a flashlight in my pocket, on my key ring."

With a deep sigh of resignation, he gingerly reached his hand toward my coat pocket as if a lion were in there ready to snap his fingers off.

"What's the deal?" I whispered, more irritated that I had to rely on others to help me when I was in high vertigo mode, than with him. "It's not like you haven't had your hand on my inner thigh with only a thin layer of Spandex between us."

"It's different now," he said.

"Different in that Magdalene doesn't want you touching me for even the most innocent reason?"

He didn't answer. Of course, I was making him uncomfortable. Maybe he was worried that he'd somehow catch my vertigo by touching me. Magdalene had voiced such a concern when she first replaced me. Initially she'd refused to work with Erik until a doctor convinced her he couldn't possibly be a carrier. Stupid woman thought it was a disease.

The flesh of my thigh, covered in a thin layer of silk underwear, a thick layer of denim, and whatever my pocket was made out of, tingled at his touch. Now that *was* different. I couldn't look at him.

He took hold of the key ring and turned on the flash-light, aiming the narrow beam at my clipboard.

The words swam along the page. The print flowed like waves rolling in and out with a tide. I tilted my head to the side, and the columns stilled.

For five minutes, I paired performers with Creekites without incident. But then I got down to Erik and one of our miming clowns. Some considered the mimes troublesome because they never broke character. "Erik and Tartuffe, you'll be staying with Mr. Win Allen."

Tartuffe clapped his hands in glee. Mr. Allen, who was a Mossy Creek restaurateur known by his alter ego, Bubba Rice, didn't appear equally excited when he stepped forward to claim his guest. In fact, Win/Bubba began scowling.

Up to this point, the local chief of police, Amos Royden, who reminded me a little of a youngish George Clooney, had been watching the proceedings with little interest. Now he smiled.

"What's so funny?" Win Allen asked.

"Just appreciating the irony." The handsome police chief arched a dark brow in Tartuffe's direction. Wicked humor gleamed in Amos Royden's eyes.

"Is there a problem?" I asked. "Something amiss with my mimes?"

"No, ma'am," Mr. Allen and the chief said in unison, like two boys caught talking in class.

I proceeded quickly down the rest of the list until I was interrupted by Magdalene. She flounced up to us in a rush of spicy floral cologne. My nose clogged, and my eyes started to water. How could Erik stand it? Magdalene's perfume was more overpowering than her make-up.

"Quinn," she said, spreading her full, glossy lips in a

fake smile. "Can you please put me in the same home as Erik?"

The muscles in Erik's arm tightened. Was he signaling me? Was that a, 'Please, say you will,' or a, 'No, don't you dare?' I couldn't risk trying to read his face. With the way the vertigo was intensifying, I could barely read the names in front of me, even with my head tilted.

"Let me see," I said tightly. I'd placed Magdalene and the rest of the single women acrobats with the Cliftons, a middle-aged married couple from a local community named 'Yonder.' Chief Royden said it was quite some distance outside town. Not only did the Cliftons have three guest rooms available, they'd told me their daughter, Rhonda, was a former Miss Bigelow County. I figured if anyone could handle a house full of women who liked to primp and prance, it was the Cliftons.

"You and the ABC posse already have rooms for the night," I told Magdalene. The ABC posse was comprised of Ann, Cherie, and Brigitta. Brunette Ann was the nicest. Blondes Cherie and Brigitta weren't even close to nice unless a man was to be won. Cherie favored t-shirts emblazoned with provocative suggestions of what she was willing and able to do for a man. Brigitta countered by going braless and wearing her street clothes two sizes too small to show off her recently acquired breast implants.

I scanned the columns on my clipboard and saw that next door to the Cliftons were the Finches, who had just one room to offer. I'd placed Tartuffe's partner-in-mime, Orlon, with the Finch family.

Magdalene stomped her *Ugg* boot. "Can you hear me, Quinn?"

"Mag, leave her alone," Erik growled.

My ears perked. Maybe he didn't want to be housed near 'Mag.'

Win Allen was waiting for Erik and chatting with Chief

Royden. I could ask him to trade Erik in for one more clown. Not that I wanted to do anything nice for Magdalene. I would do just about anything for Erik, though. We were buddies, tingly feelings not withstanding.

Magdalene tossed her hair and added, "It is Valentine's Day this weekend. And I should be near to *my* valentine. Unless you have some reason you don't want me to be happy."

A hush fell over the performers and Creekites, who recognized a verbal gauntlet being thrown down when they heard one.

I made the mistake of tilting my head so I could see her taunting face, ugly in its beauty. She knew I was infatuated with Erik. Probably everyone else here could see it as well. Could Erik? Would she tell him? I dug my fingers into Erik's arm until he cleared his throat. He didn't say anything so I decided he did want to be with Magdalene.

Mortified, I could do nothing but surrender to her telepathic blackmail. Of course, I'd rather tear her hair out. Fine, I'd give her what she wanted. No, what *they* wanted, to be near one another for this stupid holiday. "Sure, no problem, Magdalene."

"Mr. Allen!" I shouted. "Could you come here, please?"

Win Allen, who had been frowning at Tartuffe as Tartuffe mimed carrying invisible luggage, walked over. He towered above the semicircle of performers. "What can I do for you, Ms. James?"

"I hate to ask you this, but would it be possible for our second mime, Orgon, to stay with you? Erik and Magdalene want to be near one another for the holiday. Would hosting a second clown be a problem?"

Chief Royden made a strangled sound. Several other Creekites openly snickered.

Win Allen's face went darker. Then he sighed and

tapped Orgon on the shoulder. "Can I put you work at my restaurant as a waiter tomorrow night, along with Tartuffe? I'm booked solid for the Valentine's dinners, and I need the help."

Orgon nodded and bowed with great flourish.

Amos Royden, clearly enjoying himself, said, "Put me down for that table you mentioned, Win. I want to watch your new waiters at work."

Win Allen chortled. "Table for two? Since when do *you* have a date? I've already got Ida booked. She's coming with Del Jackson."

The police chief's cool look made Tartuffe and Orgon clutch their chests in mock—or maybe real—alarm. But what was I doing worrying about domestic dramas among the locals? I had my own love triangle to deal with.

"Okay, okay," I said, realizing I was sounding like Mr. Polaski. "Erik, since Orgon is staying with Mr. Allen, you can stay at the house next door to the Cliftons. Is there a Mrs. Nancy Abercrombie Finch here?"

"Awww, man!" A little boy's disappointed voice rose above his mother's 'Yes.' "I wanted the *clown*."

Relieved when I read off the last name on the list, I smiled at Erik, who wasn't smiling back.

"What about you?" he asked, only with his accent "what" sounded like "vhat." I loved his accent. "Where are you staying?"

"Me?" I said, wanting to curse instead. The low ringing in my ears rose to a higher decibel. Of course I'd left myself off the list. "Don't worry about me. I'll sleep on the bus."

"No, you won't," Erik said, this time careful to pronounce the "w" the way I would.

"It's no big deal."

"I'll sleep there," Erik said with finality.

Magdalene glared at me.

Mrs. Finch cleared her throat to get our attention. She

had one of those sleek, short hairstyles that didn't move when she'd turned her head, following our verbal volleys like we were in a match at Wimbledon. I had no idea why she was so intrigued by our mini-argument.

Her little boy kicked the blacktop with his shoe. He was miffed that he didn't get a clown.

"Miss James, I won't hear of either you or Mr. Aelbrecht sleeping on the bus," she said with a spark of mischief in her blue eyes. "You can *both* stay with us. Now won't that be nice, Charles? We'll have two circus people."

Magdalene nearly went up in flames.

The little boy looked at me. "Are you a clown?"

"No. I'm the lady in charge. That's better than being a clown." Except now I was dealing with vertigo and an angry red-haired Belgian who saw my former partner as her sole property. Maybe I was a clown, or something far worse . . . a fool.

Hannah

"He's headed this way, Mrs. Longstreet," my intern Linda Polk announced from the glass front door, which she was *supposed* to be cleaning. "He's, like, three blocks away now."

I scowled at her from behind the circulation desk. "He who?"

"You know who." Linda faced me with a self-satisfied smile. She'd gotten cocky ever since her dad had helped me catch the "library ghost." "Mr. Crogan has a thing for you, you know. That's why he comes here after he's done for the day."

"He comes here because he likes to read," I said firmly as I keyed in an interlibrary loan request and tried to ignore the silly skip in my pulse at her words. "He comes here because there's little else to do in Mossy Creek at night when you're staying at the Hamilton House Inn. To my knowledge, it doesn't have cable."

"He could go to the movies down in Bigelow. Or watch a basketball game on the big-screen TV at O' Day's Pub. Shoot, he could even read in his room, instead of hanging out here whenever you're working. Or hadn't you noticed?"

Of course I had. Every night for the past three weeks, the New York photographer had entered the library precisely at sunset, like some reverse vampire who hid when the sun went down. He'd chosen a book, lounged on the couch to read it, and then checked it out right before closing. I could only assume he finished it back at the inn, since he always returned it the next night promptly at sunset. "Maybe he doesn't find his room comfortable."

Linda snorted. "He's got 101, the biggest suite in the whole hotel."

"You've been to his room?" I exclaimed, thoroughly shocked.

"No!" She shot me a superior glance. "Katie Bell told me."

Katie Bell, the gossip columnist at the *Mossy Creek Gazette*, was definitely the person to go to for gossip. "I see." I worked hard to sound nonchalant. "And I suppose she told you plenty of other information about Mr. Crogan."

Linda was no fool. With a little smirk, she sprayed cleaner on the door. "Maybe."

When she said nothing more, I gritted my teeth to keep from begging her for info.

After a moment, Linda cut her eyes at me. "Mr. Crogan is a hottie, don't you think?"

A hottie? Absolutely. And I lusted after every lanky,

dusky-skinned inch of him.

It was mortifying. Mothers of middle-school children were supposed to limit their lusting to the latest Kenmore appliances and brand-new Beemers, not photographers with gymnast physiques. Which was why I wasn't about to admit my weakness to Linda.

Bad enough that my eleven-year-old, Rachel, had also been on my case lately about starting to date again. Just tonight, she'd ragged me so hard I'd had to banish her to the break room, where I knew she'd get engrossed in playing computer games on my laptop. Valentine's Day was fast approaching, and it was infecting every female in sight, even my daughter.

That was my only explanation for why she was so adamant about pairing me off. All right, so her dad *had* been dead for over eight years now, and I *was* a bit too prone to bury myself in my work, but that didn't mean I was itching to find another mate. Between my work at the library and my determination to maintain a safe and comfortable home for my clumsy daughter, who had time to date?

Too bad I couldn't tell Rachel that. Or Linda, for that matter. "Don't you leave at five?" I told my intern irritably.

Setting the cleaner aside, Linda planted her elbows on the circulation desk. "Katie Bell says she's pretty sure Mr. Crogan isn't married. He doesn't wear a ring."

"It doesn't matter. A man like that has to have a girl-friend somewhere." Probably several, all of them young and buxom photographer's models. Why should he even look at a modestly proportioned librarian, even one who kept in shape with biweekly workouts?

"Katie Bell found out that he's in town taking stock photos."

I'd heard that already. I just didn't believe it. Sure, he did spend from dawn to dusk snapping shots of people and fields and even our famous Sitting Tree, but he did it with a large format camera. I'd read enough to know that most photographers these days had gone digital. Hardly anybody used ten-thousand-dollar Hasselblads with massive tripods and actual film that had to be Fed-Exed to some lab for dark room printing.

I'd even Googled his name, along with the words *photographer* and *Hasselblad*, but if there were any professional photographers named David Crogan, Google couldn't find them. That alone made me suspicious. Not to mention even more obsessed.

"How old do you think he is?" Linda asked.

"I couldn't begin to speculate." I'd heard guesses anywhere from twenty-five to thirty-five. I prayed it was the upper end, because the idea of my lusting after a guy more than ten years my junior was worrisome in light of the gossip-fest that erupted when our fiftyish mayor and thirty-fiveish police chief were caught kissing last month.

"Well, I don't think it matters." Linda surveyed me up and down. "You're really pretty, you know, even with the glasses and the khakis. And I bet that if you asked Jasmine Beleau, she'd be happy to give you a few tips on—"

"Thank you, but I'm not looking for a makeover just now."

The door swung open, and we both froze as the object of our speculation entered. Blessedly oblivious to Linda's not-so-subtle wink in my direction, he approached the circulation desk and slid a copy of Poul Anderson's *Time Patrol* into the Return Books slot.

"Good evening, Mr. Crogan," Linda chirped.

"Evening, Miss Polk," he answered in his deep, whiskey-rough Scottish brogue. Then he acknowledged me with a nod. "Mrs. Longstreet. I hope you're well this evening."

"Fine, thank you," I said in my professional librarian's voice.

Meanwhile, my knees were going weak. I admit it—I'm no different from any other American female. I'm a complete sucker for a British accent. Make it Scottish, and you might as well douse the guy in pheromones. It even trumped the red-brown dreadlocks he wore tied back with a strip of black leather.

"Has that interlibrary loan copy of *The Smoke Ring* come in?" he paused to ask.

"Not yet. I suppose you've read the rest of our Nivens?"

Amusement made his unusual grey eyes gleam like freshly polished silver. "You ought to know the answer to that. You're the one who introduced me to his works."

Linda's winking was practically a twitch now, which I determinedly ignored. "I'm sorry we don't have more of his books. But you could always try something other than hard science fiction. Perhaps some Terry Brooks?"

"Thanks, but fantasy isn't my cup of tea." He pronounced cup as "coop." He leaned one leather-jacketed arm on the front desk in a move that curled my toes like raw potato chips hitting hot oil, then added, "Don't worry about it, luv. There's a Heinlein over there I haven't read in a long while."

Luv. I turned to mush. Or *moosh*, as he would probably say it.

"How's the photography going?" Linda asked before he could leave the desk.

He clammed up tighter than a book with new binding. "Pretty well," he said tersely. "The light was good today." Then shoving away from the desk, he headed off to his usual spot on the worn couch in the reading area.

"*That* was rude," Linda muttered under her breath.

"He doesn't like talking about his work." And I should know, since I'd tried questioning him about it a few times. Invariably it got me the cold shoulder, though he was more than happy to discuss books and art and music.

A mysterious man, our Mr. Crogan. Unfortunately, that did nothing to subdue my rampant interest.

"I guess I'd better go," Linda said, handing the window cleaner over the desk. "Sorry I can't stay until closing tonight."

"No problem. The place is practically deserted anyway."

But that was fine by me. To tell the truth, I preferred the library to just about anywhere else in town, especially when I had Rachel with me. It was safe and bright and blessedly devoid of sharp objects, so I never had to worry about her getting hurt. Knocking stuff off shelves, yes, but not getting herself hurt.

Minutes after Linda headed out, the front door opened again, and Mossy Creek police officer Sandy Crane hurried in, towing a thin blond woman whose wan cheeks showed the strain of late nights and long hours. "You haven't changed your mind about taking in one of the *Cirque d'Europa* people, right?"

I stifled my groan. I'd completely forgotten about our phone conversation earlier. "Of course, not." I managed a smile for the thin woman, who returned it tentatively. "Rachel said she'll give up her room and sleep with me for as long as necessary."

"Good." Sandy turned to the woman. "This is Mrs. Longstreet. You'll be staying with her and Rachel."

"Rachel. Yes," the woman said.

Sandy frowned. "No, Rachel is her daughter. This is—"

"Hannah," I corrected her, wanting to put the woman at ease. "Call me Hannah."

"Hannah?" The woman looked confused.

Sandy's cell rang, and she answered it. "Yes, Chief. I'm headed over there now."

As she pocketed the phone, she glanced at me. "Gotta go. This lady's name is Monique Laplante. That's about all I can tell you."

"But what—" Too late. Sandy had already sprinted out the door, leaving me with a circus performer who was starting to look a little panicked.

"I can't leave until closing," I explained to Monique, "but until then you're free to read or use one of the terminals to check your e-mail." I noticed Mr. Crogan listening in on the conversation as the woman just stared at me. "Are you hungry? Have you had anything to eat?"

Her lips quivered. "*Parlez-vous Francais?*"

My heart sank. Sandy had conveniently neglected to mention that the woman didn't speak English.

"*Je parle Francais*," said Mr. Crogan, unfolding his angular body from where it was sprawled on the couch.

"You speak French?" I said as he headed for us. "You told me you were born and raised in Scotland."

"Yes, but my mother was originally from Burundi, where French is the state language. I grew up bilingual."

"I grew up uni-lingual, I'm afraid. Would you mind telling Ms. Laplante that she's staying with me and my daughter?"

"You and your daughter and . . . er . . . your *husband*?"

Oh, Lord. It had never occurred to me that Mr. Crogan might not know I was a widow. "My husband passed away some years ago."

"Ah," he said with what I would have sworn was relief. "I wasn't sure."

I liked that he didn't say he was sorry, as if it could possibly be his fault. I never knew how to answer people who did. Luke's aneurysm wasn't anybody's fault . . . not even Luke's.

I lifted my left hand and wiggled my fingers. "No ring. I guess you didn't notice."

"Oh, I noticed. But divorced women don't usually go by Mrs. these days and you're so young to be a widow that—" He halted, as if realizing he'd just revealed how thoroughly he'd considered the matter. "Anyway . . ." he mumbled, and abruptly turned to Monique.

He said something in French, and she nodded vigorously, casting me a shy smile as she replied.

"She says to call her Monique," Mr. Crogan explained.

"Would you ask if she's eaten?"

A short conversation ensued between him and the Frenchwoman, in which the only words I picked out were "McDonald's" and "café."

Mr. Crogan turned to me. "It seems she and her companions stopped for a bit of lunch, but the poor lass has had no more than coffee since then."

"That won't do." I gestured toward the back of the library. "There's yogurt in the refrigerator in the break room. That might hold her until the library closes. Rachel's back there—she can show you where I keep the potato chips."

He arched an eyebrow. "Potato chips and yogurt? Quite the interesting diet you have there, Mrs. Longstreet."

"The potato chips are for Rachel."

"A likely story." His eyes glinted with mischief. "Are you sure you don't dip them in yogurt whenever no one's looking?"

Oh my God, he was flirting with me. Wasn't he?

I struggled to keep my tone light. "Hey, the only weird food I will admit to is my dad's toasted peanut butter and ketchup sandwiches."

"That's certainly a vile-sounding combination."

I shrugged. "They're not as bad as you'd think. Besides, don't you Scots eat haggis and kippers?"

"Ah, but haggis and kippers are delicious, something you'd realize if you ever tried them. In fact—" He cast me a challenging glance. "We should do more than speculate about our respective cuisines. If you'll agree to try kippers, I'll agree to try your horrible sandwiches."

"You're on," I said blithely.

"Really? I expected to have to do a bit more convincing."

I laughed. "You'll never find kippers in Mossy Creek."

The sudden devilish grin transforming his dusky features gave me pause. "I wouldn't lay odds on that if I were you." He lifted one eyebrow. "So it's a date, is it?"

My heart began to pound. "Sure. A food-tasting date."

"I won't forget," he said, then winked as he led Monique to the back of the library.

Mr. Crogan had winked at me. And flirted. And asked me out on a date. Well, a sort of date.

I wiped my clammy hands on my slacks. I must be out of my mind. He was in town temporarily. Nothing could come of this.

Freelance photographers can live anywhere.

I groaned. That line of thinking was dangerous. And here I'd thought that the library was safe—apparently sharp objects came in more than one guise.

For the next hour or so, I tried not to feel left out as sounds of a party going on in the break room wafted out to me. My daughter's high-pitched Southern accent mingled with the low rumble of Mr. Crogan's Scots English, which was interrupted by bursts of melodious French in both his and Monique's voices. It was like listening to a multinational orchestra from outside the auditorium.

But I didn't dare leave my post. Someone had to man the desk. Besides, I had work to do.

For one thing, I had to Google "David Crogan" and the word *kippers.* Unfortunately, that led me in every direction except the one that told me more about my mysterious photographer.

With a sigh, I glanced at the clock. Almost closing time, thank God. Remembering what Linda had said about a makeover, I whipped out my compact and put on the lipstick I rarely used, then finger-combed my spiky blond hair.

My daughter suddenly dashed from the break room. As I whisked my makeup away, Rachel stumbled over a chair, reeled toward a bookshelf, then caught herself before she sent books flying. She finished off by rushing breathlessly up to the desk. "Mom, did you know Mr. Crogan's dad is Scottish?"

"Is he?" I said, trying to sound cool and professional as he and Monique emerged from my office behind Rachel.

"Yep! And Ms. Laplante is from Provence. Isn't that cool?"

I eyed Rachel askance. "Do you even know where Provence is?"

"Well, no, but it sounds really pretty. Mr. Crogan shot pictures there for a month, and he told me all about it."

Provence. Something else to Google with his name.

I winced as I glanced over to where he chatted in French with Monique. The man was turning me into a cyber-stalker. "I hope you had Mr. Crogan explain to Ms. Laplante that our house will be nothing like Provence."

Mr. Crogan heard me and smiled. "She won't care—she's grateful for the place to stay. They feared they'd have to spend the night on the tour bus."

"Ms. Laplante is a knife-thrower," Rachel exclaimed, fairly bouncing on her toes at the prospect of having a circus performer in our house. "She says she'll show me how to throw knives, too."

"Wonderful." I stifled a groan at the thought of my clumsy daughter sending any kind of missile flying through the air, much less one with a sharp edge.

"And I told Mr. Crogan that he has to come home with us for dinner," Rachel added, "so he can explain things to Ms. Laplante in French."

My heart snagged in my throat before I got hold of myself. "Now, Rachel, I'm sure Mr. Crogan has better things to do this evening than spend it interpreting for us."

"Truth is," he broke in, the burr of his brogue humming along my senses, "I'm happy to work for my supper. Though I do hope you're serving something more traditional than peanut butter and ketchup sandwiches."

"You eat pb-and-k sandwiches, too?" Rachel exclaimed. "Cool! Mom, now you *have* to make—"

"We're having pizza, Rachel, and that's final. Why don't you show Ms. Laplante to the car while I close up and talk to Mr. Crogan for a second?"

As soon as my daughter had tugged Monique out the door, I turned to the photographer. "Pay no attention to my daughter. She's always eager to impose on people, and I don't want you to feel as if you have to indulge her, Mr. Crogan."

"I don't. And call me Dave. Please."

My mouth went dry. "All right. But only if you call me Hannah."

His smile dazzled me. "The name suits you."

"Does it?" I said inanely, feeling as if I were thirteen again and sitting tongue-tied while Bobby Jackson, the most popular boy in school, asked me the time in study hall.

"Besides, I'd be the one imposing. Much as I enjoy Rosie's fried chicken, I'm ready for a change. I'll even pay for the pizza."

"Pay?" I drew myself up with a mock sniff. "I'll have you know, sir, that we make our pizza from scratch."

"You must be joking. No one does that anymore."

"Well," I admitted, "we don't have any choice. Domino's doesn't exactly carry the ingredients we like to eat."

He groaned. "Please say you don't make them with peanut butter and tomato sauce."

"Don't worry," I teased. "You can always order the standard old boring pizza if you don't like our version. But you *will* like it, I promise."

"I will?" he echoed, obviously skeptical.

"Trust me."

Sagan

Emily says I have a restless soul. That's why I studied anthropology, why I roam through the past. I'm always searching for something. I wish I knew what it was. Until I do, I probably won't find it. I think I'm just curious. That's what I tell myself.

My parents were restless, too, always on the move. When I was fifteen they were killed on a mountain climbing expedition, leaving me in a nerdy boarding school, totally on my own. They must have expected some kind of disaster because they carried large insurance policies, enough to put me through college, earn more than one degree and support my vagabond lifestyle. I thought that if I found my past, I'd understand why I searched. But you can't buy a peaceful heart.

Over a year ago, I came to Mossy Creek looking for my Cherokee ancestors and found my Salter pioneer roots instead. For several generations, being a Salter in Mossy Creek was an automatic ticket to destruction. After being part of the group of founders after the Civil War, the Salter clan gradually diminished until there were only two of us left—my distant cousin, Sue Ora Salter Bigelow, whose family has lived in Mossy Creek for over a hundred years, and me, Sagan Salter, part Cherokee Indian, part Scots Irish, part who-knows-what, returning to land my Cherokee family occupied until the Trail of Tears led them to Oklahoma.

Before I knew it, I'd bought a house and even formed a comfortable relationship with Emily, another loner who came back home to live in her grandmother's house, which is just down the mountain from me. She's made it clear that she's open to taking the relationship further, but I'm not certain I'm ready to settle down that way. I either have to commit or move on. That's why I took a little sabbatical back to Oklahoma recently.

I've been working on a book, a historical piece about mysticism and Native American beliefs and the white man's lack of acceptance. I needed to do some research. At least that's what I told Emily.

I was more honest with myself. I don't know what I want. I just know I'm drawn to Mossy Creek, the solitude of the mountains and the trees and the townspeople. But that isn't enough. Something's missing.

So I spent Christmas with Emily in Mossy Creek and New Year's in Oklahoma visiting some of my Cherokee family. They welcomed me with a Stomp Dance, where stories are told, stories that sound too grand to be real. The spirit has remained but times have changed.

No matter that the ceremonial rattlers are now metal cans and bottles filled with river gravel, and the ankle amulets are jar lids strung on twine. After enough liquid refreshments, we all believed the stories and joined in the dancing.

When the year rolled over into February, I left the flat, desolate plains where I'd grown up, called back to the green mountains of north Georgia by a need I could neither understand or explain.

As I rode my Harley into Mossy Creek that chilly Friday evening, I thought I was in the wrong place. My heart gave a lurch and I came to an abrupt stop. Instead of the tranquil town square that usually lived up to its motto, "Ain't going nowhere and don't want to," a man on sparkly stilts, wearing a silver mask, nimbly stepped over my Harley, leaned down and shook his head at me as if in disapproval. I pealed off my helmet and studied the town before me. Sequins sparkled in the glow of the street lamps. A bevy of strangers seemed to have turned the square into a fairytale fantasy. In the time I'd been to Oklahoma and back, Mossy Creek had turned into *Brigadoon*.

"Welcome home, Sagan," Katie Bell yelled across the town park. The *Gazette's* journalistic snoop, advertising sales rep and keeper-of-all-secrets in town gave me the provincial hug required upon the comings and goings of all Creekites. "Glad to have you back, Sagan. Guess you can see we have a few visitors."

I was at such a loss for words that I could only nod. My Cherokee heritage opened my mind to many things I didn't understand, but this was beyond explanation. Several local kids were practicing handstands and cartwheels under the guidance of a woman in spangled Spandex. A crowd of Mossy Creek's more adventuresome adults were juggling huge hearts and sparkling balls.

"What's going on, Katie? I seemed to have taken a wrong turn at the North Star."

"Well, so did we," she said, looking at me with a big, cat-that-swallowed-the-canary grin. "Park that thing and I'll bring you up to date."

Twenty minutes later, after interruptions from elderly Ed Brady and his son, Ed, Jr., who were carrying tool boxes, Mutt Buttoms, who was dragging a large sheet of plywood, and Bert Lyman, carrying what looked like part of his radio station's sound system, I finally understood that a small European circus, *Cirque d'Europa*, had settled in for the weekend until repairs could be made on their tour bus.

"We found rooms for everybody," Katie Bell told me, "but this group voted to camp out on the square."

"I guess they come from *cold* parts of Europe," Ed, Jr. said. "Our nippy weather seems to feel like springtime to them."

"Crazy foreigners," grumbled Ed, Sr. "We offered 'em warm baths and heat."

Katie flipped her notebook closed. "They told me they'd rather share a 'universal celebration of love' with us, since it's Valentine's weekend."

That was too much for me. "You mean Mossy Creek is turning into Woodstock?"

Katie shook her head. "Don't be silly. Sunday's Valentine's Day. They're just in a holiday mood."

Amos pulled up in his patrol car. Our police chief looked a little worse for wear, to me. Something tight and unhappy around his eyes. I'd heard the rumors about him and the mayor before I left for Oklahoma. Obviously, their romance hit the rocks as soon as word spread about Ida's significant other catching them in a major lip lock in Ida's front yard. Amos nodded brusquely to me. "Sagan."

"Chief."

"Welcome home. You got back just in time for the entertainment." He arched a brow at the square. A performer back flipped across the park in front of the granite statue of our old Confederate general. "Acrobats. Lots of them."

"Well, I wouldn't want to miss this," I commented, still trying to wrap my mind around the activity before me. Music wafted from a boom box—a soft, magical flute, a violin and bagpipes provided a lyrical accompaniment to two women pirouetting on the porch rails of the park's big gazebo.

Amos cleared his throat. "Katie, do me a favor. Ask around and see what our visitors can tell you about a boy named Nikoli. He may be missing. There's no need to panic, yet. He has a history of hiding."

"Missing?" Katie's reporter instincts sprang into action. "What's that name again?"

"His name is Nikoli. He doesn't speak much English. In fact he doesn't even belong with this troop. Seems he was with a family of animal trainers who are being returned to Russia. The boy decided he didn't want to go back home to the youth facility he was being sent to. His relatives left him with a friend in the *Cirque d'Europa* troop in the hope the Russian authorities would forget about him."

Katie was nothing if not a defender of the lost and wounded. She folded her arms across her chest as if she were daring Amos to argue. "Youth facility?"

Amos nodded. "Nikoli has other talents, including picking pockets and petty theft. The owner of the animals was tired of the trouble Nikoli caused after his mother died. Arrangements were being made by immigration on this side and the Russian counterpart on the other. He's too old to go to a children's center so it's a military training facility for him."

"And 'military facility' in Russia means becoming a soldier," I said. "I've heard about those facilities. Can't our government do something to help him?"

"Problem is, he's helping himself. Last week he stole a bird from a pet shop in Atlanta. He also took a box of Valentine candy and the heart-shaped necklace the shop's owner had hidden in the candy for his wife. The parrot's on the endangered species list. And Nikoli seems bound and determined to add himself to that list."

Katie scribbled madly. "Poor kid. How did they know that Nikoli was the thief?"

"He left a trail of candy wrappers and bird seed to the *Cirque d'Europa* bus."

"Why don't you just forget about it?" I asked. "Once their bus is repaired, he can go with this group and Russia will have one less youth to corrupt."

"Breaking the law is breaking the law," Amos said. "Besides, what I would or wouldn't do doesn't matter. I don't think Dwight Truman will ignore the fact we have a thief running amuck in Mossy Creek." Dwight was the local Chamber president. Not a relaxed guy. The chief eyed Katie for a moment. "Word is bound to get out. I'm not going to find him without some help."

"You're darned right." Katie gave me a conspiratorial look and slapped her note pad shut. "I'll pass the word," she said and started toward the newspaper office. She stopped and turned back to make one last comment to Amos and me. "Don't forget, we expect both of you at tomorrow night's Sweethearts' Dance. Bring Emily, Sagan. Amos, bring . . . uh, well, uh . . . whoever you can think of. " As Amos's expression went grim she clamped her mouth shut and hurried away. Amos nodded curtly to me and drove off.

Sweetheart's Dance? Bring Emily? That was one of the things I was struggling with. I'd spent the last month on sweat-lodge vision quests and wilderness medication searching for answers. I liked Emily and we'd become sort of a couple. But did I want to spend the rest of my life with her?

In a city, we'd simply move in together and see where it went. Here, everyone would start planning our wedding. The good-natured pressure would mount until Emily and I gave up and set a date. Mossy Creek already had one notorious pair of live-in's in the Salter clan, Sue Ora Salter Bigelow and her husband, John Bigelow, who were officially separated but continued to see each other frequently. Creekites accepted their situation.

Maybe it was because of their son, Willie, who seemed content with the part-time arrangement which allowed John's car to remain parked at Sue Ora's house overnight about once or twice a month. Maybe being married made their avant garde relationship okay, but I doubted Creekites would let me and Emily off the matrimonial hook.

I cranked my Harley, replaced my helmet and headed for Colchik Mountain where my little house clung to a ridge. If anyone has asked, I would have denied the warm feeling that came over me when I saw my cabin. But an unmistakable sense of peace settled inside me. I was home.

Louise

I *do*, therefore I *am*. I realize that's not precisely what Descartes said, but he was a *man*. He could sit around all day thinking, because Mrs. Descartes was going to the market for his food and fixing it, cleaning up after him, washing and ironing his lace ruffs, and bearing his children. I could go on, but you get the idea.

If there *were* any little Descartes, Mme. Descartes was also running around after them telling them not to make noise because Daddy was *thinking*. How nice for him.

While I'm misquoting, here's another. Some are born to nurture, some become nurturers, and some have nurturing thrust upon them. I don't know whether I'm misquoting Benjamin Franklin or Stevie Wonder, actually. I just know I belong in the third category. I definitely had nurturing thrust upon me.

I am good at it. I've been married for nearly forty years, and the other day after Charlie came in from a wintry golf game down in Bigelow that ended in an ice-cold downpour, he asked me how to turn on the washing machine, so he could toss his filthy golf socks in. A whole load for one pair of socks. I ask you.

Charlie is a graduate engineer. He can create production lines where none were before, but he didn't know how to turn on the washing machine?

Whose fault is that? Mine, of course. He still sets his dirty dishes on top of the dishwasher instead of inside, and when he reaches for a clean shirt in his closet, he expects one to jump into his hand.

He does put his dirty clothes in the hamper. I picked them up off the floor for six months after we were married, then one day I decided to leave them where they were until he ran out.

When he reached for that clean shirt and found nothing but empty hangers, he had a fit. I told him I'd done the laundry already. I showed him the empty laundry hamper, smiled sweetly, and went to lunch at Hamilton Inn with Eleanor. She and Zeke have been married for years. She's full of good advice on husbands.

When I came home, his dirty clothes were in the hamper. Not washed, of course, but picked up. I should have continued with the lesson, except that he would have washed my coral pink linen shirt in with his shorts and been furious when he had to wear peach undershorts. So I took the line of least resistance and did the wash myself.

Men have figured out through the millennia that if your mate asks you to do something you don't want to do, screw it up. She'll never ask you again.

Maybe things have changed. My daughter's big ol' husband can do the laundry, even run the vacuum cleaner. But only after she asks him. My generation, however, the peri-Betty Friedan group—wants to be equal, but feels guilty about it.

Because who would want us around if we didn't *do*? And keep doing?

I worked as a secretary, complete with coffee-making and toting duties, until our daughter was born, but Charlie reminds me from time to time I've never had a *real* job since. I suppose he means I haven't been paid to run General Motors.

During those years, however, I have been president of the Altar Guild and the Women of the Church at least a dozen times, been room mother at my daughter's school for ten of her twelve grades, run the PTA and the garden club, baked enough oatmeal cookies and chocolate chip cupcakes and coconut sheet cakes to give the entire state of Georgia a sugar high. That's just for starters.

I've also been the perfect corporate wife for Charlie.

The second year we were married I also took over our finances. Charlie would leave the mail unopened on the end of the piano. In my family we do not open mail addressed to other people—not even spouses or children.

Because I was home all day, I was the one who had to field the irate calls from the utility company and the telephone company and the car company because the payments were overdue. I considered letting the phone and the utilities get cut off and Charlie's car get repossessed, but I lost my nerve.

So for nearly forty years I have paid the bills, kept the checkbook, and desperately tried to keep track of Charlie's expenses. He never writes check stubs. He says we'll have copies of the checks at the end of the month. He can keep track of millions of dollars of other people's money, of course. He's only cavalier with ours.

To his credit, he never questions what I spend. He isn't a lazy slob, either. He builds beautiful wood cabinets, mows the yard, changes light bulbs. You know, guy things. Now that he's retired, however, he mostly plays golf.

I know this has been a long preamble. I promise there's a kicker.

I recently had my yearly mammogram, always a fun event.

And on Friday morning, the Friday of Valentine's Day weekend, I got a call. Something didn't look quite right. Could I come back for another mammogram and an ultra-sound? Possibly a needle biopsy? First thing Monday morning?

Probably nothing, but . . .

I don't think I actually choked until I hung up the phone, then I sat down on the floor and shook. My adrenaline was pumping so hard I'm surprised I didn't have a stroke right there. My skin felt dry and clammy at the same time, and every nerve jangled. I never knew what that meant before. Now I do. The electrical current was like being hit with a Taser.

When you hear "probably nothing," you think "undoubtedly something," don't you? Of course you do. Me, too.

I know we all have to die. We all want to die with a minimum of fuss and pain and with mind and body intact at say—a hundred and ten. I've nursed the dying. Dying is nasty, brutish, ugly, undignified, and smells bad. Those who are in the throes of chemo or radiation throw up, use bedpans which have to emptied, mess up sheets that have to be changed, and frequently get crazier than Cooter Brown from the drugs.

Oh, if I were dying Charlie would talk a good game, and he'd try desperately to be nice to me, at least in the beginning. Pretty quickly, however, he'd toss my ugly butt into a hospice and visit me regularly once a week while he surfed the net for twenty-year-old mail-order Russian brides to take my place. It's not that he doesn't love me. He loves the *me* I am now. If I became another me, I think he'd be horrified.

I'm being flippant because I'm scared. The reality is that Charlie could never handle looking after me, psychologically. A couple of years ago the wife of one of his golfing buddies had a radical mastectomy. Charlie said the guy sat in the clubhouse and sobbed because every time he looked at his wife's wounds and scars he ran to the bathroom to throw up. He couldn't bear to touch her, even to comfort her. And she knew.

She's doing fine now, but I think all that guilt is why he died of a massive heart attack a year afterwards. I don't want that to happen to Charlie. He would try to look after me, try to keep me from seeing how appalling he found cleaning up vomit or worse, changing dressings, even helping me to the bathroom.

My daughter? She already has her hands full with her big husband and those two wild boys.

My friends? They have their own families. We can't afford nurses.

If I can't *do*, then what good am I? Who do I become if I have to be done *for*?

While I sat on the floor shaking with my hand still on the phone, the darned thing rang. I snatched it to my ear. *Please, Lord, let it be the clinic calling back to say they made a mistake in the X-rays!*

"Louise, honey, Ida is bringing over your houseguest as we speak."

"House guest?" Oh, Lord, I had forgotten. That weird bunch of circus types who were stranded in Mossy Creek for the weekend. Had I actually agreed to house one of them for two days? *These* two days?

I wanted to say, "No, I can't do that, I'm probably dying." Then, I figured having someone under foot that I actually had to look after might keep me from thinking too much about Monday. "When?"

"I'm guessing she's pulling up in front of the house now. Look out your front window."

I hung up the phone and went to greet my guest.

Peggy

I have been celibate since my husband died several years ago. I never expect a man to make love to me again. I don't miss the sex per se. After all, there are perfectly good alternatives. Sex isn't all there is about making love, however. I miss the touch of his hand, his scent, that wonderful feeling of closeness afterwards when I snuggled against his shoulder, and he held me. I think those tender moments are the only time men really let down their guards.

One of my male friends says all men really want is to

roll over and go to sleep. I never felt that.

Since he died, I've missed the casual touch of his hand on my hair as he passed behind my chair, the comfortable kisses in the morning and evening, knowing that I could reach out at night and touch his sleeping body. Fireworks are delightful, but fleeting. The constant awareness of another human being to whom you matter, and who matters to you, is not.

I miss the shared memories most of all.

I've decided this is a normal stage of my life. I am over sixty, after all. How much over is none of your business. Men my age are bedding twenty-five year olds. I am a grandmother, an incompetent but enthusiastic gardener, a voracious reader, and I have a wonderful circle of friends, mostly widows or what used to be called *spinsters*. Nasty word.

At my age in most societies I would either be considered fodder for the wolves and leopards or a wise woman imparting arcane knowledge to my tribe.

Wise I am not. And the last time I checked, north Georgia was fresh out of leopards and wolves, thank God. So I have taught myself contentment.

Or so I thought.

Why Carlyle Payton couldn't leave me happily doddering toward my grave, I don't know. He is, after all, a good ten years younger than I am. An old friend, a colleague I knew casually when I was still teaching at the University of Tennessee. He is a world-renowned botanist. We met again over the Bigelow County garden club contest, in which my poison garden beat out Ardaleen Hamilton Bigelow's illicit opium poppies and won the contest for Mossy Creek.

When Carlyle called me a couple of months later and took me to dinner, I figured he was being kind to a lonely old lady. We had a great time, and have continued to enjoy dinners, movies and plays at the university. We have become real friends. I thought that was enough.

Not that I feel old. Inside, I suspect we never age past sixteen. If I look younger than my age, it's not by forty years, so I don't fit into those twenty-somethings men are after.

The age difference isn't actually that important. The gulf between thirteen and twenty is as wide as the Grand Canyon. Between forty-five and sixty-five—once we are all adults—the gulf is more like a tiny creek that can be stepped over.

I am not concerned with the morality, either. We are both consenting adults. My issue is esthetics. I have a friend who spends two weeks each year in a nudist club. She is my age and probably wears a size twenty-two. The other nudists are equally ordinary. She says it doesn't matter because the naked human body is a beautiful thing.

Not necessarily. Frankly, the mind boggles. I probably look pretty good for my age, but I do not look twenty. My belly is not flat, my boobs are not perky, and I have enough cellulite to stuff a mattress—well, at least a sofa cushion.

I am amazed when women on television and in the movies strip and jump on men they met twenty minutes earlier. They are absolutely certain the guys will be receptive. Granted, the women are generally young and beautiful, but even at twenty I would never have had the nerve.

Now, frankly, the thought of revealing my naked body to a man, any man, goes way beyond boggling my mind.

Not that Carlyle's a great beauty, either. He's a couple of inches shorter than I am, and although he's not what I would call fat, he's *burly*. Good word.

He wears an aging tweed jacket and rotates a couple of silk *Repp* ties that have been cleaned so many times the stripes are downright pastel. He doesn't trim his gray beard often enough, and what hair that remains on his head is tonsured like a monk's.

But men never seem to be concerned about their looks. Someone, I think it was Noel Coward, said, with regard to sex, that things should have been organized better. I have never understood voyeurs. I've seen my share of porn—it was all the rage on the campus for a while. I think watching other people have sex is hysterically funny. Like viewing copulating frogs.

Unfortunately, the last time we had dinner, I was stunned to discover that my friend and colleague had undergone a sea change in some mysterious way. When he took my hand, and stared too long into my eyes, I found that my juices still flowed, my heart was capable of speeding up on its own, my throat could still tighten, my skin could still heat up, and I could indeed want him to touch more than my hand.

I bolted like the lily-livered coward I am.

He, however, was amused and delighted by my response. And wise enough to let me go. For the moment.

I agreed to see him on Valentine's Day. He planned to fix me dinner at his apartment. We all know what *that* means.

What was I thinking when I agreed? Victoria's Secret can only do so much. It was Friday. Valentine's was Sunday. Could I lose twenty pounds and have my thighs liposuctioned in two days?

To top it off, I had to spend the weekend hosting a young man from the stranded circus. He did something that entailed soaring around on ropes. When Ida called to solicit my guest room she said he performed aerial ballet. It's not trapeze. The fact that a young man should be billeted on me, a single woman, showed that our mayor and everyone else in Mossy Creek thought of me as sexually safe.

No doubt he would, too.

Eula Mae

The old gas stove heated the kitchen to a comfortable eighty-five degrees, and I sat snugly against it in my favorite chair, silver mixing bowl between my knees, my great granddaughter Estelle looking intently into the bowl.

Big Band music filled the room with cheery melodies that always lifted my spirits, interrupted intermittently by Bert Lymon on the radio. WMOS, the Voice of Mossy Creek, dictated much of my afternoon activities.

I loved the music but my personal highlight was the Bereavement Report. Bert or his wife, Honey, read the weekly obituaries from the *Mossy Creek Gazette* and the *Bigelow Daily Reporter*. Between those two they covered the newly dead from one end of Bigelow County to the other. There was always a good funeral to attend, although now my friends were mostly dead and those that were left were dropping like flies. Man, was I jealous.

Today I was especially perky because I had two viewings and a memorial service to attend, so I was baking twice my usual amount of buttermilk biscuits, and Bert had just said he was going to play some Louis Armstrong. Life didn't get any better than saying 'See ya, later,' to dead friends and listening to songs from dead Louis.

Estelle's head got too close to the bowl and I shook my spoon at her. She jumped back to her side of the table.

"Great Nan." She'd taken to calling me that. "I can't

determine how much you put in if you won't accurately measure."

"You can't write down a recipe, Estelle. You have to learn how to cook first, then duplicate it by cooking it again and again."

"Great Nan, I'm preserving history. Now what'd you just put in there?"

"About a cup of flour, then a little bit more, about a teaspoon of baking powder, a pinch of salt, a quarter or so of baking soda, a bit of sugar, a third cup of milk, and fold. Then I got to double it 'cause I got two funerals and a service to go to today. Oh, it was a fine day when you could sit aroun' that old TV set and watch Great Louis." I laughed, remembering how we used to push and pull to get the good seat. "Those were the good old days."

"Did you ever get to see him, Great Nan?"

"Like in person?" The thought made me blush like a schoolgirl. "Well, naw. I just can't imagine me seeing Great Louis in person. But I sho' used to dance to him. When I was in my thirties I used to move like water."

Estelle laughs, not mean like she's thinking what I'm saying is impossible, but like she just can't imagine me dancin' at all. "You, Great Nan? I thought you went to strict church. That you weren't allowed to dance."

I nodded, understanding where she was coming from. Her grandmother, my daughter, was still coming from there. Still kneeling at the church all day and night, but missing out on the precious afternoons of life. We used to be devout like that until I realized God gave us those afternoons, too.

"Chile, we worked all week and prayed everyday, and on Saturday night we put that hot comb to our hair cause we was goin' out on the town. Mayor Ida's grandma, Big Ida, would give us a few dollars for helping with her chores and she'd loan me her . . . well, never mind." I started dropping thick, bumpy dough onto the baking sheets.

"Loan you what? The gun? Her gun? What's the story behind that?"

"One story at a time, Estelle! You act like you're seven. Now pay attention. The stove can't stop itself. Did you set the timer?"

"No, ma'am."

"Well dead peoples don't like when they relatives get served burnt biscuits, I promise you that." We shoved them in the oven and watched them start to flatten before I took my seat again, the egg timer in my hand.

Bert is a man of his word and he starts playing Louis. "We'd go down to this little hole in the wall called the Backdoor. It was a *roadhouse*." I gave the word some drama.

"You weren't offended by that?" Estelle wanted to know, her eyes earnest. Youngun's are so curious about everybody hurting everybody else's feelings now. Back then, that was all we had and when me and Chicken and the rest of my girls got together, all we wanted to do was visit and dance.

"No, Chile. It was like a great big birthday party every weekend. I paid my twenty-five cent admission and I would dance until my feet hurt."

Estelle rubbed my hand, her smile reminding me how pretty mine used to be. "Great Nan, that sounds absolutely lovely. I bet Mossy Creek was never the same."

"Yes, Chile, it was a special time and place then and now. Not many places back then where a girl my color was able to fit in so easy and feel that comfortable. I always say there's magic in the Creek. Magic in the water. Oh, Bert. What's gotten into him, interrupting Louis?"

"All right, folks, who among you can host a guest in your home this weekend? We've got the *Cirque d'Europa* bus broken down on Bigelow Road," Bert announced. "And unfortunately, it's going to take a day or two to get the parts needed to fix it. Being the neighborly Creekites that we are, we need good citizens to open their homes and welcome these slightly different, but harmless strangers into your homes. So if you're willing and able to accommodate a pair of performers, please come and collect your houseguests. Mayor Ida and the town council thank you, and Happy Valentine's Day this Sunday."

Being that I'm 101, I can't move as fast as I'd like, but I feel quite springy most days, although all my movements have about scared Estelle to death. I sprang out of my chair.

"Great Nan, what are you doing? Having a heart attack? Do I need to drive you? What's going on?"

"Shhh, Estelle. Nothing is wrong. I'm just going to get me some circus people. I always wanted to be in the circus. This is a great day in Mossy Creek history, and I'm not about to miss it."

Why did Estelle look like the eagle statue that had tipped over at the post office during the blizzard of 1922? 'Cept she kept blinking and her lips were moving. "Circus people, Great Nan? Grandma isn't going to like this one bit."

"Aw, my daughter's a stick in the mud. She won't be happy about it, no. Especially when she finds out they're sleepin' in her room."

The buzzer went off for the biscuits. "Hurry. We got to drop these off and get to that bus before all the good ones are gone."

"Great Nan, they're people, not apples." Estelle moved quickly while she talked, transferring biscuits to packing bowls. "You wanted to be in the circus? Why? The elephants stink, people walking on stilts. The whole idea scares me to death."

"Girl, be scared when you know you got the wrong end of a gun chasing you. People with makeup on, handing you balloons? I say hidey ho! Where's my coat and hat? I'd better call Mr. Wiley and remind him Sunday is Valentine's."

Estelle's grin was mischievous. I do wish she'd get a boyfriend. If I can get one, anybody can! "Great Nan, you called him yesterday."

"So what? I'm trying to line up the right present. Now you stay out of grown folks business and get the car. Today just went from being nothing special to right nice."

Harry

The sun had already disappeared behind Colchik as I wended my way home. The mountain's shadow crept eastward across the valley toward Mossy Creek. Dusk was settling beneath the mountain's thick blanket of hardwoods, though it was still more than an hour before full dark. What little warmth the mid-February day had provided was vanishing, quickening my footsteps. As if I needed a reason to hurry home besides the sure knowledge that if Josie wasn't already there, she would be soon.

I'd worked all day with an abstracted air of anticipation. Valentine's Day was Sunday.

The holiday had never meant much to me. Scientists are not the most romantic of men, generally speaking. This, however, was Josie's and my first Valentine's as husband and wife, and I knew what it meant to her. She'd been bustling about happily all week. We hadn't made any specific plans, other than promising to not let work, family or friends interfere. We were going to spend the entire weekend alone. Together.

The possibilities made my blood sing.

As I rounded the last bend in the trail, I saw no smoke wafting from the chimney rising above the white clapboard farmhouse nestled at the edge of a mountain meadow. Josie hadn't made it home yet. Part of me was disappointed, though she wasn't due for another half hour.

Oh well. Now I could have the small, drafty old house warm when she walked through the door.

After our honeymoon cruise last June, we'd settled into Josie's grandparents' house at the western-most edge of the McClure farm in Bailey Mill. The four-room house had been built by Josie's great-grandfather around 1895 for his bride from Dahlonega, Josephine Mayfield, Josie's name-sake. The house had been updated somewhat through the years. The most notable addition being a bathroom at one end of the back porch. Even so, the house had been empty since Josie's grandmother died three years ago. According to Josie's father, John, the house wasn't worth the money it cost to keep it up. So even before she died, Granny McClure's house had started a slow descent into just another of the decaying structures that dotted Southern landscapes.

One of the puzzling oddities about Southern culture, to me. Why not tear the structures down instead of letting them turn into rotten, snake-infested rat traps?

Our old farmhouse wasn't to the rotting stage yet. At least the plumbing and electricity still worked—on good days. Because my work is on the mountain and Josie's work is in town, we had to live somewhere in between. This house was convenient and free, so we'd decided to live here until we could find one more suitable. We did what we could to make it livable, but Josie deserved better.

Much better. Something with a Martha Stewart-inspired kitchen, at the very least.

Reminded of one surprise I'd planned for the weekend, I smiled smugly as I stored my backpack in the utility box on the back porch, then went back down the steps for a load of firewood.

I'd just lit the fire in the Franklin stove—the only source of heat for the house—when I heard Josie's SUV speeding up the drive. By the amount of gravel I could hear flying, I knew all was not well in Josie's world. Which mean all was not well in mine.

I closed the door on the stove and hurried outside. Josie's car door slammed as I reached the screen porch.

She saw me and planted her feet, arms akimbo, her purse swinging from her wrist. "Have you heard?"

I let the porch door close and headed down the worn wooden steps. "Heard what?"

"Valentine's weekend is shot!"

"Shot?" I stopped short and studied her flushed face. "Who shot it?"

"Mayor Walker!"

"Ida? I didn't know she hunted Cupids."

Her brown eyes narrowed. "Make fun if you want to, but we'll see how hard you're laughing at the clowns who are about to invade our house." With a huff, she pushed past me.

Or tried to. I grabbed her and pulled her into my arms. "I'd never make fun of you, my love. You're just so cute when you're angry."

"Cute? Me?" She was genuinely startled. "I've never—"

I smothered her words with a kiss.

She struggled against me for an instant then sank into my embrace.

Gratified that my touch could distract her, I ended the kiss and smiled down at her. "Explain, please, about the mayor shooting our weekend. Has she asked you to decorate town hall? With clowns?"

Reminded of her ire, she scrunched her face again. She pulled out of my arms and started up the steps. "I'm talking about real clowns, Harry. Circus clowns."

"Circus clowns?" I followed her. "What on earth are you talking about?"

"Mayor Walker called up to Swee Purla's shop about an hour ago. Something called '*Cirque d'Europa*' is touring the country. They were on their way from Atlanta to Tennessee when their bus broke down just outside Mossy Creek." Josie placed her purse on a rung of the coat rack beside the back door, then hung her red wool coat over it. Even with her dander up, she remained organized. "The performers have no place to stay, so the mayor is calling around town, asking Creekites to put them up until the bus is repaired. That could take all weekend."

"So you volunteered us for a couple of clowns." I was not surprised that my Josie had stepped forward. Southern hospitality was mother's milk to her. "*Cirque d'Europa*? That's a high-class act, as circuses go."

"Actually, I don't know who we're getting. I told the mayor that we don't have much room, but she was so grateful for any bed, she didn't mind. I couldn't bring myself to say no."

I pulled her back into my arms. "Of course you couldn't."

She lifted her chin. "You don't know how badly I wanted to tell Mayor Ida where she could stick her old clowns. Or bearded ladies. Or lion tamers. Or whatever it is we'll be getting."

"Josie!" I was truly shocked. I had never heard my

wife speak like this. Usually, she was the first one to offer hospitality. "Y'all come" wasn't just a platitude. It was a way of life.

"Well, it's Valentine's, Harry! Our first together as a couple. And our house is so small. Where are we going to put them?"

"In the guest room you decorated so beautifully."

"Yes, and that guest room is just a thin wall away from the head of our bed. We won't be able to. . . I mean, they would certainly hear if we. . . Goshdarnit, Harry, it's Valentine's! I made *plans*."

I tightened my arms around her protectively. I would rather tear my own heart out than see the beautiful spirit of my wife in distress.

Even so, I was torn. Ever since the gracious people of Mossy Creek had shown me what the true spirit of kinship means by sacrificing their time and gardens so my Josie would have flowers at her wedding, I had thrown myself into that spirit of kinship. Josie and I attended church every time the doors opened. We went to town meetings, festivals, parties, and nearly every other function the town promoted. I wanted to do my part for the town that had given so much of themselves to us. I wanted to *be* part of it. For so long, I'd been part of nothing but my loneliness and my research. Then a whole town had opened its arms to me.

Now that town was asking us to share our home for a few nights to strangers passing through.

"How can we say no?" I asked softly.

I saw complete understanding in the soft brown eyes that searched mine. Josie knew me intimately, every hope and fear and secret I'd ever harbored.

She drew her hand down my face. "Harry. . ."

"How about your parents? They have several empty

rooms, now that you're gone."

Josie shook her head. "I already thought about that. They're sick."

"Sick?"

"Stomach flu. Mama called me this morning at work, to warn me not to come over this weekend. Daddy was sick all last night, and Mama was coming down with it this morning." Josie made a rueful face. "To my utter shame, I felt the tiniest bit glad when she told me, knowing it meant there would be no danger of them dropping by this weekend. Talk about instant karma!"

I squeezed her gently. She saw no dichotomy in being a steadfast Presbyterian who studied Zen philosophy. And to his credit, Reverend Hollingsworth didn't, either. They'd had several lively discussions.

"Do we need to bring them anything?" I asked.

Josie shook her head. "They can't keep anything down. I talked with Mama just before I left work. She doesn't want us coming by. At least not tonight. I'll drop by tomorrow to check on them. I'm sure I can slip away from our guests for an hour or so."

"Josie, if you really don't want guests this weekend, I'll call the mayor and make some excuse."

She sighed heavily and shook her head. "Mama would kill me."

"Sounds like LuLynn is too sick to kill a cockroach."

Josie smiled lovingly as she took my face between her hands. "Oh, Harry, I do love you. But you know as well as I do that I can't let you make our excuses. Neither one of us could enjoy a romantic weekend, knowing we were letting everyone down."

"You're sure?"

She kissed me and let go. "Mama didn't bring me up to turn my back on anyone who needs a good dose of

Southern hospitality. Why, if I did that, I might as well be a *Yankee*. Besides, when I hold up my mantra beside the decision, I know I have to put a smile on my face and fluff the pillows on the guest bed."

"To which mantra are you referring? I've heard you mention about five million."

She raised a brow at my exaggeration. "My hospitality mantra, of course. 'What would Martha do?'"

I couldn't resist teasing her more. "Martha Stewart is a Yankee."

She shook her head patiently, as if gently setting a child straight. "Not in her heart-of-hearts, Harry. Where it counts, Martha is as Southern as cheese grits casserole."

I grinned. "Where are we picking up our clowns?"

"Mt. Gilead Methodist Church. And we need to get going." She turned toward the bedrooms. "Give me just a minute. I want to change into my jeans."

"And fluff the pillows."

"All right, then, *two* minutes."

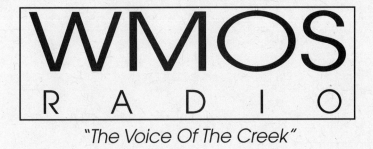

"The Voice Of The Creek"

Bert Lymon, here, with the latest news update on the stranded circus folks. It's gonna be a cold February night in Mossy Creek, but I'm happy to report our visitors have been parceled out to friendly homes for the evening. Only a few more are waiting to be picked up at the church. Take good care of them, Creekites!

FRIDAY NIGHT

The Circus Settles In

Chapter 2

Louise

My first thought was that this crazy *Cirque d'Europa* troop was circumventing the child labor laws. The tiny person who got out of our mayor's red Corvette couldn't be more than ten. Then she turned toward me with a broad smile on her face. And crinkles at the corners of her eyes. Her almond eyes. She swung her wealth of straight black hair away and reached out her hand to me. She was probably closer to thirty than to ten. But what a thirty! I wasn't in that good a shape when I was ten.

Mayor Ida nodded from the guest to me. "Louise, this is Wang Zhen. Zhen, meet Louise."

Oh, lord. "*Nihau,*" I said. The only word I know in Chinese is hello.

She laughed. "Actually, I answer to Lisa Wang. So kind of you to open your beautiful house to me for the weekend." She sounded like an English duchess.

"Oh—"

"I was born in Hong Kong," Lisa said and took my hand. "English was my first language. My family lives in Vancouver." Her hand felt like a chicken's foot. Tiny, but rough and muscular. She picked up a duffel bag almost as large as she from the tiny back seat of Ida's vintage Corvette. Ida and I traded an arched look. Mossy Creek's mayor was a young fifty, gorgeous, lean and able to leap tall buildings in a single bound, yet Lisa clearly impressed her. Even in the chill of a wintry mountain evening Lisa wore a sleeveless athletic shirt and jeans, and her muscles bulged.

A gymnast, then? I hadn't seen the circus, but I'd heard their acrobats and gymnasts were made entirely of elastic.

Then she pulled out a bundle of what looked like six-foot-long ivory sticks. She apparently intended to carry both them and the bag, but I took the duffel. I would undoubtedly bash the porch steps if I tried to carry the sticks.

She saw me looking at the sticks. "I'm a spinner as well as a gymnast," she said.

"Oh." What on earth was a *spinner*? Whatever it was, the equipment in the duffel weighed a ton. I managed to make it as far as the front hall, but I didn't attempt the stairs to the guestroom.

"May I leave my poles here?" Lisa asked. She leaned them carefully against the wall beside the door.

"Sure."

She picked up the duffel and looked at me expectantly. I led her upstairs.

"Oh, my, what a beautiful room!"

It was, actually. Charlie and I had redone my aunt's old Victorian cottage from top to bottom, nearly killing ourselves in the process. I told you Charlie wasn't lazy.

Our new master bedroom bath, kitchen, and den were downstairs. What had been the master bedroom upstairs had a brand new bath next door to it. I had furnished it in Victorian antiques, including a gigantic Lincoln bed.

From the foot of the stairs, Ida called, "Louise, I'll leave you and Lisa to get acquainted. Thanks again."

"Thank you so much, Mayor Walker," called Lisa from the doorway of her room.

I heard the front door close. Now it was just me and this tiny little woman with black hair that hung below her waist. Said waist being about the circumference of my forearm. She moved as though she hadn't a bone in that teensy body, but I'd seen her muscles. Spinners must apparently be strong enough to kick butt.

"You must be hungry," I said. "I admit I have no idea what to feed you, or what your schedule is, or even what you do. Does that sound too awful?"

"Not at all. Tonight I must rehearse if I can find someplace big enough. As to food, I eat anything."

"Even pimento cheese sandwiches?"

"I have no idea what pimento cheese is, but as I said, I am an omnivore. Like bears."

She was going to be the kind of houseguest I prefer. She moved into my kitchen as though she were coming home to her family from college. I pointed out the silverware drawer and the glass cupboard, and made the sandwiches. I made her two. She probably ate like the proverbial horse. Most athletes do.

"Please tell me what a spinner does," I asked after she had devoured one sandwich and started on the second. I was ready to start making her a third.

"This sandwich is wonderful," she said. "Your South has many wonderful dishes. Your barbecue is different from ours, and I could eat my weight in fried chicken."

"In your case, that would be *half* a chicken."

"I weigh more than I look. It is all muscle, you see."

"I'd barely noticed," I said, looking down at my ever-increasing stomach. And boobs. Two of them. Big ones. Was I soon to lose one? I had the crazy thought that if I were on chemo and radiation, I'd probably lose weight.

"A spinner puts up poles," Lisa explained, "then spins plates on top of them."

Ahah. "Oh, I've seen that. You keep running from plate to plate to keep them all going."

"We are a bit more complicated. I spin my poles on the soles of my feet and my chin and my forehead and my arms and my belly while I lie on my back. And I spin other objects, not simply plates. We wind it all into a story. The theme of our current show is life. *La Vie*, in French."

"Amazing. I could never even keep a single top going when I was a child."

She laughed. "I have been spinning and doing gymnastics since I was three-years old. I have practice."

"Three? In Hong Kong?"

"At first, then in Shanghai when I was five."

"Forgive me, but your parents moved from the Crown Colony to Shanghai on purpose?æ

"Not exactly. I moved. They remained. They acquired British passports, you see. We had been planning to move to Vancouver when the Communists took over Hong Kong."

"But meanwhile, you went to school in Shanghai? At five? Left your parents?" I'm sure I sounded as appalled as I felt.

She lowered her head. "I do not say it was not difficult. I saw my parents one week a year, but they wrote me often. They wanted me to succeed, you see, and they knew I had talent."

I thought of letting my daughter, Sarah, go off for fifty-one weeks a year at five. I would have slashed my wrists. Lisa sounded casual. "Didn't you miss them?"

She sighed and ate another quarter sandwich, then washed it down with iced tea. "Of course. I cried a great deal. It was extremely difficult. I was terribly lonely the first years, but young bones must be made flexible before they solidify or they will not be able to do this."

She put down her sandwich, and right there in my kitchen she bent over backwards until her head was between her legs. "The spine, you see. Sooner or later I will grow too old to do that. I am only twenty-seven."

I had figured she was maybe twenty. "I couldn't put my head face-backwards between my knees when I was a fetus."

"Ah, Louise, one of my teachers was nearly eighty. She could still do that, but someone had to help her up afterwards."

"I can't even touch my toes."

She laughed. Lisa and I seemed to have made an immediate connection. We sat at the kitchen counter while she wolfed down another couple of sandwiches and we split at least a gallon of iced tea.

She saw the pictures of my family on the wall, so we talked about family.

She was divorced from one of the backstage crew at the circus. No children. "I would like children before I am too old," she said. "Every Chinese woman wants at least one son to look after her in her old age."

"In this culture it's the daughters who look after the old folks," I said. Then I burst into tears.

"Louise, what have I said?" She slid off her stool and came to me. "You do not feel well?"

Sometimes it's easier to talk to a complete stranger.

So I told her. Not just about the mammogram, but about my worries about Charlie.

"But you say he loves you. Surely he would not desert you."

"He won't want to, but he's totally helpless when it comes to dealing with the scutwork of life. He could never discipline our daughter, either. He throws up at the sight of blood. Everybody told us when we put in the new master bathroom downstairs we needed two sinks. Charlie said we didn't need but one because we don't even brush our teeth together. Last year when he got stuck in the toilet—that's a whole other story—he nearly died from embarrassment even to have me try to get him out. I didn't think he'd survive having half the fire department dislodge him."

Lisa's eyes grew wider with my every word. I could tell she was dying to ask about Charlie's getting stuck, but was too polite. "What did he say when you told him about the mammogram?"

"Good grief! I haven't told him, and I don't intend to."

"Louise, if you go into hospital, you will have to tell him."

"I know that. But not until then."

"So you bear this burden alone? How will you continue to be cheerful?"

"Don't you say 'the show must go on?'"

She continued to shake her head. "He will be very angry that you did not tell him."

"Only if I *have* to tell him."

"He will be very angry that you do not trust him. And even more angry that you are sick. I think you have allowed him to believe you are indestructible. He will not like to think you could die."

"So this is my fault?"

"You have spoiled him. Now if worst comes to worst, you must teach him to be alone."

"What about teaching myself how to die? How come I even have to train Charlie when I'm about to kick off?"

"You are not. But do you not see that this is a wake-up call? If you love him, then trust him."

I just sighed and fixed her another sandwich.

Peggy

His name was Marcel Desjardins, and he was possibly the most beautiful male creature of any genus and species that I had ever seen. He wasn't tall, but if the Michelangelo *David* and the Apollo *Belvedere* were combined and made flesh, they wouldn't hold a candle to Marcel. His hair was long and waved well below his shoulders, and his eyes were a strange, dark chestnut flecked with gold. I supposed he must shave his body for his act, because so far as I could tell, he had no hair on his arms, not even down. That's all I saw of him, or expected to see.

When we were introduced, he bent over and kissed my hand.

"Madame, you are so kind to take me in," he said. No French accent, despite the French name. That surprised me. The French generally pride themselves on maintaining their accents even after forty years in the United States. I figured he was probably Canadian, since the accent was nothing like Cajun.

I simpered. I know I did. I could feel my face turning puce.

Dashiell, my evil cat, and his three adopted cat children eddied around Marcel's ankles purring like lawnmowers.

They usually hid under the sink with strangers. I explained to Marcel that they are indoor cats. Too many things outside can make mincemeat of them. I also told him about my daughter and granddaughter.

"Such a beautiful house," he said. "And the garden! I do miss my garden."

The house is an old mock Tudor with dark woodwork and too many bookshelves that hold too many books. It's shabby, but comfortable.

"I wouldn't think you'd be able to have a garden, the way you travel," I said. I had offered him iced tea or a beer.

"Tea, please. I don't drink, except the occasional glass of wine." He thumped his six-pack abs. "I must keep in good shape. My wife would be extremely annoyed if I fell from the rope and broke my neck before I could get home to her."

"Where is home?"

"Could we sit on your deck? It is not too cold here for the middle of February. You have crocuses blooming. We still have snow."

I grabbed my jacket and followed him outside. He sat on the glider, leaned back and seemed to savor the air. "My home is in Montreal."

"Your wife doesn't travel with you?"

"Usually she does, but we are expecting our first baby in a couple of months. She thought it better not to travel so much."

"My dear man, your wife is seven months pregnant and you're not there?"

He shrugged. A very Gallic shrug. "One must make a living. I am very good at what I do. Jeanne works in the circus office. She is a chartered accountant. A C.P.A. That's where we met. She's on a leave of absence until after the baby comes. Next season, we won't be separated."

"The baby will travel with you?"

"It is always like that in circus families. Most everyone who is with it is second, third, some even fourth or fifth generation. For us there is no other possible life. By the time I am too old, perhaps I shall have child to take over for me and I can become a coach."

"But you have a house?"

"For the off season. Then I am a gardener. I grow orchids and sweat."

"Orchids? I am impressed. I have problems growing zinnias."

He slipped off his loafers, then glanced up at me for belated permission. He was wearing heavy socks.

I nodded. "Although you may get frostbite."

"This is practically summertime."

"I grew up wearing shoes only during the school year," I said. "The soles of my feet were tough as leather when I was a child."

"Mine, too. I am like a dancer in the air. My feet are always miserable. I remove my shoes every chance I get." He leaned his beautiful head back and closed his eyes. "Orchids aren't much more difficult to grow than zinnias, actually, and the blooms last much longer."

Having absorbed all my lore about orchids from *Nero Wolfe* mysteries, I didn't believe him for a minute.

"I do have lilac bushes as tall as your house," he said.

"Too balmy in Mossy Creek for lilacs, I'm afraid. Our summers are very southern."

"But you have a beautiful lawn, and azaleas. I should like to see them in bloom."

"Not for at least another month, maybe longer."

"Would you mind showing me your yard? Where the

flowers will be?"

I was delighted, if a bit overwhelmed. He, for his part, seemed to be genuinely enchanted by my little walled secret garden, once the site of my poison plants, now seeded with wildflowers that my granddaughter planted in place of the deadly nightshade and death-angel mushrooms.

He wandered over the yard. "Our garden is very small. This is nearly a farm."

"Tell me about it."

"We do not have such trees as these," Marcel said, as he patted one of my giant water oaks.

"I thought Quebec was covered with trees."

"Oh, it is, but not these monsters. A great many pines. And no magnolias at all. Nor hollies."

Suddenly he took hold of the trunk of the tree and walked up it like a Tongan warrior up a palm tree to sit on a fat branch above my head. I gaped up at him.

"I loved climbing trees when I was a boy," he said with a laugh. "Not that much different from climbing a tent pole. A bit rougher, perhaps, and not as straight." He straddled the branch. "Lovely view, Madame. You should build a tree house for your granddaughter."

Now it was my turn to laugh. "I've been trying to get a swing hung up for her for nearly a year. My son-in-law never seems to have time to hang the chains, and Lord knows I don't dare do it. I don't climb ladders."

He casually swung from the branch and dropped at my feet. "Then let that be my housekeeping present to you, Madame. I will be delighted to hang your swing."

"Oh, I couldn't ask you . . . "

"Please, it would be my pleasure."

Actually, I had all the fixings for the swing in my garage. I'd had them for months—heavy chains, the already drilled and painted wooden seat, the eye bolts and such. Since

I seldom used the tools my husband left me, the electric drill was always charged, so that was no problem.

"In a small circus, everyone helps maintain the tents and equipment," he told me as he hunted up the long bit that would drill through the limb of the tree. "Each performer checks his own rigging. That way, if I fall, the responsibility is mine and no one else's. We have no performing animals to tend, but we have an enormous quantity of rigging. Ah, this should do it." He came up with the perfect bit. "A big branch will have to be drilled from both top and bottom." He hefted the chains. "And this should hold a small elephant. How old is your granddaughter, Madame?"

"Four-and-a-half."

"Then I will find a branch strong enough so that she can swing safely until she leaves for college."

"I certainly don't want anything to break."

"We will test it afterwards."

"Huh. You can test it. Not me."

"Of course you will test it."

"Young man, I haven't been on a swing since I was twelve years old."

He shrugged. Another very Gallic shrug. It showed his French background more than his syntax did. "As you wish."

I helped carry the tools down my yard toward my largest water oak.

He pointed. "There. That branch should be perfect."

"Lord, no," I said. "It's higher than the Empire State Building."

Again that shrug. "But the chains you have are more than adequate. The branch is straight and very strong. It will not bend or break."

"She's four-and-a-half, Marcel," I said. "I was thinking a

nice, dinky little swing that barely clears the ground."

This time I didn't get a shrug, I got a frown. "Nonsense. She will grow. She will want to fly . . . "

"She will fall off and break her four-and-a-half-year-old neck, young man. She's my only grandchild."

"I promise you she will not fly too high. Let me try, Madame. Then if you don't like it, we'll pick a lower branch." He glowered up at the tree as though challenging it to dispute him. "But that is the only truly perfect branch for the balance."

I threw up my hands.

He climbed the tree with the same casual ease he'd used before. Once he'd straddled the branch, he dropped a rope down. I attached the drill and up it went. In a moment he began to drill.

It was the middle of winter, the sunlight was fading, and I had a barefoot Adonis up in my tree.

"Mother, what on earth are you doing?"

With the noise from the drill, I hadn't heard my daughter, Marilee Bigelow, and my granddaughter, Josie, walk around the house. I must have started like a guilty thing disturbed. As I recall, Hamlet said that about his father's ghost. I suspect parents have been starting guiltily at the sudden appearance of their grown children since Neanderthal days.

"Grammie, Grammie, it's my swing!" My blonde, leggy grandchild flew at me and yanked the wooden seat I'd been holding out of my hands. "You're fixin' it."

"Indeed we are, Miss Priss," said I.

"Way up there?" Marilee said. "Mother, that's too high. Are you insane? It's February! And who is that up in your tree, anyway?"

Marcel leaned down and saluted. "Marcel Desjardins, Madame, and Mademoiselle. *A votre service.*"

"Oh." I have seldom seen my daughter struck dumb, but the sight of Marcel with his hair tumbling and his smile flashing would have struck the Delphic Oracle dumb. Then, I swear to God, she simpered.

"It's set very high off the ground," she said, but without much emphasis.

"But one doesn't have to swing very high on a high swing, does one, Mademoiselle?" He winked at my granddaughter.

Josie clapped her hands. "I wouldn't swing too high, Mommy. I promise I wouldn't. And not without you or Daddy or Grammie here to push me. Oh, please, Mommy, please! I've wanted my swing forever. You promised."

"You see?" Marcel said. "You have a most obedient *petite fille*." Since Marcel hadn't used one bit of French before Sarah's appearance, I knew he was trying to charm my daughter, but do you think I interfered and told him to knock it off? Hardly.

And if he thought the *petite fille* was obedient, he didn't know my grandchild. She's a sweetheart, but she is both opinionated and obstinate. I wonder where she gets that?

I could tell Josie was ready and willing to launch into whine-and-wheedle mode, but with Marilee so mesmerized by Marcel, it wasn't necessary.

What was necessary, however, was for me to practically shoe horn her and Josie out of the yard, and only with a promise that Josie could come back after church on Sunday to swing, but only under adult supervision. She didn't want to go, but she did.

"What did you want, Marilee?" I asked as I leaned against her open car window.

"What? Uh—I swear I can't remember."

She drove away, with Josie waving goodbye merrily.

Eula Mae

The bickering in the backseat between the circus people was like riding through a field of onions. They look pretty from the side of the road, but once you're among them they stink so bad you just wish you were dead.

The woman, Roxie, seemed especially upset. She kept screeching at the man, her partner, named Cowboy, in some language that sounded like a duck honkin'. I couldn't turn around anymore on account of Estelle had me strapped into the front seat with the seat belt that doubles as a strait jacket for super senior citizens—that's us seniors over a hundred.

Wind from the long-legged woman's hand kept creating a breeze on the back of my head and I was getting quite upset. I have some pretty dandy wigs I'd inherited from Harriet Mobley when she'd passed on two weeks earlier, but I'd forgotten to put one on in all the excitement. When I die I sure do hope God recognizes me with the thirty-six strands of hair I have left, because sometimes I'd look in the mirror and don't know myself.

I turned just enough to see Cowboy scrunched up in the corner with an expression on his face that said he'd rather be shoveling manure than in the car with Roxie. I had to shout over Roxie, who had now started to count some kind of list on her fingers—his shortcomings, I suspected—when I realized what was going on between them.

Although Cowboy looked like he got stuck in the bottom with a pitchfork, his eyes said he loved her. But he was holding back and it was obvious she didn't feel too happy about that.

"She wants to get married and he doesn't," I said to Estelle.

"Great Nan, how do you know? They've been in the car all of ten minutes."

"I've been in love five or six times, Estelle. Might not have no degree in it, but I don't have to speak their language to know what they're talking about. Besides, she keeps pointing to her third finger, and she ain't got no ring."

"I think it'd be better if we just stayed quiet," Estelle said, unconvinced. "Would you mind terribly if I sped up just another five miles per hour? If we stay at a steady twenty-five like we're going, by the time we get home we'll have missed the Bereavement Report on WMOS and *Oprah*."

"Oprah!" they shouted from the back, and I was able to see them nodding, because their heads were right beside mine in the rearview mirror.

Estelle and I turned our heads slowly, staring, as if a dead person had come back to life.

"Oprah," they repeated together.

"Well, how do you like that?" I said to Estelle. "I'm changing my name to Oprah."

"Oprah," they screamed again as we turn into the driveway.

I couldn't help being just a little miffed. Here I was, doing the Lord's work and taking circus people into my home and how do they show their thanks but by yelling another woman's name?

Now I know Oprah is a big who-ha lady with all her giving, but I bet she ain't never had circus people stay in her house *and* fed them buttermilk biscuits made with her own hands.

To be honest I know I got her beat there. I heard down at the Press-N-Go she don't even know the way to the kitchen in her own house. Yessiree, that's what I heard.

My house, *all* five rooms, including the bathroom, is built right around the kitchen. You can't miss it! I know I'm luckier than her.

I decided to try an experiment. "Eula Mae!" I yelled at the top of my voice.

Roxie and Cowboy didn't make a peep.

"Eula Mae," I belted.

Again, nothing.

"What kind of people are they, Estelle?"

"I don't know. Some kind of Asian and African, possibly. Since they don't speak English, it's not like we can ask."

An African circus performer named Cowboy and an Asian girl named Roxie. I shook my head in wonder. I'm an old black lady who's seen it all. The world sure is gettin' smaller.

The arguing escalated again.

I'd had enough. "You two are the darndest people I've ever met. What language do you speak, boy?"

"Great Nan, you don't have to shout at him. He can hear, he just can't understand you."

"How do you know he can't understand me, Estelle? He might speak that clicking language like that man in that movie, and I understood *him* pretty well."

Estelle looked at me skeptically and wisely kept her opinion to herself.

"I knew when he was going to run or jump," I went on.

"He ran and jumped through the whole movie, Great Nan. He was a bushman."

Cowboy and Roxie's voices escalated again and I turned around in my seat. "Stop it right now. You might want to marry him and he might not want to marry you, but you don't have to wake the dead to get your point across. Now, shhh!"

They understood enough to stop, but the second

Estelle parked the car in my driveway they were out and the woman went up the tree in the front yard.

It always took me a few minutes to get myself out of the car, but watching Roxie, I had to say I was right jealous. I didn't bother to stare long because I had two things on my mind and one was sitting on my porch with some pretty red roses.

"How you, old girl?"

"Right fine, Mr. Wiley. It'll be just a minute before I can receive company."

Estelle knew my first pit stop after a trip is the ladies room, and we got me there in record time. When I came back, I had on one of Harriet's wigs and some lipstick that I got in my Christmas stocking last year.

Unfortunately, my circus guests were really showing off. They were *both* up my tree by then, arguing like banshees, but as they argued they swung from limbs, making what seem to be impossible leaps possible, and landed like butterflies on branches.

"Shhh," I said loudly. They got quiet but they didn't stop flinging themselves around, Roxie moving effortlessly, Cowboy following her higher.

"He loves her," Mr. Wiley told me, but I already knew that. "He keeps reaching for her, but she moves away."

"She's tired of waiting. Women get like that, Mr. Wiley."

"You trying to tell me something, Ms. Eula Mae?"

"Ain't no trying to, Mr. Wiley. If I want you to know something, I will sho' spit it out. I'm a hundred and one. I can't save things for tomorrow. Right now, I've got to get these people out of my tree and patched up."

Estelle came out on the porch with glasses of sweet tea. It was cold, getting dark, but she brought out the iced tea.

"Why do you have to do it, Great Nan?" Estelle handed

Mr. Wiley a plate with a buttermilk biscuit on it. We both looked at his hands and they were steady. Sometimes they move so quickly with the Parkinson's, I'm reminded of a hummingbird's wings, but that evening they were steady, just like Mr. Wiley's temperament, no matter his condition.

I decided to let them in on my plan. "I got to get them together because we gon' have a wedding Sunday at four, and then I'm leaving town with the circus."

Mr. Wiley gave me the biggest grin, and I thought the Lord done made the sun rise twice in one day. But then I looked at Estelle and she was all drawn up and pinched just like her grandmother. "Great Nan, this is your worst idea ever."

Then there was a piercing scream and branches started to hit the ground.

Being that I'm a hundred and one, I can't take too many surprises, so seeing Roxie hanging from Cowboy's hand from high-up in my tree is like being thirty all over again and seeing the man I shot with Big Ida's gun telling me to give him my pocketbook. I gave it to him and a hole in his kneecap for his trouble.

But when you add my sixty-six year-old granddaughter, Clara, screaming at the top of her lungs at my guests, well, every creature great and small should take cover.

I got up and used my walker to go down the handicap ramp. "Clara, quit that caterwauling'. You done scared the rain back into the clouds."

"Call the cops!" She said it so loud, you could see her tonsils flappin'.

"Come on down, Cowboy, Roxie," I said. "She's harmless."

"You know these people?" Clara asked me, her face saying I better not. That's the thing about Clara. I enjoy annoying the heck out of her.

I poked my chest out. "I got one better. I've invited them to stay with us for a couple days."

"We don't have room for company, Nana. The extra bedroom has a leak and the house isn't ready for guests."

"That's all right. They gon' stay in your room, so we don't need the guest room."

"What!" she screeched.

Cowboy and Roxie dismounted the tree with barely a sound.

Roxie stormed off around the side of the house with Estelle running after her, leaving Cowboy with the rest of us. He walked along as if he was invited into our family disagreement.

Clara kept looking at him strangely, but Cowboy didn't get the fact that he was unwanted. He nodded along, his hands caught behind his back, his face very sympathetic. Clara couldn't speak; she was so stunned. I just loved this guy.

"Mr. Wiley done fell asleep, so there's no time like the present for me and Cowboy to have a good long talk. Clara, make yourself scarce. I got business to tend to and not a lot of time."

Suddenly I went blind for a second, then realized Harriet's wig shifted. Her head was bigger than mine. I used my fingers to put the wig back in place and was grateful the incident wasn't a test run on death. It's just rude to go mid-sentence.

"Cowboy, why won't you marry Roxie?"

The man started speaking in a language I don't understand. It sounded foreign not something where I could pick up a few words, but he did do some of the clicking and I sho' do get *that*. I listened to his tone and heard the melody of his words, and I began to understand his heart. "You can't marry her but it's not 'cause you don't love her."

He nodded and sighed and hugged me. Finally, someone understands.

"Son, life doesn't always give you fifth and sixth chances."

Cowboy walked under my apple tree and found some dried-up winter apples. He pried the seeds out. He buried them and began to gesture and show me how love grew the seeds and now it's a blooming tree.

This was his love for Roxie. He loves her with his heart, but for whatever reason things with them have to remain the same.

"The tree grows, Cowboy. It bears fruit, but when it's not nurtured, eventually it will die. You can't expect it to stay the same. Nothing does, unless it's not real. Is your love for her real?"

He didn't answer. I got tired and gestured toward the house. Cowboy helped me inside and when he didn't see Roxie, he went in search of her. By then it was getting dark.

I found Estelle at the kitchen table writing on her computer. "Where's Roxie?"

"She mumbled something about 'being a good wife' and went to get her bag out of the car."

"So she speaks English?"

"Great Nan, that's a major overstatement. She says a few words here and there. I think she understands more than she speaks. I was thinking we'd get dinner started and then maybe they'd get tired and want to settle down for the night. This whole thing will probably blow over by morning."

I really do love Estelle. She's reasonable, just like me.

"Where's your grandmother?"

110

Estelle looked down at her computer. "She said she's not wanted here so she went to Ms. Mary Kathleen's house down the road."

"Good," I said. "No room for her negativity anyway. We have a lot to accomplish and a wedding to plan. Do you notice Oprah never has anybody on her show that tells her no? Maybe I should write to her and get a few tips."

"Or call," Estelle encouraged, smiling.

"I think I'll do just that. I'm sure she can use some tips from me on how to live to be a hundred and one. All those fancy pants doctors and none of them can tell her that."

"You've got them beat there, Great Nan."

"You bet your socks I do."

"What are you going to say to her about chewing snuff?"

"That was just a phase. Those ladies in the home were doin' it and it was peer pressure, pure and simple."

"So you won't do it again?"

"Naw. Those girls died. Ain't no fun doin' it alone."

"I guess I'd better go wake Mr. Wiley before he gets frost on his head." Mr. Wiley was dozing on the porch, still holding my roses.

"Definitely." I looked for my lipstick. "I still ain't got my Valentine's Day sugar yet."

At this moment, Estelle is like her grandma 'cause she covers her ears and goes outside.

I don't care. I got a boyfriend and none of the other women in my household do.

That makes me the prettiest peach in the bowl and I like that just fine.

Mr. Wiley comes inside and hurries to the bathroom. When he comes out, I can tell he's been in my Efferdent. He's smelling minty fresh. I give him a squinty eyed grin and shake my head cause I know what's comin'. Course

Harriet's wig shifts and I have to readjust again. The wig's red. Harriet was the tackiest red-headed old white woman in Mossy Creek. This wig's a mood killer as far as I'm concerned and probably the reason poor Harriet died a Miss instead of a Mrs.

The curtain flaps against the kitchen window and we see Cowboy and Roxie by my apple tree.

"He's holding her, but she's so stiff, she reminds me of my daddy's Sunday shirt," Mr. Wiley says.

"I think he's explaining his side, but she don't want to hear him."

"How you gon' get them married in two days, Ms. Eula Mae?"

"Mr. Wiley, that question's got a complicated answer. You see, the love is already there. I just got to get to the bottom of the why he won't. Lawd, this don't look so good. She's mad now."

Just as I think Roxie's going to walk away, they start doing mid-air flips and spins, running and jumping. This is where the real talking begins. They are doing something like an acrobatic ballet and it's quite pretty.

I don't think there's any rhyme or reason to it when suddenly Roxie slips, Cowboy catches her and they begin again. Every once in a while she falls or he slips, and I catch my breath. They push off each other, angry like, and I know this is how it has to be between them. They don't realize they won't get their rhythm until they agree on the course of their relationship.

They stay out in the yard still full dark settles and a cold moon rises. I call for Cowboy and Roxie, but they don't come.

"What are they doing?" Estelle asks, eating the bell pepper as fast as I can cut them up.

"Trying to come to an understanding," I tell her. "Now

look, you got to stop eatin'. Groceries don't fall out the sky."

The moon comes out from behind a cloud and I can see them again.

I make sweet potatoes, cabbage, cornbread, neck-bones, and we pull out a pie we'd made yesterday. The aroma of food brings the two inside, and they sniff the air like children.

Estelle hurries Roxie to the guest room and Cowboy heads to the toilet. That leaves me and Mr. Wiley alone to celebrate Valentine's Day. Even if it's not for two more days, we like to start early.

Finally I get my sugar, and boy is it sweet.

When the girls emerge from the guest room, I hardly recognize Roxie. She had war paint on her face before and was in a stretchy outfit. Now she's got on a regular dress. Heels and no make-up. Her black hair is down her back and she seems almost shy. Cowboy stares at her. When we all sit to eat, they are quiet, then Roxie pops up and starts to serve food to everyone. She's so graceful, and Cowboy notices every movement she makes.

Mr. Wiley and I watch this couple and he squeezes my hand under the table.

"She's a nice girl. Why won't you marry her?" Wiley asks Cowboy. "Do you love her?"

Roxie eats a little cabbage and puts her fork down, her gaze trained on Cowboy. "Do you love her?" Roxie repeats Wiley.

"Me?" Estelle says, helping her.

Roxie nods. "Do you love me?"

Cowboy seems intent on finishing his vegetables. "Yes."

We all clap. I don't know why. You can love a fish and not want to marry it.

"Marry me," Wiley says.

"Marry me," Roxie repeats.

"No, you, Eula Mae."

"No, you, Eula Mae," Roxie repeats, although she has the good sense to look confused.

"Mr. Wiley, are you doing what I think you're doing?" Estelle says, rising from her chair.

"Yes, Ms. Estelle. I'm asking for your Great Nan's hand in marriage and I'm waiting for an answer."

Mr. Wiley set the ring box on the table, and when Roxie sees it, her eyes fill with tears and she runs into the bedroom, closes the door and cries her eyes out.

I don't care. I'm grinning.

Harry

Full dark had fallen when we pulled into the parking lot of Mount Gilead Methodist Church. The broken-down bus was nowhere to be seen, but several trucks and a tractor-trailer I'd never seen before were lined up side-by-side in the parking lot, probably carrying all the equipment necessary to run a circus.

The church was lit like evening services were about to begin. Evidently Reverend Phillips had opened the doors so the poor stranded troupe could wait in relative warmth while they waited for townspeople to pick them up. Several stood outside the doors, smoking.

As I eased the Explorer into a space near the walk, the Abercrombies left the church with a young couple in tow.

"I wonder who Zeke and Eleanor have," Josie mused as she unhooked her seatbelt.

I switched off the ignition. "There's no way to know by

sight, is there? Circus performers look just like everybody else when they're out of costume." I smiled at her. "Let's go get our clowns."

"Harry, I told you—"

"I know, I know. We might have lion tamers."

"Well, no, Mayor Ida said the circus didn't have any animals."

"Bearded ladies, then?" I waggled my eyebrows. "Kinky."

Josie giggled. "Oh, Harry."

"Let's go in. I'm dying of curiosity."

I came around the SUV and opened Josie's door, then swallowed her hand in mine as we walked into the church.

The mayor was busy talking to Jayne Reynolds, who held her toddler, Matthew, in her arms. A young lady I didn't recognize was included in their circle. Most of the other people in the church sat wearily in the church pews. There weren't many circus people left, I noted with satisfaction. Creekites always come through.

Josie pulled me toward the mayor. We stopped just shy of the group to wait our turn, but Ida turned to beam at us.

"Ah, the newlyweds! Most gracious of you to volunteer!"

"Volunteer?" Josie asked sourly.

I squeezed her hand, then offered my other one to Ida. "We're happy to be part of it, Mayor."

Josie moved to Jayne's side, clucking Matthew under the chin. "Who do you have?"

Jayne looked down at the paper in her free hand. "Inga and Brigette Karlson. Ms. James says they're dancers. Swedish, right?"

The young woman nodded. She looked slightly akilter, as if dizzy. Mossy Creek has that effect on strangers. "That's right. They speak fluent English."

"Josie and Harold Rutherford, this is Quinn James," Mayor Ida said. "She's the manager of the *Cirque d'Europa*." Quinn, a pretty woman with tired eyes, smiled at me.

"Inga and Brigette have already gone outside to get their bags," Jayne said. "I'd better go collect them."

"See you later," Josie said.

"Thank you again!" the circus manager bid. She smiled wearily as she turned to us and shook Josie's hand, then mine. "Thank you for extending your hospitality. I know it's an imposition, especially since it's Valentine's weekend . . . "

"Don't think twice about that," Josie said. "We couldn't be happier to help. Our house is small, but certainly more comfortable than a church pew, even if the Methodists' *are* padded."

Ms. James nodded. "Mayor Walker told me about your house. That's why I'm assigning only one troupe member to you." She turned and called, "Yuri! Your hosts are here!"

The head of a middle-aged man with thick black hair appeared above one of the front pews, where he'd obviously been resting. He waved with a weak smile and stood slowly, looking as if he bore the weight of the world.

"Yuri Filakov is half of an antipodist act," the manager explained.

"Ant—" I said. "I'm sorry. What kind of act?"

"He's a foot juggler. Yuri is the porter. He lies on his back in a chair and holds his legs up in the air. The other part of the act is known as the flyer. The flyer is juggled, more or less. They balance on Yuri's feet, lying horizontally or sitting, and then flip and spin in a series of increasingly difficult maneuvers."

"Wow," I said sincerely. "I've never seen that. Sounds very athletic."

"I saw the *Cirque du Soleil* do it on an HBO special," Ida said. "It's amazing."

"It *is* amazing, and extremely athletic," Ms. James agreed. "Yuri is as strong as a bull. He does speak English, though his accent is a little thick. He's good-natured about it, though, and doesn't mind repeating anything you don't understand. Right, Yuri?"

The man who joined them was nearly as tall as me, and his shoulders were several inches broader. What made his appearance even more remarkable was the fact that he was *hairier* than me. Josie didn't call me Harry for nothing.

Our guest had a long face with a broad, flat nose. His black eyes were dull with exhaustion and were topped by the bushiest eyebrows I'd ever seen. He was more or less clean shaven, but at this time of day, his stubble would put a hobo to shame.

"I shall speak clear as bells in San Petersburg Cathedral, Miz *Queen*," Yuri assured her. His mouth curved upward, but the smile didn't reach his eyes.

"Yuri, this is Mr. and Mrs. Rutherford. They're offering you accommodations until our bus is repaired."

Yuri snapped his heels and bowed. "I yam most humbly grateful, Meester and Meesus Rutherford."

I held out my hand. "Please call me Harry, and my wife's name is Josie."

Yuri shook my hand with strength. "Tank you. Please to call me Yuri."

"You're Russian?" I asked.

His face lifted. "I yam Russian. So good of you to know it."

"I was in Moscow a number of years ago for a conference," I said. "Very interesting place. I've never been in a colder place in my life."

"Ah, Moscow. Not Mother Russia's most beautiful city. Too bad you did not see San Petersburg."

I shrugged. "We flew in and out of Moscow. Didn't venture outside that city."

"You went all the way to Russia and didn't do any sightseeing?" Ida asked in amazement.

"He probably didn't see much more than the inside of his hotel," Josie said. "My Harry is very . . . focused when he's working."

I peered down at her. "I unfocused long enough to see you when you wandered onto my mountain."

"Oh, so Colchik Mountain belongs to you now." She turned to our Russian guest. "Follow me, Yuri, if you please. Our car is just outside."

Ida and Ms. James thanked us again and said they would keep us apprised of the bus repairs. We gathered Yuri's duffel bag from the dwindling pile in the parking lot and headed home.

Josie plied Yuri with questions about his native land, which Yuri answered with politeness but not a lot of enthusiasm, which I put down to weariness from a long, hard day. We learned he'd been born in St. Petersburg, which had been Leningrad at the time. When he was twelve, he ran away to join the famous Moscow Circus. He began tending the circus animals, then developed an affinity for bears and worked as bear trainer until the Iron Curtain fell and he joined *Cirque d'Europa*.

That's as much as Josie gleaned from Yuri by the time we pulled up at the back door to our humble farmhouse. Josie settled Yuri into the guest room, then made a delicious meal of fried brookies—what she called brook trout. I'd caught them in the stream near the cabin. We also had field peas which she and her mother put up last summer, and seasoned rice.

Yuri showered while Josie and I prepared supper. I fried the fish while Josie handled the more complicated dishes. She humored me every now and then, when we were having something simple, like fish. Before she'd found me on the mountain, I'd pretty much survived on trout and venison stew.

Mostly she shooed me away, claiming that I was too big for such a tiny kitchen and just got in her way. She'd grown up in world where the kitchen was a woman's domain. John and LuLynn McClure were decidedly old school parents. I was doing my best to change Josie's perception of marriage to one where chores are shared rather than divvied up. Not only did I enjoy cooking, I enjoyed being with her, and I certainly enjoyed bumping into her in the small kitchen.

To show her just how much, I pulled her into my arms and kissed her so thoroughly we didn't hear our guest leave his bedroom.

"Ah, forgeeve me."

We jumped apart, which made me feel silly.

Yuri looked up at the ceiling. "I vait in the—"

"No," Josie and I chorused.

"Sit down, Yuri, please." Josie pointed toward the kitchen table, the only one we had. "Harry will join you. I just have a few things I need to finish up, and then we can eat."

Left with no choice, I sat in my usual place at the head of the small table. Yuri sat facing the kitchen.

Josie had supper on the table in five minutes. She sat across from Yuri and we dug into the bowls of food. Josie never served plates from the stove. She always insisted on eating family style.

"So, you juggle people with your feet," Josie commented as she passed Yuri the peas.

He shrugged his massive shoulders. "That is what I did, yah."

Yuri's answer was so cryptic and his voice so heavy, Josie and I glanced at each other.

"'*Did?*'" I asked. "Am I misunderstanding your English, or do you mean to use the past tense?"

"I do not know this tents," he said. "What I mean iz my . . . how you say . . . career as an antipodist iz kaput."

"Over?" Josie exclaimed. "Why?"

A shadow fell over Yuri's dark face. "I have lost partner." His fork clattered against the plate as he set it down hard. "Her name iz Tatiana Nikulin. Beautiful woman. Strong. Young."

Josie gasped. "She died?"

Yuri shook his head. "She run away from circus. Two days past. Tatiana alvays vanted to be American. A beeg strong young buck fall in love vith her vhere ve vere veek ago. He show up in Atlanta and ask for her to marry him. So she go." He lifted his shoulder again, and dropped it heavily. "Who can blame her? He has own land. Lots of land. And dairy cows. She vill have lots of American babies and grow fat on American cheese."

Even I was touched by the deep sadness in his voice. Josie—who is far more sensitive to raw emotions than me—reached across the table and covered his hand with hers. "Oh, Yuri, I'm sorry. Can't you find another partner?"

He attempted a smile. "Vhere am I to find a partner such as Tatiana? I yam too old to train another."

"She wasn't just your partner in the act, was she?" Josie asked softly.

Yuri peered across the table at her, then finally admitted, "Yes, ve vere lovers. She vas much younger than me. A . . . how you say . . . strong lover." He threw a wry smile toward me. "I yam too old for such nonsense, yes?"

I'd keenly felt the difference in years between Josie and me when we first met, but she'd shown me that age didn't matter. "A man is never too old to do what he wants to do. Especially when he finds the right partner."

Yuri conceded the point with an expansive shrug, but didn't look convinced. "Even so, vith no partner, I yam useless for circus. They vill send me back to Russia vhen they see it."

"It sounds as if that's something you don't want to do." I said.

He nodded. "I have traveled much in my life. I do not know where 'home' iz. Mother Russia iz not my mother. I don't know vhere I vould go. Or vhat I vould do."

"Surely the circus can find something for you to do," Josie said.

He smiled sadly. "Perhaps."

Josie turned her gaze to me, and I held it until Yuri pushed away from the table.

"If you vouldn't mind, I vill go to bed. I yam most tired."

Both Josie and I stood.

"Of course," she said. "We'll see you in the morning."

He bowed crisply, then left us to our supper.

Win Allen

When you can't trust your friends, it's time to get out of Dodge. Well, technically I could trust them—to mess with my mind. Or my mime. Sure. I could have refused these particular houseguests. I probably would have if Amos and Hank Blackshear, the town veterinarian, hadn't been standing there. You can't let those boys see you sweat. You can't let them know how to get to you. Not if you're going to play baseball with them in the spring. I know this because I'm as bad as they are. I've been needling Amos over the whole Ida deal since the moment I found out he'd lost his mind and laid one on her. So I sucked up my aversion to all things "clown" and said, "It would be *mime pleasure*."

Which of course is a bald-faced lie.

Etienne Decroux is known as "the father of modern mime." I can't help but wonder how much better the world would be today if he'd done the responsible thing and gotten a vasectomy. If I sound a little politically incorrect, please accept my sincere apologies. I grew up in the Deep South in the sixties, ingrained with the inborn prejudices that went along with those times. Over the years, I've outgrown ninety-nine percent of the ignorance that is prejudice. My remaining biases are focused in two directions . . . clowns and mimes.

They can live in my neighborhood, but I'll be damned if my daughter is going to marry one! Wait, I don't have a daughter, but you get the idea. So, I'm certain that it is for this reason that I've been assigned, sentenced, if you will, to house two members of the circus that is stranded in town. You guessed it. Clown mimes. White faced, juggling clown mimes. Kill me. Kill me now.

How do you kill a mime? Wait until they're trapped in a glass box and shoot 'em. I'm sorry; I just had to get that out of my system.

Since most of the town is opening up their homes to the traveling band of entertainers and since Ida is almost impossible to say no to, I just told her that I had room for two. *Note to self, next time, be more specific. Two NORMAL people.*

But, it's too late for that now. It won't be so bad, I mean, it's only for the weekend, right? And, surely these guys don't stay in character when they're not working, right? They're probably just normal guys, *right*?

If a mime is arrested, is the officer obliged to inform him that he has the right to remain silent?

Coulrophobia is the fear of clowns and clown-like characters, such as mimes. I'm not losing a minute's sleep over the thought of sharing my house for the weekend with a couple of mimes. However, Ida informs me that the manager of the circus insists . . . the whole crew intends to work for their keep. Clown mimes . . . in my restaurant. Relax . . . take deep, cleansing breaths . . . think calm thoughts . . . go to your happy place . . .

OK, maybe it won't be so bad. I can always use some extra help around the restaurant. It never fails, around any special occasion like Valentine's Day, someone calls in sick, something goes wrong in the kitchen, someone has to go out for "whatever it is that we didn't order enough of." A couple of extra hands would be a good thing. Even if they are wearing white gloves.

I learned from the circus manager, Quinn James, that their names are Tartuffe and Orlon. I also learned on Friday night that once a mime applies face paint, he is in character until the face paint comes off. So, my hopes for "normal" house guests were not to be. But, simple human needs are pretty easily communicated without words.

Orlon immediately running to my kitchen, opening my refrigerator door and pointing was a pretty good indication that they were hungry. Tartuffe hopping up and down with legs squeezed tightly together was my clue that he needed quick directions to the bathroom. Orlon eyeballing my bottle of twenty-one-year-old Chivas Royal Salute was a cry for assisted suicide. And, since neither of them took off their makeup before going upstairs to retire for the night, not a cross word was spoken.

Amos

Jayne Reynolds still lived above the coffee shop. I stared at her apartment door for a long time. I knew that it was time to try something new to get Ida's attention. Jayne was a good soul. Easy to look at and would remind Ida that I hadn't "settled" for her. There were other fish in this Mossy Creek fish bowl. Hopefully she'd realize that Jayne looked as wrong at my side as Del looked at hers.

The door opened. I scared Jayne half-to-death but she still managed to throw her bag of trash in my face and slam the door. Then a quiet voice said, "Chief?"

"Yeah. Unless I didn't get the memo about my move to Sanitation."

She laughed. The door opened again, grimaced as I lifted a banana peel off my shoulder and brushed what I sincerely hoped was coffee grounds off my trousers. Jayne covered her mouth. "Sorry, Amos. I just got home from the church. Want to meet my Swedish dancers?" She grabbed some tissues off a credenza beside the door and shoved them at me.

"I give you an 'A' for self-defense but your instincts need work. Come down to the station sometime and Sandy'll give you some moves you can use when you don't have garbage handy."

"I'll do it. I'll feel safer when I travel with the baby. Matthew's not old enough to protect his mother from much of anything except boredom. What can I do for you? Besides pay your cleaning bill?" She left the door to swing wide and backed up into the apartment. "The dancers are eating dinner downstairs. Leave all that. I'll get it later. You just come in."

"I don't think so."

"Come on. I have a baby. My carpet has seen way worse than a little garbage. I feel bad."

"Bad enough to do me a favor?"

"Sure." She flicked her hair back and I realized it was wet. The woman didn't have a shred of makeup on. Her t-shirt was worn thin, oversized and said, "It takes balls to play golf the way I do." That wasn't Jayne's t-shirt. She still got ready for bed and wrapped herself in memories of her dead husband at night. Amos wondered how long Ida had done the very same thing. Or if she still did.

"Amos?" she prodded. "In or out. "

"Out. And I'll be quick. Two friends. Dinner. Saturday night."

Jayne snorted. "You're tired of the *will they* or *won't they* speculation. You're tired of Katie Bell's incessant questions, and you're using me to annoy Ida."

"What's your point?"

Surprised, she thought for a minute. "I don't have one." She smiled. "I just liked saying it."

"Jayne. You threw garbage on me. I can ticket you for littering the Chief. Don't mess with me. Will you help me out or not?"

"I can't abandon my guests." She sucked in some air through clenched teeth. "Plus Ida's hosting that circus family and she's going out with—" We both knew who Ida would be out with. "Well, I'm supposed to go be her hostess while she's out Saturday night."

One of those conversational lulls dropped with a thud into the room. I filled it by saying, "Maybe another time."

"No." Jayne closed the distance between us, hatching a scheme with each step. "Come to Ida's with me. That'll be perfect."

"Not if the hounds of hell were chasing me and Ida's porch meant everlasting life. No."

"What do you mean, no? Seriously, Amos. I know what I'm doing. Who do you think got Harry to take that last step toward Josie? I'm good at this."

"I'm good at avoiding trouble. You know how those young girls wear jogging pants with *precious* and *hot stuff* written on their butts? Well, trust me, there's a sweet young thing among that juggling family at Ida's who thinks I'm the second-coming of Rhett Butler, and she has trouble written all over her. In four languages. So, no. Thank you."

"Coward."

"Where crazy romantic young things are concerned? You betcha. I prefer my women aged long enough to have some sense."

Quinn James

I supervised as the last of the performers met their weekend hosts. When everyone was safely parceled out, Erik escorted me to Mrs. Finch's van. He helped strap me into the seat like I was a child. I tried not to resent it. He sat next to me, so that he could care for me, which I also shouldn't resent. He was being sweet and kind. All I wanted to do was hit him. My bad.

As Mrs. Finch put the van in motion I braced myself for another surge of vertigo. It didn't look dignified for the manager of the circus to wobble drunkenly all the time. I held tight as the parking lot of Mount Gilead Methodist receded behind us. Her little boy leaned forward in his seat behind me and yelled in my ear. "Hey, lady, are you sure you aren't a clown? Why else would you walk so funny?"

With her foot still on the gas pedal, Mrs. Finch whipped her head around from the front seat captain's chair; she shook her finger. "Charles Albert Finch! Where are your good manners?"

"I'm using them, Mom. My teacher says it's good to ask questions when you don't know the answer." He snuffled his nose. "I'm in the first grade."

"It's okay, I don't mind explaining," I said, earning a sympathetic pat on the hand from Erik. His touch brought back that tingly feeling. Best to ignore it. Answer the kid. "Sometimes my brain doesn't work right, Charles, so it looks like the ground is tilting up at me when it isn't. If I hold my head to the side, I don't get as dizzy."

"Oh. So it's like the Tilt-a-Whirl at the Bigelow County Fair."

"Yup. But no one else is riding," I said.

"Sweet."

"Not exactly. You wouldn't want to ride the Tilt-a-Whirl for two days straight all the while going to school, doing your homework, and feeding your dog." I felt Erik looking at me and Charles.

"We don't have a dog," Charles said, sadness infusing each syllable. "Mom won't let me have one. We have a cat."

"But you understand what Miss James is saying, don't you Charles?" Mrs. Finch asked, taking a left at a traffic light onto a darkening two lane road.

"Yes, ma'am. I guess I wouldn't feel good either, if I wanted to get off the Tilt-a-Whirl, and no one'd let me."

After that we were all quiet. Charles began singing *John*

Jacob Jingleheimerschmidt over and over, so much so that I burst out laughing. Charles stopped singing to join in the laughter, as did Mrs. Finch. Erik didn't laugh, but his lips curved in a smile. I contemplated how they'd feel curved to mine until Mrs. Finch pulled into a subdivision of Mc-Mansions with landscape lighting. She must have sensed my surprise at such a suburban scene in the middle of forests, fields and Appalachian mountains.

We were greeted by a tall man with salt-and-pepper hair, who I presumed was Mr. Finch, and a little girl, Mary Alice, older than Charles, who wore her dark hair in a braid. She rushed to the van.

"Mama!" Mary Alice pointed at a gangly teenage boy I hadn't noticed before. He was standing by the hedge between the Finches' yard and the Cliftons', where he had an excellent view of Magdalene and her ABC posse stretching their legs over their heads in the driveway. "Randy had his binoculars out. He was looking at the circus girls across the way."

"Na-uh," Randy said, eyes glued to the sight before him minus the binoculars. I suspected the show was for Erik's benefit. Magdalene had hoped to lure him, not the Finch's teenage son.

Cherie and Brigitta might have been fishing for Mr. Finch or Randy. But seeing as how Randy was under the limit and Mr. Finch was a protected species, I figured the ABC posse would soon realize their bait was no good in McMansionville.

"My oldest son is incorrigible," Mr. Finch said. "Randy! Come help with the bags."

Mrs. Finch gave her husband a peck on the cheek. "He's a teenager. And you were probably just as. . . hor. . . bad when you were his age. We have a special mission to discuss later."

I wondered if the mission involved hanging a black-out curtain over the neighbors' windows. If I weren't so swimmy-headed, I'd offer to help.

Randy sulked his way over to the van, while Erik helped me out of my seat and along the driveway.

There was a minor skirmish involving my luggage between Randy and Charles. Something about the wheels on my bag. Charles won.

I entered the Finchs' brightly lit foyer and stopped for a moment to get my bearings where the wooden floor ended and the carpet began. A beige cat lying across the back of a brown sofa meowed at me.

Randy saw this as his opportunity to embarrass his parents further. "So, like, are those girls naked under their costumes when they perform, or do they wear thongs?"

Mr. Finch's face turned purple. Mrs. Finch said the boy's name like an expletive, and Charles sang, "Randy's getting in trouble, Randy's getting in trouble."

Their imperfection reminded me of my own family.

"I am so sorry," Mrs. Finch said.

"No need to apologize, my brother John asks me similar questions every Christmas."

Erik seemed surprised that I'd mentioned my family. I guess I didn't speak about them often, not like he talked about his. It wasn't that I didn't miss seeing Mom, Dad, and John; it was that I'd feel homesick if I talked about them, so I didn't. I might be living my dream of running away to the circus, but I missed my family.

"Is there anything we can do, other than get you to bed?" Mrs. Finch asked. "A cup of tea or warm milk? I made some peanut butter cookies . . . "

"No, thanks," I said.

"That's good 'cause there aren't any left," Randy added.

"That's not fair," Mary Alice whined. "Mom, he eats everything good in this whole stinking house. You have to make him stop."

"That's enough," Mr. Finch said in a scary voice that was close to a growl. The fat beige cat scooted across the top of the couch, thudded onto the carpet, and ran into the kitchen in a furry blur.

"I get to take the luggage up the stairs!" Charles shouted, as if he needed to call dibs.

Erik took me as far as the hand rail. As I waited for the spinning in my head to slow, Mrs. Finch showed him the study. She figured I should be closer to the full bath upstairs.

"I'll bring down a blanket and some pillows for the couch," she told Erik. "There's a powder room next door, but you'll have to go upstairs for a shower."

I tried not to think about Erik showering. I had enough to do to get up the stairs. I could hear Charles wheeling my case back and forth on the floor above.

Once I arrived in Randy's room, which fortunately didn't smell as much like dirty socks as my brother John's did, I tilted my head to the side to take in my Hawaii-meets-skateboard surroundings. If I had a smile on my face, I'm sure it faded when I saw that Randy had one of those low lounge beds. What I needed to soothe my dizziness was a high four-poster.

Charles rolled my bag into what would be my room for the next day or so. He grinned, exposing half-grown-in front teeth with pronounced saw points.

Mrs. Finch smiled. "The bathroom is the first door on your left."

"Thanks."

"So, I was wondering," Charles said, still grinning. "What's that guy downstairs name again?"

"Erik."

"Yeah, Erik." Charles smirked and said Erik's name in a singsong manner that let me know more mischief was coming. "You like Erik, don't you? Quinn and Erik sitting in a tree, K-I-S-S-I-N-G."

"Shh!" I said. Maybe Erik hadn't heard the schoolyard ditty.

So Charles sang even louder. "First comes love, then comes marriage, then comes Quinn in the baby carriage."

Heat rose up my neck. I decided leveling might be my best option for keeping him quiet. "He doesn't know, and I'd like to keep it that way."

"Why?" Charles asked.

"Now, Charles, you're asking too many personal questions," Mrs. Finch at long last piped up. "She doesn't have to answer them if she doesn't want to." But Mrs. Finch didn't cut him off completely. I suspected she wanted to know the answer, too.

"Because Erik likes someone else."

"Is that because you tilt your head to the side?"

"No. You know the girls your brother had his eye on next door? Well, the redhead is Erik's girlfriend."

Charles snuffled his nose. "She's kinda scary looking."

I knew there was something likeable about Charles. "Well, you and I might think so, but not everyone agrees."

Mrs. Finch tried to scoot Charles out the door. "Good night, Quinn. Sleep well. Charles, Quinn is exhausted, and you sound like you're getting a cold. Let me check your temperature. Do you have a fever? And will you please stop snuffling your nose? There's tissue in the bathroom."

He put his hand out, and I shook it. "So Charles, you

and I are friends, now. After all, I did explain vertigo to you *and* I let you wheel around my luggage."

"Yeah, I guess so."

"Let's keep my crush on you-know-who on the down low, okay?"

Charles giggled, which was better than a maniacal laugh, but I wasn't exactly reassured. Especially when his mom didn't chime in with "of course we will."

Sagan

I wasn't expecting to see smoke coming from the chimney. No one lived in my house but me. I had no animals to be fed so no one had a key, and I had not invited guests, unless raccoons and field mice knew how to build a fire. I wheeled my cycle into the shed, slung my backpack over my shoulder and picked up a section of tree limb from the wood pile. I could have called Amos, but this was my house to defend. I did glance over at Emily's place. No smoke. No lights. Apparently she was either working late or out of town.

The door was closed but unlocked. I pushed it open. The most horrendous squeal I ever heard split the silence as something hit my shoulder, knocking me to the floor with a thud. An Australian boomerang with feathers? Then it was gone. I didn't know what it was but I could surmise that Amos's missing bird thief was occupying my quarters.

I got to my feet, turned on the light and groaned. Apparently my house guest had been there for several days and was unfamiliar with a dishwasher or a garbage can. The place was a mess. I slung my backpack into the washroom, opened the blinds and shook my head. Had I not returned, nobody would ever have thought to check here for the runaway. I reached in my pocket for my cell phone and started to punch the numbers.

Then the boomerang with feathers shrieked again and a huge feather floated gently down and settled on my arm. I looked around. A cool breeze snaked through an open window. Okay, a Russian kid with a giant attack parrot was hiding in the shed or barn, and I'd catch both of them eventually.

Maybe I'd just wait and see what happened. If the kid came back, I'd deal with him. If he didn't, he was on his own. But that was easier said than done. It was cold in the mountains of north Georgia in February. People in Mossy Creek were known to quietly call the month 'Uglywary.' But they said it with pride, particularly if it came with a bit of snow. Even the hint of white brought the tourists, which were a nuisance and a blessing. I laid my phone on the table and went to the door.

"Okay, Nikoli, if you can hear me, you'd better come back inside. This isn't as cold as Russia but you can still freeze your . . ." I hushed. He probably couldn't understand me, anyway.

I waited a while then turned back to the kitchen. By the time I'd restored it to its normal state of order, a cold, dark winter night had settled in fully. That's when the knock came on the door.

"Come in. It's not locked."

There was a hesitation then a blast of wind pushed the door open. "Sagan?"

It was Emily, not the kid.

"Yes." My heart leapt. I had missed her so much. "Who'd you think it was?"

"Eh, nobody. I mean, I've been in Atlanta for the last few days. Did you see those circus performers in town?"

"Yep."

She was still standing in the doorway as if she was waiting for an invitation to come inside. "Did you have a good trip?" she asked but I could tell she really didn't want to know.

"Well, motorcycle travel in the dead of winter isn't the best way to go. But yes, I suppose you could say I had a good trip."

"Did you . . . Did you find what you were looking for?"

"What makes you think I'm looking for something?"

"I've watched you, Sagan. You go up into the mountains and stay for days at a time. I don't know what you're doing, but I know you're waiting."

I didn't answer. She was right.

"Do come inside, Emily," I said.

"No, let me get it said. I have something to tell you and I might as well get it off my mind right now."

"Is there something wrong?"

"Yes, and I think you know what it is. I care about you, but I don't want to spend the rest of my life waiting for you to know what you want, so I'm selling Granny's house and moving back to Atlanta. If you change your mind about us, do it soon."

I don't know what I thought she was going to say, but that wasn't it. My first reaction was dismay but not such distress that I could say what she wanted to hear. She was waiting for my reply and I had none.

"I never wanted to hurt you, Emily. I don't know what to say."

"You already have, Sagan." She came inside, kissed my cheek, then turned and left the house.

I let her go.

I morosely stoked the fire while pausing periodically to

check out the window. The darkness was no longer solid. It was like gray watercolor, running from the sky down the thick growth of trees making a surrealistic painting that surrounded me. Through the gray I could see that Emily's car was gone. I didn't know how I felt about that. Solitude was what I'd wanted but now I was alone, me and my white feather. The boy knew I was here and that Emily was gone. If he was smart, he'd get into her house and stay warm.

If I were smart, I'd call Amos and tell him I'd found the runaway. Or maybe not.

That's when I understood that I'd come back home to see the vision I'd searched for in vain elsewhere. Now I had to wait for it to direct me. I leaned back in a chair by the fireplace and closed my eyes.

I dreamed one continuous dream that night. I was aware of the fact that I was dreaming, and in some strange way I was trying to interpret what was happening as one scene fed into another. But I couldn't understand. The only thing I was certain of was that I was flying, not as a child flies when he fears falling and tries to catch something to hold onto.

No, I was looking through the eyes of something . . . a creature that I'd joined with. We flew through the clouds, the trees, swooping down to the silver ripples of a stream that cut through the rocks and disappeared for long stretches before reappearing. There was an urgency about my actions, a fear that sliced through me. I had to hurry, else I'd be too late.

And then my alter self cut sharply around and headed back toward the cabin. It, no, *we* flew inside and I slid to the floor with a thud. The same raucous cry sliced through the stillness of the night. Suddenly I was awake. For a moment I thought I had dreamed the cry, too. I heard the shriek again and I knew this was no vision; this was real.

I turned on the small lamp on my desk, punched up the fire and considered what had just happened. It was real. I was wearing my usual tee shirt and boxers, which were damp and cold now, and my feet were bare. The squawk came again, accompanied by a rustle of wings as the cabin door opened and the creature flew into the house, perching once more in the rafters.

It was huge, spreading its wings and turning around angrily. Even in the shadows I could see its eyes, a golden glare of light that seemed to be frowning. Suddenly, it came back to me. I'd had this dream in Oklahoma, when I'd been on my vision quest. As if I'd walked fifty miles and my feet were bare. I'd thought when I woke the next morning that I'd failed, that I'd fallen asleep. That's when I packed my knapsack and headed home, disappointed in what I'd done and in my inability to keep awake.

I heated a container of water and a hand warmer in the microwave and dressed quickly, finding a pair of thick socks and waterproof boots. I packed my knapsack with dry clothes and a blanket and finally, I added powdered coffee to the hot water. At the last minute, I pushed a small flask of medicinal vodka into my supplies and pulled the pack over my shoulders.

A pair of fur-lined gloves and a wool hat with ear flaps and I was ready. Finally, I reached for the staff I always carried when I climbed and headed out, trusting that my feathered creature would show me the way.

The woods were silent, giving me no clue as to which direction to take. Which way? I heard nothing, nor did I see any signs of someone having run through the brush. The bird and the boy were connected. Find one and I'd find the other. I called out, "Hello? Hello? Nikolai?"

No answer. As I stood at the foot of a path I normally

took up the mountain, an icy fog wafted down to the ground, completely covering the mountain, leaving only me in the center of a circle of silver gray.

Then it came toward me, the bird I'd called a boomerang with feathers. It swooped down, circled me and headed off toward the mountain top. I couldn't see it, but I knew where it was. And I followed. The higher I climbed, the colder it got and the stronger the wind surged.

I seemed to walk for hours when I suddenly stepped out of the mist into a clearing. The sound of water rushed passed me and disappeared as if it had never carved a downward slice from the earth. As I stood, watching the waterfall, the mountain went silent.

"Hello? Is there anyone here?

No answer.

Why had the bird led me to this place? Was the boy here? Could he be hurt? Carefully, I made my way upwards. The bird flew back over and up, landing above a point where the water exited the other side of the ridge and plunged into a small pool below. I pointed a flashlight. That's when I saw him, the boy crumpled beneath an overhanging rock. He'd made a clumsy attempt to cover himself with leaves but when I finally touched him, he felt like ice. A few feet away were the remains of a fire. On the wall behind him was a shadowy drawing that seemed to wave in the mist. Gusts of wind blew leaves and sticks against the wall behind the boy.

I covered him with an insulated blanket while I set about building a fire. If my Cherokee forefathers had sheltered beneath this rock, so would the boy and I. Snow began to flurry; it would be melted and of no consequence by morning, but it made the night feel much colder.

I rubbed the boy's hands and his face with the hand warmer but he didn't respond. I fished the vodka from my bag and forced some of it down his throat. Moments later he coughed and sputtered, then spewed out a few words in Russian.

He pushed himself up on his elbows, gazing at me wildly. I moved back a few steps and sat down cross-legged beside the fire. Slowly he calmed down. He drew the blanket tightly around him, scowled, sighed, then sat down across the fire from me, rubbing his hands and arms. He suddenly reached out and grabbed the thermos of coffee I'd set nearby. He drank it down without stopping for breath. His eyes drooped. He slept.

I built up the fire and covered him with the second blanket, wondering where the bird had gone, wondering if it was the stolen parrot or a figment of my imagination. Sleep wouldn't come. I felt as if I was in a silent world, alien to me, yet protecting me with its seclusion. Finally, I inched my way over to the wall so that I could shine a flashlight on the drawing I'd seen earlier.

The etching depicted a campfire much like ours with three men sitting around it. The curved wall around them had vein-line lines with irregular patterns along the bottom. Obviously, the picture was not one of the exact place we were camped. There were no boulders, no waterfall. But the place was familiar. There was no suggestion of fear or flight.

I huddled beside the fire again, watching the boy sleep. Finally, I slept, too.

WMOS
R A D I O

"The Voice Of The Creek"

Here's old Bert again to tell you it looks like all our visitors survived Friday night, despite some escapades reported from Miss Eula Mae's front yard and rumors that Sagan Salter has found the runaway Russian boy. Some of the *Cirque d'Europa* performers have offered to put on a little show tonight at the new high school gym. It's free and everybody in town is welcome to drop by. Just remember to dress warm, since the gym's not quite finished and the heat's not on, yet. Yep. It's February in the mountains.

Saturday

More Fun Under the Big Top

Chapter 3

Ida

Like I needed another attractive man in my life. The kind of man who makes women jump through hoops while juggling her heart at the same time. On top of all that, he was charmingly French.

Americans who sneer at the French have never read a history book. France is no bigger than one of our largest states, yet its brave people have survived centuries of bloody attacks from their neighbors plus two devastating world wars (World War I wiped out an entire generation of young French men.) Not to mention giving us Quiche Lorraine and Yves Montand.

Speaking of strong, handsome Frenchmen . . .

"Pardon moi," Philippe Chu said in a deep voice as he stepped into my kitchen at Hamilton Farm that Saturday morning wearing a snug pullover and tight, faded jeans.

His French-Vietnamese heritage made for a tall, lithe, honey-skinned slice of *cake de beef*. He was in his mid-forties by my guess. Silver wings dramatized his shoulder-length ponytail of jet-black hair. His Anglo Asian features included deep, green, almond-shaped eyes. I pirouetted from the kitchen sink and found him smiling at me the way a tiger smiles at a gazelle. "I'm up a little early for my morning training routine," he went on. "May I join you for coffee, first?"

"Absolutely. That would be wonderful." My gazelle body, clad in slender charcoal slacks and a form-fitting white sweater with tiny onyx buttons, zinged with pleasure. Ah, the harmless thrill of being chased. I set fragrant cups of dark roast Columbian on a heavy oak table, followed by a platter of extra-crispy raisin bagels glopped with overdoses of pineapple cream cheese, which my young housekeeper, June McEvers, had left under a clean dish towel on her rush out a side door.

She'd arrived two hours before her normal eight a.m. schedule, zoomed through a few cursory chores, then bounded outdoors into the frosty backyard. Where, by no small coincidence, Philippe's gorgeous twenty-two-year old son, Jean, had promised to teach her some juggling techniques.

Funny, I'd always thought June was more the Scottish poetry-and-museum type. Now she was outdoors tossing large silver hoops among my freeze-dried winter azaleas.

"Tell me more about your juggling act," I said as Philippe and I sipped coffee. "Besides flinging glittery Hula hoops, what is your family's specialty?"

Philippe smiled. "Imagine my twin sons—Jean and Maurice—atop a platform suspended fifty feet above the stage. Imagine Maurice's delicate little wife, Lien, balanced upon a tall pedestal barely wider than her feet. Imagine my reckless teenager, Camille, perched very carefully upon *my* shoulders. Imagine all five of us madly whirling dozens of flickering hoops back and forth." He paused. "Blindfolded."

I smiled. "That sounds truly magical. How did you learn that? How many hoops have ended up around the necks of audience members?"

He laughed, a deep, musical sound. "Quite a few, actually. But they're light and harmless. We've found that people love the risk of our act. Danger and surprise have a powerful allure." His eyes shifted slightly, taking all of me in with one glance. *Care to duel with rose-tipped swords?* "Don't you agree?"

"I prefer to be the tosser, not the *tossee*. Don't fling any hoops *my* way. I'm not fond of being on the receiving end of unexpected complications."

"*Mon Dieu!*" He feigned shock. "Such timidity behind your glorious *joie de vivre!*"

"Do I *look* timid?" I tilted my head just so. Flirting is second nature to some men and women, me among them. The art of it has little to do with tawdry come-on's. Great flirting was born in the ancient ages of gallantry, a substitute for forbidden sex, a graceful parlor game. Men love a woman who makes them feel, hmmm, *effective*. She doesn't have to be beautiful or young, slender or firm. It's about the tilt of her head, her smile, her attentive gaze. What's the harm in that?

"You, timid?" Philippe said, leaning toward me. "Never! Afraid to take risks? *Impossible!* Such a shame. I can't fathom it!"

Beneath the teasing he seemed genuinely amazed. I sank back in the silk-padded security of my kitchen chair. "You don't ever feel any pressure to . . . *act your age?*"

He stared at me. "Do you? Act your age?"

"Maybe I should. I'm fifty-one."

"Such a vibrant woman, talking as if a mere number can define the passion and promise of life. Tell me it isn't true."

"You tell *me* something, first, Philippe. Last night, over dinner, one of your children mentioned that their mother died a few years ago and you've been alone ever since. I understand grieving for a lost spouse, believe me, but I assume you have plenty of gorgeous young women from which to choose. At least to have, shall we say, companionship."

He looked at me wryly. "Ah, 'companionship.'"

"All right, *Frenchman.* You know what I mean. *Sex.*"

"I have had companions. I adore them. But I don't need or want a replacement for my wife."

I waggled a finger at him. "A bit stuck in your ways, eh? What happened to the 'passion and the promise'? Maybe you're older than you think."

"*Mais non*, my darling hostess." His smile grew wistful. "I am whatever age my birth certificate claims, but my heart sees nothing but love. My wife was far younger than me. More than twenty years younger. I'm sixty-one years old, Ida."

I was seriously flabbergasted. When I recovered, I said, "Mais non, my handsome, unwrinkled guest!"

He gave a soft chuckle but his eyes took on a sad, distant gaze. "Life was difficult for me, growing up in Vietnam as a half-white child. So my wealthy French father sent me to a Catholic boarding school in Paris. I didn't return to Vietnam until I was nearly forty years old. I was an acclaimed gymnast by then, a performer with the most elegant juggling troupes—and I had won a bronze medal in gymnastics at the Olympics, as a very young man. I was a celebrity.

"Important Vietnamese families, their fortunes ruined by decades of war, were anxious to curry favor with me. To offer me their daughters in marriage—their *pureblooded* Vietnamese daughters, offered to me, a mongrel. Imagine. In my pride, I chose a beautiful, well-educated girl the way traders choose a prize cow. She was barely eighteen. I never intended to love her, and I told myself I didn't care whether or not she ever loved me. I *owned* her, this . . . beautiful, innocent, barely grown child. I had *earned* her. Nothing else mattered."

I sat there, hypnotized, my coffee mug cooling in my hands. "There's a nice surprise ending to this story, I'm guessing."

He nodded. "Yes. We fell in love. We had the most soulful marriage two people could ever wish for. Despite our differences, we became best friends."

I set my coffee down. "I see. You're telling me it's easy to find a new companion. But not to find another soul mate and best friend. Those cannot be predicted or planned."

"Indeed. You understand."

"I've been alone since my husband died, twenty years ago. Despite an ample supply of male companions since then, no other man has ever . . . " I stopped. A needling sensation on my skin told me I was about to tell a lie. What lie? *You know what lie*, the angel of my conscience hissed. *And you know who it's about, too. Who that special man is. The one who could stand side by side to equal Jeb's place in your life.*

I fumbled with a bagel mounded with cream cheese. "No other man," I repeated grimly, and aimed the bagel for my lips. When cornered, hide behind food.

Philippe stopped my hand. His fingers were long, supple and callused. They closed gently around my wrist.

"I am hearing what you're *not* saying," he accused. "Ahah. There *is* such an amazing man in your life. So, tell me, what stops you from pursuing him? From accepting this incredible second chance at happiness? Is he married?"

"No."

"Disinterested?"

"No."

"Horribly humpbacked? Covered in festering leprosy sores?"

I couldn't help laughing. "No."

"Then what could possibly be the problem?"

"He's only thirty-six. I'm fifty-one."

Philippe frowned. His fingers splayed on the tender underside of my wrist, as if searching. "And?"

"That's fifteen years' difference. He's a man. I'm his older woman. And no, it's not the same as an older man and a younger woman. Not like you and your wife. You know that. I keep trying to explain the biological reality to him."

Philippe clucked his tongue at me. "So you're telling me this reckless *boy* of thirty-six surely cannot know what he wants? Why, of course. He's barely old enough to shave. You cradle robber."

"Be serious."

"I cannot be serious when faced with such absurd reasoning." He removed the bagel from my hand then cupped my hand in both of his. Leaning toward me intently, Philippe said in a low, graveled voice, "Never turn your back on passion. We will all surely grow old and die some day, but our love, our passion for life, makes us young at heart forever. Love is eternal. Love is not about age, my beautiful new friend. It is about lust and friendship, courage and faith and hope." He raised my hand to his lips and kissed it.

I sat there with tears in my eyes.

He kissed my hand again.

We heard footsteps on the hall rug only a few seconds before Del stepped into my kitchen doorway. Philippe, being a Frenchman, calmly refused to release my hand. And me, being a Southern woman not given to panicking, looked up at Dell's grim face and said, "This is my houseguest from *Cirque d'Europa*. Philippe Chu. He's a palm reader."

"Does he read palms with his *mouth*?" Del growled.

"He's near-sighted. Philippe, this is Del Jackson. Lieutenant Colonel, retired, United States Army. Who *is* glad to meet you, regardless of his scowl."

Philippe released my hand, stood, and bowed slightly. "My pleasure, *monsieur*."

"All yours, I'm sure," Del said coolly. My heart sank. The Del I knew had never been inhospitable, sarcastic or given to cheap retorts. His churlish mood was my fault.

I stood. "Let me fix you a cup of coffee."

"No. I've got errands. I just dropped by to talk about tonight." We had plans for a pre-Valentine's dinner at Win Allen's restaurant. "I'll be waiting in your office." Del pivoted with the crisp authority of a recruit on the drill ground and walked out.

My shoulders slumped. I felt Philippe watching me, and I faced him. "Yes?"

"I take it," Philippe said gently, "he knows he's not the man you love."

I could only nod.

Sandy

I had read myself to sleep Friday night, listening for a call from Mutt at the jail, telling me Sergei and Mariska had chopped each other up with some plastic knives from the break room. Even though no call came I woke up Saturday morning tired. I wasn't much of a reader until I met Jess, and he introduced me to fantasy novels. Now I love to read about magical creatures and mystical places, like unicorns, fairies, wizards and elfin kings and queens performing heroic deeds. I dreamed of a feisty little girl with blond ringlets and fireflies in her hair. Me in Camelot or some such place.

After I fortified myself with coffee, I did some house work until mid-day. I used to clean houses for a living before Amos hired me to be his dispatcher. I always liked to keep things tidy, but lately I'd been on a serious cleaning binge. I thought about how much I missed Jess and wondered how he was enjoying his camping trip. His solo camping trip. I hoped he was as lonesome as I was. Really, really lonesome.

About eleven-thirty I went to pick up lunch at Bubba's for the circus folk. Turns out they still had not kissed and made up. And I still couldn't figure out exactly why Mariska wouldn't let Sergei throw knives at her anymore. Well, not anymore than *anybody* with a lick of sense wouldn't let their husband throw knives at them.

Even though the cells in the jail house weren't exactly five-star accommodations, I had thought that a night of privacy away from the rest of the troupe would give them a chance to talk things out. Evidently that hadn't happened because they were just as out of sorts as they had been yesterday. But at least they liked the food. I consider myself a good Southern hostess, so it was nothing but the best for them as far as I was concerned.

"Dis—how you say—*burrito*, ees very good," Sergei said between bites. "It ees both crispy and spicy. Very different from food in old country."

"It *is* quite bodacious, isn't it?" I drawled.

I had gotten a burrito for myself as well, so I joined them for lunch. It seemed like the neighborly thing to do. "What *do* you eat in your country?" *Moose and squirrel, I bet*, I thought, and stifled a giggle and a burp.

Mariska was busy sampling Bubba's flan. "Porridge," she said. "Much porridge."

"My wife is from poor family," Sergei explained and immediately looked as if he wanted to take it back. Mariska gave him the old skunk eye. He'd obviously hit on a sore subject.

"That's too bad," I said, and took a big swig of Bubba's hand-squeezed cherry lemonade. I mean, he squeezed the lemons, not the cherries.

A long and uncomfortable silence ensued in which Sergei squirmed and Mariska pouted. I waited patiently. It was a quiet weekend at the jail; they were the only tenants. Our jail is kind of like the jail in Mayberry, only we don't have an Otis the drunk to come and go. So they had the place to themselves. When Sergei finished with his bodacious burrito, I gave him a fresh towel I'd brought from home and directed him to the shower down the hall.

"Do you vish to join me, darlink?" he suggested hopefully to Mariska.

"I vil vait," she said coldly, and finished off the flan she had been picking at.

Sergei sighed and entered the shower room alone. When the door closed behind him, I asked Mariska, "So, what's the story with you and Sergei? Is he such a bad knife thrower? Do you really think he'll skewer you?"

"My husband is excellent knife thrower," Mariska said. "But I still do not trust him."

Trust issues were quite a challenge in domestic conflicts, I noted. "What did he do to cause you not to trust him?"

"It started weeth the broken promises," Mariska said. "I was very young wheen I left my first troupe with heem. I grew up in tiny town in countryside. Was dismal place, so I was desperate to see outside world. So I run away to join the circus."

It made me kind of sad to hear her talk that way about the place she was born. I thought about our Mossy Creek slogan—"Ain't going nowhere and don't want to." But I guess not everybody feels that way about the places where they were raised. Not every town is Mossy Creek, and I reckon there're some towns young folks just can't wait to get shed of. I just couldn't imagine living anywhere else but here.

It's mostly the people I love, of course, but I think I'm just a mountain girl at heart. There's just something about the mountains—the evergreens, the views, the rambling, babbling streams like Mossy Creek itself. The creek circles the whole town like a hug. We feel protected, here. Simply put, there was nothing not to love about my home town.

"My first troupe was very small also," Mariska continued, "but I was beegest star. So wheen Sergei came along with hees handsome looks and hees charm and fell in love weeth me, he promised I would be star in his much beeger troupe. I felt myself most lucky to be leaving old troupe with heem. But after we marry it turns out that his troupe does not have job for aerialist. So I have to start career over as lion tamer's assistant. Theen the lions were taken away and now we have to start over again."

"You trusted him when he was a lion tamer, didn't you?"

Mariska made a little sound of disgust. "I trusted those old, *toothless* lions," she said. "They were about as dangerous as your peeing Spanish rat-dog."

"Mexican," I corrected.

Mariska shrugged. "I do not like the rat-dogs of Mexico as much as their burritos."

"Me neither," I agreed. "But there's got to be something else. What was the straw that broke the camel's back?"

"Camels? I know nutting of camels. Only lions."

"I mean, what is it that Sergei did that makes you angry with him?"

Mariska sighed and looked away. "It ees not really heem. It eez me. I have received offer from another circus. They are going to train me once again to be aerialist." She looked back at me and smiled wistfully. "I could fly, you know? Fly like bird on wing. Now I tink my skeels are what you Americans call . . . rusty."

"Why couldn't Sergei learn to be a trapeze artist like you? That way you could become an aerialist again and you could form a trapeze act."

Mariska shrugged. "He eez—how you say—*afraid of heights*."

He was afraid of heights but not afraid of lions. How do you like *them* apples? I could sympathize with Mariska wanting to reclaim her dream of being a trapeze artist. I mean, as soon as I knew I wanted to be a law officer, I made it my goal and gave the Mossy Creek Police Department one hundred percent until Amos hired me. I had worked my way from being dispatcher to being a full-fledged officer of the law. I achieved it. But Mariska's thinking still bothered me. And I thought I was beginning to sense why.

"So," I said. "Are you picking a fight with Sergei so it'll be easier to leave him?"

"Eef I get fired from troupe, then eet will be easier to break away from Sergei. He can go back to old country and get more lions. Lion taming ees hees first love anyway."

She waved a dismissive hand as if Sergei losing his job because of her was of no consequence.

I was beginning to think that Sergei would be better off if Mariska *did* leave him. "So he gave up his first love—lion taming—so that the two of you could be together. And now you want to leave him for a better job offer? Do you even love him?"

Mariska had the decency to look taken aback. "Of course I luff Sergei," she said and sniffed. "But all good tinks must come to end. There ess many other fish in sea. Besides, I catch him keesing acrobat *beetch* behind tent two veeks ago."

Ahah. All righty, then. Now we were getting down to brass tacks. "Did you confront him with what you saw?"

"Yes, but he told me I was beink rideeculous." Mariska said, "He vill see who ees rideeculous when I vill be leaving as soon as written offer arrives."

Before I had time to ponder this, Sergei came out of the shower room naked except for the towel I'd given him to wrap around his waist. His broad, straight shoulders seemed to go on for miles and his chest and biceps rippled with well-defined muscles. And he was hairy—my land, was he hairy. Now, I know some women are turned off by body hair, but to me, a nice mat of dark chest hair is my idea of real manliness. Yes, indeed, I love me a fuzzy man. My Jess has a hairy chest, and there's nothing I like better than snuggling up to him at night and letting those little crispy curls tickle my cheek. Well, almost nothing.

My lips puckered up for a long, appreciative whistle at Sergei, but I caught myself just in time. Mariska wouldn't have appreciated that and I wouldn't blame her. It was a sensitive enough situation already. Besides, I was starting to identify with her a little bit more—for obvious reasons.

Mariska's breath caught, and she looked away like she wasn't affected by the sight of her gorgeous, half-naked husband, but her ruse didn't fool me. There might be other fish in the sea, but the one she'd already reeled in was a keeper and deep down, she knew it.

"I will take shower now," Mariska said tersely and brushed past her husband.

Sergei looked very sad as he headed toward the cell to get dressed. I picked at the rest of my burrito and asked myself what Dr. Phil would do in my situation. Could this marriage be saved? *Should* it be saved?

Sergei came back a few minutes later as I was clearing away the take-out containers from lunch. I like to keep the station as clean as a pin. Dressed in clean jeans and a checkered shirt, he sat down forlornly in one of the office chairs and stared at the floor. "I am losink her," he said.

"She said you kissed another woman," I stated. No use beating around the babushka. Time was short and I had to get to the heart of the problem.

"Eet vas nutting," Sergei said with a wave of his hand. "LuLu-san is like seester to me. I kiss on her cheek. Mariska knows thees. She is being reediculous."

"Is that what you told her? That's she's being ridiculous for objecting to you kissin' someone else?"

"Of course! I would not let her speak to me of such foolishness."

"There's your problem, Serg," I said. "You should never ignore a woman's feelings, especially when she has you dead to rights. Besides, Mariska is what we call a *high-maintenance* woman."

Sergei's dark brows arched upwards. "What ees these 'high mainteenance?'"

I could tell I had his attention. Good. "That's a woman who needs you to tell her—and show her—how you feel about her. Every single day."

"Show her?"

"Yes. Words are not enough. And sex is not enough either, if that's what you're thinking."

Sergei tried to keep a poker face at this news, but he was a man. Of course that's what he was thinking.

"I am curious," he said with the hint of a smile. "Are *you* a high-mainteenance woman?"

"Me?" I thought about all the nights I went to bed alone, nobody to tickle my cheek or any other part of me for that matter, while Jess sat at his computer tapping away at his latest novel. And then there were these last couple of weekends when he left me home alone while he went camping. All this I have endured without complaint with nothing but Bubba's Bodacious Burritos to comfort myself with.

"Of course I'm not a high-maintenance woman," I declared. "Don't be *rideeculous*."

Quinn

I woke Saturday morning feeling the breeze from a heating vent beside the bed but not hearing the white noise it must be creating. Phase two of vertigo was in full swing.

Imagine, if you will, that beyond the world tilting and a low ringing in your ears, you now are proceeding with minimal hearing like right before your ears pop when you're on a plane.

For a moment, I wondered where I was because it smelled like home, then I recalled. In the suburbs of Mossy Creek, Georgia—the Yonder community, to be exact—at the Finch household, and even though I might have lost some of my hearing, my sense of smell was still keen. What smelled like biscuits and sausage urged me to get my butt out of bed and sate my growling stomach.

Being lower to the ground on this lounge bed was going to make getting out of bed more tricky than usual. I rolled to the side and placed my feet on the cool floor. I had nothing nearby to hold onto, so I attempted rising by pushing up from the low mattress. The next thing I knew my face was meeting that cold, hardwood floor.

Heavy footsteps hurried upstairs and down the hall. "Quinn?" Erik called out. The door opened, and I saw bare feet and masculine legs with well-defined calves. February is not shorts season. Was he standing in my room naked? Maybe I was dreaming.

"I'm fine," I said, my voice sounding feeble and unconvincing.

He lifted me up, and he smelled good and clean, like Zest soap and shaving cream. I tilted my head to the side, and he came into full view. Half-shaved face. Bare chest. Washboard abs. And towel firmly tucked around his waist.

"Do you need some help getting dressed?" he asked.

Heat flooded my face. He didn't even think me enough of a girl to realize helping me get dressed was inappropriate? Indignant, I pulled up the loose waistband of my oversized flannel pajamas decorated with flying monkeys. "I can manage."

"Like you managed to get out of bed?" he challenged.

"Look. I can dress myself, and I need to do my vertigo exercises before I go downstairs. So if you'll leave . . . ."

"Excellent," he said, "I'll be back to help in a couple of minutes. I need to put some clothes on."

I couldn't help but think it might be more interesting if he didn't.

"That won't be necessary," I called to his muscular back. Heat flooded my face again when he poked his head back in the doorway. "I didn't mean don't get dressed. I meant I can do the exercises myself. It's not like I'm lifting weights or anything. You go ahead and do whatever."

What if I reacted to his touch, and he noticed and he got embarrassed? If there was anything more pathetic than liking someone who didn't like me in that way, I didn't know what it was.

He didn't listen to my protests and returned fully clothed. Not that clothes helped. He had on that sandalwood aftershave I liked, and he was wearing those low slung Levis worn nearly white in all the right places. Plus I had that picture of him in just a towel in my spinning head.

Pure torture. That was what this therapy was going to be.

He helped me down onto the lounge bed, and I turned to my side so I wouldn't smell his minty fresh breath. I probably had morning breath. "I can do this on my own," I mumbled. "All I have to do is turn my head to a forty-five degree angle."

His hand gently guided my jaw until the back of my head rested against the futon-like mattress, and I imagined him guiding my jaw to better plant a kiss on me. My lips burned just thinking about it. I hadn't felt like this since seventh grade when Michael Tolliver sat next to me at lunch.

Focus, Quinn. The exercises. "Has it been thirty seconds?"

"Mmmm, hmmm."

"Okay, help me sit up. Now, we do the same thing to the left side."

How was I going to make it through five repetitions?

My phone rang. I knew it was Mr. Polaski, so I ignored it. I also ignored it the second and third time it rang.

We'd made it nearly to the end of the session, when Erik said words that made my palms sweat.

"Quinn," he said. "I have something I need to talk to you about."

Please no. He couldn't be sharing his feelings about Magdalene with me. I'd have to lie and say she was great. I wiped my sweaty hands on my pajamas.

He helped me sit up and turned me back to the right. "There's someone I care for deeply."

My gut clenched. They were getting married. I couldn't let him see my pain, so I forced my mouth into a brittle grin. "She's a lucky girl. I wish you all the happiness in the world. I'm sure she'll say yes."

"Yes to what?"

"To whatever it is you want to ask her."

I noticed he was scratching his head like he was confused. I guess he'd expected me to react differently.

"How's the dizziness now?" he asked.

"Not bad," I lied, tilting my head more to look directly into those troubled hazel eyes that Magdalene would spend the rest of her life gazing into. "You're lucky it's Valentine's Day eve. Magdalene's the kind of girl who'll appreciate the drama of a proposal on such a romantic holiday."

His brows drew together. "Proposal? Magdalene?"

Unable to look at him, I attempted to stand. I had to act like I didn't care, just as I'd acted like it was no big deal to give up performing. Pride alone enabled me to hold my wavering ground. "I don't know about you, but I'm starving. You going for your run?"

After I said it, I realized he must have gone running earlier. Why would he shower and shave before a run? He must know I was in love with him, and he wanted to break the news of his upcoming proposal to Magdalene gently. But I didn't want to know any more about it, and I wasn't helping him plan their romantic evening.

"Quinn, I think you misunderstand me," he said.

I threw a robe around my shoulders and hobbled down the stairs, desperate to get away. "Is that biscuits I smell? There's nothing I love more than a good, flakey biscuit."

"Quinn!" He called out. "I must say what is in my heart."

"Later. We'll talk about it all later," I snapped back. If he could see that the news was going to be difficult for me to take, he could also see that I was in no mood to hear it right now. And if he wanted my opinion on an engagement ring, I'd scream.

I found my way to the kitchen as Erik slammed the front door. He muttered in his native tongue all the way outside. Maybe he was heading over to see Magdalene. I didn't care.

Since I didn't care, the Finches' sunny yellow kitchen should have brightened my mood, but it didn't. I sat down at the table with the rest of the clan, who were eyeing me suspiciously.

Mrs. Finch placed a plate with fried eggs, biscuits and sausage in front of me. Amazed that she knew how I liked my eggs, I could only form the word "How?"

She winked at me. "I asked Erik."

I took a bite of the biscuit; the soft insides melted in my mouth as Mrs. Finch took her place in the chair next to me.

Charles sniffled. "When can we tell her?"

"I guess now's as good a time as any," Mrs. Finch said, smiling like we were in an episode of the *Brady Bunch*. "We took a vote this morning and decided we're going to help you."

My phone rang. Damn it; I hadn't called Mr. Polaski back. I hadn't heard from the mechanic at Peavey's Garage, either. I pushed my plate aside.

How was I going to get Mr. Finch's watch back from Erik? Better yet, how was I going to face him now that he knew I loved him?

There is a good reason to hate Valentine's Day, I thought as I leaned back in my chair at the kitchen table. I contemplated how best to salvage the wreck that had been made of my life. I glanced out the kitchen window. Here came Erik. A blur of red hair and red velour was following him to the back door. Magdalene. Great.

"Erik!" Magdalene called as he entered the kitchen. Magdalene didn't ask to be invited in. She barged. "I expect you have a gift for me, as well."

As well. So she'd given him something. Something I hadn't yet seen. Please no plush toys with treacly sentiments embroidered on their bellies. I might throw up what breakfast I'd managed to eat.

Before I could inquire as to whether there was a problem at the Cliftons, implying I didn't want her here, the front doorbell rang.

"I wonder who that could be?" Mrs. Finch said, as she departed for the door with a mischievous gleam in her eyes.

A delivery girl with kind brown eyes carried in two bouquets and set them on the kitchen table—one, long-stemmed red roses and the other an arrangement of bright yellow, orange and red flowers, which must be from me to Erik. *Just shoot me now.*

"Oh, Will, you haven't given me roses since Charles was born," Mrs. Finch gushed, smiling broadly and looking like a woman still very much in love with her husband.

Mr. Finch looked uncomfortably from the dozen reds

to his happy wife. "I didn't."

"Sorry," the delivery girl said and tiptoed back to the front door. "I'll let myself out."

How I wished I could follow, but Mary Alice blocked me from leaving the table.

Mrs. Finch took the card in hand. Her blue eyes widened as she read it. "They're for you," she said, handing Erik the card.

Magdalene looked like the proverbial cat that swallowed the canary. "I sent them, Erik. The card says, *I'm passionate about you.*"

"The other bouquet is for you, too, Erik," Mrs. Finch said, and made a point of nudging me.

I calculated the distance between my seat and the passageway to freedom, but I couldn't knock a child to the floor to get there. God only knew what Mrs. Finch wrote. If only I were a superhero who could turn myself invisible.

"Who is sending you flowers?" Magdalene stamped her foot oblivious to the tension in the room. "I must know."

Erik frowned as he read the message attached to the bright bouquet. "Thanks," he said.

"I . . . um, I'm glad you like them," I managed to spit out. I hated this awkwardness between us. I missed the ease we'd shared in each other's company. Maybe if I made a joke about the card and flowers, we'd be able to move past it.

"Quinn? Quinn sent you flowers? What does the card say?" Magdalene asked, reaching for it.

"Nothing that concerns you." Erik tucked it away in his pocket.

Ouch. So my feelings weren't anything for her to worry about.

"The bouquet is pretty, Quinn," Mary Alice said, now blocking me and Magdalene. Magdalene glared at the child, who held her ground. Mary Alice lifted her chin. "They're different. They show imagination."

"Magdalene," Mrs. Finch said, heading past me. "I've got a fresh pot of coffee. Why don't I serve you in the den?"

As the Finch children surrounded and herded Magdalene out of the kitchen, she tossed her mane and gave Erik one of those smoldering looks that runway models use. "I'll be back."

I guess the time had come for Erik and me to have an excruciating talk. "Look, Erik, about the flowers. I can't take credit for them or for whatever Mrs. Finch wrote on the note. They were her idea."

Erik rubbed his jaw, and I recalled how he'd looked in the towel, half-shaven, half-naked. My face burned.

"Thanks for the chocolates," he said, softening the "ch" into a "sh," which made me tingle all over.

"My guess is they weren't Belgian," I said.

"Guess?"

"Yeah, they weren't my idea either. Nor was the choice of messenger, though Charles can be adorable."

He smiled briefly and removed Mr. Finch's Rolex from his pocket and placed it in my palm. "I suspected this belonged to our host."

"Erik, I appreciate so much that you haven't launched into the I-only-want-to-be-your-friend talk. I'm sorry that the Finches got a little overly enthusiastic about this silly crush of mine." I didn't think it was possible, but my face grew hotter. "That's all this is—an infatuation. I promise I'll get over it soon. And I'm sorry if any of what happened this morning causes problems for you with Magdalene."

Erik's lips moved like he was saying something under his breath, or maybe he didn't. It was hard to tell with my hearing worsening.

"If things were different," he said in tones I could hear, "and you hadn't had the Finch family's help, what sort of gift would you have chosen for me?"

I shrugged, which was hard to do with my head tilted. "I don't know. I think Valentine's Day is pretty cheesy. Besides what's the point? You have Magdalene."

"I don't *have* Magdalene."

"Okay, okay. You *love* Magdalene. I get it."

"What?" Magdalene shouted from the den. "I heard my name."

I heard what sounded like tackle football going on in the den.

Bravely, I met Erik's gaze. "It was bad enough losing you as a partner. I don't want to lose your friendship, too. I miss you enough as it is."

"Quinn, I don't think you understand me. Sometimes friendships only last so long, and then—"

My phone rang. "I need to call Mr. Polaski." I certainly wasn't going to sit here and listen to him tell me that we couldn't be friends. Rather than cry, I bit the inside of my cheek.

"You realize this conversation isn't over," he said.

"Yes, it is," I said a little too forcefully, knowing he'd find me alone at some other point that weekend, and he'd have his say. By the time he did, I'd have the pain in check. He'd never know how much I hurt.

Sagan

When I woke up Saturday morning Nikoli was still dozing and we were both covered in a slight dust of snow. But the sky was bright blue and the wind had stopped. I was laying on one side of the burned-out fire and Nikoli was on the other, our heads and feet almost touching in a circle. In the dry leaves beneath the boulder there was a large white feather. As I studied the irregular pattern along the bottom of the feather I realized that the ground outside of our shelter had been swept clean.

"Nikoli?"

He woke with a start and scooted back against the boulder, staring at me, his eyes wary and filled with questions.

"Nikoli?"

I held out the feather and pointed it at the drawing, then held it out to him. He looked at the feather, at the wall and back at me. Then, with a shriek, he scrambled out onto the path and began to whistle. At least that was the only thing I could call it because it was sound unlike any I'd heard before. Vision, or reality? I might never know, but at that point I was certain that the frightened boy was communicating.

I looked up at the sky. There was nothing there.

He spoke. I had no idea what he said. Then he gave a frustrated groan and motioned that I should follow. I did, and in a much shorter time than it had taken me to climb the mountain, we were in sight of my house. I waved him inside, shivering. Within ten minutes he'd opened what appeared to be the last box of crackers in the pantry, stuffed a handful in his mouth then politely held out the rest to me. I opened the refrigerator. Empty. It appeared that we'd have a choice of crackers, popcorn or grits for breakfast.

Any other Creekite would take a guest to town for a hearty breakfast. I considered it. Why not? And afterward we'd stop at the library for a book on Russian and at the Piggly Wiggly to restock the pantry.

Simple. All I had to do was avoid Amos and Katie Bell

while I decided how to keep Nikoli hidden from the immigration authorities. I didn't want either our police chief or the town's gossip columnist alerting the circus managers. Better take some time to think about it.

"Grits," I said to the kid, wagging a container at him. "That's about it, for food. We'll hang out here today while I make some discreet phone calls and try to decide how to help you." I put a pot of water on the stove to heat. "If your pet bird is still around, you can feed him grits, too. My guess is, he's either a frozen bird-cicle by now, or he's roosting in my shed. Either way, I hope you and he like grits."

Nikoli stared at me, obviously trying to translate my intentions, if not my words. Finally, his face relaxed a little. He exhaled. "Grits," he said in heavily accented English. "Okey dokey. Grits."

I set out bowls, spoons, butter, salt and pepper. When the grits were ready I spooned a large serving in Nikoli's bowl. He sat down, tasted it, made a face, went to the fridge, brought back my ketchup bottle, and turned the grits into something resembling buttery red mud.

He then ate happily, nodding at me.

I sighed and shook my head.

Win Allen

After a quiet night, the mimes and I arrived at my restaurant, Bubba Rice's Diner, at 5:30 a.m. to open up for the breakfast crowd. I assigned Tartuffe and Orlon some simple tasks, and we made it through the morning without incident. The customers even seemed to enjoy their antics as they "mimed" their way through their tasks.

Thanks to Marcel Marceau, most of us know the classic mime routines like "man in a glass box", "man pulling a rope" and "man walking against the wind." Did you know that mime for *"Fire!"* is . . . *"Fire! Fire! The kitchen's on FIRE!!!?"*

These were the first words that I heard spoken by my house pest . . . uh, *guests* since their arrival on Friday night. Tartuffe came running out of the kitchen, hands waving in the air, screaming at the top of his lungs like a baby girl whose doll had just been ripped to shreds by rabid dogs. Then, realizing his cultural *faux pas*, he stopped, did his best Charley Chaplin "holding onto his head and jumping up and down" routine, pointing all the while at the smoke pouring out the kitchen door.

When you shoot a mime, do you have to use a silencer? Just kidding. Really. Maybe not.

As it turns out, it was only a small fire, confined to the oven. Ever see bread burned so badly that it actually caught fire? I hadn't either, until now. And, while the oven wasn't damaged by the fire, it needed a serious cleaning before we could use it again. On Valentine's Day Eve . . . when we needed to start making a half-dozen cakes for desserts on the dinner menu. We had a lot to do and no time to do it. I didn't want to face Saturday night Valentine's Eve without chocolate. We redoubled our efforts.

I'm not sure how long it had been going on before I became aware of the fact that I was miming my instructions to Tartuffe and Orlon. And, I'm not sure which one of us was the first to laugh out loud, but once the silence was broken, the mime routine was over, at least as long as we were out of sight in the kitchen.

When they went out front, they returned to character. I didn't bother trying to convince them to drop the mime routine with customers. Most of the folks who'd booked reservations that night would be happy little campers to get dinner *and* a special mime show.

And the ones that wouldn't be? Well, let's just say that I wasn't particularly interested in keeping Del Jackson happy when he brought Ida to dinner. Amos is my pal and I was rooting for him to get the girl. So if the mimes annoyed Del during his romantic dinner with Ida, good for them. Del's a soldier, one of those commando, bleed-red-white-and-blue-types who never really retire. He had plenty of experience negotiating *mime* fields.

Suddenly I was beginning to like mimes, and the last of my prejudices faded. Oh, wait. I forgot. Mimes weren't exactly the *last* of my prejudices. Lawyers were. Excepting Mac Campbell, one of Mossy Creek's leading legal types. He seemed a decent sort. Except for the kilt. I hoped he didn't wear it when he brought his wife to dinner.

I didn't even want to contemplate how Tartuffe and Orlon would mime, "What's a Scotsman have under his kilt?"

Harry

I rose with the dawn Saturday, as I always did, and found our guest already on the back porch, gazing up the mountain.

"Good morning," I said.

Yuri made a valiant attempt at a smile. "Good morning, Harry. Tank you for warm bed I enjoy last night. You have lovely home."

Only a Russian raised on the Siberian tundra would think so, I thought but kept it to myself.

Last night, Josie and I had indulged in a long, mostly-whispered conversation about our unusual guest. Primarily we discussed what we were going to do with him today. It was Saturday so Josie didn't have to work. My own work could be accomplished any day of the week, and I usually took off when Josie didn't have to go in.

However, since our romantic plans were shot, as Josie had put it earlier, I suggested that I take Yuri up the mountain so that I could check my data-collection sites. I had the feeling the Russian would enjoy being outdoors, even on such a cold day.

Apparently I was right. Yuri sat on the porch swing in only a flannel shirt, even though the frigid morning air bit through my own flannel with icy fangs.

"Thank you," I replied to his compliment. "Josie is fixing some breakfast. After that, if you like, we can hike up the mountain. You can see a bit of scenery and get some exercise. And I can check my data collection sites."

. Yuri brightened. "I vould like that. Riding in a bus every other day from town to town gets old. Ve only see countryside from out vindow."

We set off on foot soon after breakfast. Josie set off in her car to check on her parents.

"These data collections . . ." Yuri shrugged. "I do not understand."

As we climbed, I explained to Yuri that I worked on a grant through the University of Georgia to study the effect of acid rain on the indigenous plants of the Appalachian Mountains. I had built collection facilities all over the nearby mountains to capture the rain for analysis. After a rainstorm, I hiked to each to collect the samples, then analyzed them in the small lab I'd set up in my old cabin, which Josie and I still used occasionally. If it had been awhile between rainstorms, I would visit each one to make sure some critter hadn't gotten curious and torn it up. That had happened more than once. During the growing season, I also collected plant samples and analyzed them.

Yuri tried to show an interest in my work, but it was clear he didn't understand what I did or why it was necessary. I didn't take offense. I knew that my work wasn't the stuff of thriller novels, and that most people didn't understand it. I'd come to terms with that long ago.

Because of that and because Yuri seemed distracted, I didn't go into much detail about my work. I asked him about his position at the circus, but that was something I didn't much understand. Inevitably, we began to lapse into comfortable silences which lengthened with the morning. Yuri clearly had a lot on his mind, and I wasn't accustomed to carrying on conversations while I worked. Occasionally he would ask about some wildlife or tree, or I would point out certain mountains when we came to vistas. But mostly we just walked, enjoying the exercise and the fresh air.

It's hard to describe the magic of a winter mountain morning. The air is ethereal ice. You can feel every breath as frigid shards of nothing enter your body, then morph into a lovely cloud of steam as it leaves. Occasionally you'll hear some winter creature rustling through the dead leaves carpeting the ground, seeking what sustenance the bleak season has to offer. Mostly, however, the silence is so acute, your footsteps run up the massive trunks of hardwood trees and echo through their barren limbs.

Yuri clearly enjoyed the hike and the mountains, which linked us with a kinship few can understand. We were mountain men at heart, if not reality.

Around noon, I took Yuri to the cabin I'd built from Appalachian hardwood when I first came to Colchik Mountain. I made lunch from the supplies Josie and I kept there. Yuri loved the grits Josie had cooked that morning, so we had grits and canned beef stew.

I had a few more collection sites to check, so we

headed out soon after we'd cleaned up.

Yuri seemed to be in brighter spirits, for some reason. Maybe it was the grits. At any rate, he soon began to hum as we walked along.

"That's an unusual tune," I commented. "What is it?"

"You vould not know, I tink," he said. "It's old Russian. . . how you say . . . people song."

I stared at him hard for a second, then I got it. "Folk song."

"Yah. As you say. Volk song. '*Kak za Donom za rekoi.*'" He frowned. "How you translate. Hmmm. Don River. On other side."

"Across the Don River?" I asked. "Beyond?"

"Yah. You understand." He began to sing the words. It was a lovely song, with a lilting quality that seemed common to folk songs. His expression told me that he was far away in his mind. No doubt he was revisiting his boyhood Russia.

Suddenly he stopped both his song and his steps.

I stopped and turned. "What's wrong?"

He was at full alert, his dark eyes peering into the surrounding woods intently. "Deed you hear that?"

"What?" My gaze followed his. I could see nothing through the trees. "No, I was listening to you."

"You have bears here, no?"

I blinked hard. "Well, yes. But it's February. Bears are in hiberna—"

A honking wail moaned through the trees.

"Well, I'll be. . ." I shook my head. "That certainly sounds like a bear. But in February?"

Yuri alertly peered in all directions, trying to discern the direction from which the bear's call came. "Some bears get hungry. They vake and vant to eat. Ezpecially those that do not get fat enough in fall."

"Now that you mention it, I believe I read that some place, but I've never seen a bear up here from December to about March or early April."

The bear called again.

Yuri's head zeroed in on a point down the mountain. "He iz that vay."

I pointed in the opposite direction. "Then let's go this way. If that bear's hungry, I don't want to run into him."

I continued down the trail, not noticing for several strides that Yuri wasn't following. I turned back to see why just in time to see Yuri step off the path and head downhill.

"Yuri, where are you going?"

Instead of replying to me, Yuri began singing the Russian folk song again, this time at the top of his lungs.

Cussing, I rushed to catch up with him.

"Are you nuts?" I called. "Black bears aren't the most aggressive of the ursine genus, but they *will* attack if cornered."

Yuri paused long enough after the first chorus to say, "Not black bear. Brown."

Catching up, I pulled on his arm. "We don't have brown bears in this part of the country. Ursus Americanus is the only bear native here."

Yuri stopped to look at me. "Is brown bear, my friend. I know this."

The bear called again.

"Hear?" he said. "Is brown bear. Is Russian bear."

"Russian? No, Yuri, it can't possibly—" I broke off when he resumed his song and his stride. I watched his broad back in disbelief. Had Tatiana's desertion unhinged his mind? A Russian bear? This was Georgia, but the American Georgia, not the Russian Georgia. Even if it were, why on Earth was Yuri *singing*?

172

With a sinking feeling, I followed. Several yards later, Yuri stopped. I came up beside him and there about thirty yards away, to my utter amazement, was a brown bear. He stood on his hind legs, sniffing the air. Bears have a keen sense of smell and hearing, but their eyesight isn't all that great.

"There's a chance he hasn't seen us, Yuri," I said softly. "If we turn around very slowly, we could probably make it back to the—"

Yuri ignored me. He broke into another chorus of the folk song and continued toward the bear.

Oh, geez. A Russian with a death wish. Josie was going to kill me for feeding our guest to a bear.

The bear's gaze zeroed in on Yuri, and it let out the strangest sound I'd ever heard from a bear. I didn't claim to be a bear expert or anything. I saw them often as I trekked through the mountains, but we gave each other wide berths, as a rule. Still, this was not a sound I'd ever heard from a bear. It was plaintive and eerie.

The bear dropped to all fours and took several ambling steps toward the Russian.

Suddenly Yuri spun around and made a wild gesture with his arms.

Then—and this is when my mouth dropped open—the bear reared up and started spinning. Wailing and spinning and clawing the air with its paws.

Yuri mimicked the bear's motions, singing the whole time.

Dancing. The bear was dancing. Here in the middle of the north Georgia mountains, we'd come across a dancing bear.

No, not just a dancing bear. A *Russian* dancing bear.

This had to be a dream. Some bizarre dream.

The song and dance continued for several more minutes. When Yuri stopped, the bear released another loud wail.

I tensed, waiting to see what would happen. Just because this bear had been tame once didn't mean that it still was. No telling how many years it had been since the bear was part of a circus troupe. How long had it been, even, since they'd had dancing bears in the United States? The practice had been vilified for decades.

Standing a few yards from the bear, Yuri stood still and held both arms out in welcome. The bear hesitated, then placed his head between Yuri's beefy hands.

With a loud, joyful laugh, Yuri scratched the bear's neck.

"Someting to eat in backpack?" he asked.

"Yes, I . . ." I dropped my backpack and reached inside, fumbling for the granola bars that Josie had dropped in that morning. I pulled out three, tore the packaging off one by one, then gingerly approached Yuri, holding them as far in front of me as I could.

"Do not have fear," Yuri said with a genuine smile. "This old man is tame as kitty cat." He took the bars and offered them to the bear, who devoured them greedily.

"If you have more, give them now," Yuri said. "Our friend vill find if you do not."

I rummaged in my backpack and found two more. I handed them to Yuri, and he fed them to the bear.

After finishing, the bear licked Yuri's hand.

"How is this possible?" I asked in amazement. "I'd almost swear he was purring."

Yuri's shrugged. "He run away from circus. Or maybe was let loose when too old to dance good. Poor old man." Yuri ruffled the bear's thick fur. "Heez in bad shape."

"He is?" Never having been this close to a bear, I didn't know what good or bad shape was.

"Heez fur iz dull, thin. He has no meat on bones. No wonder he iz not in vinter lair. Heez starving." Yuri lifted the bear's head and pulled back his lips to bare his teeth. "See? Only half left."

The bear nuzzled into Yuri's leg. His need for human attention was touching. And now that Yuri had pointed it out, the bear did look bedraggled.

"I wonder how long he's been up here?" I said more than asked. "I wonder if. . ."

"Vhat do you vonder?" Yuri asked.

"I remember Josie talking about a circus fiasco here years ago. An elephant escaped and ran amok in town. Started a fire that destroyed the high school in Mossy Creek. I guess the bear could've escaped at the same time, but that was twenty years ago."

Yuri considered that. "Iz possible. Bears leeve to thirty year or more in wild. If he vas young bear. . . iz possible."

I glanced between Yuri and the bear. "Is he tame enough for me to touch him?"

Yuri shrugged. "I tink so, yes. Come close slowly, and hold out hand. Like to dog you do not know."

The bear emitted a low sound as I approached. He sniffed the hands I offered him, then must've decided he liked me because he began licking them. His tongue was thick and rough against my palms. Then I remembered I'd handled the granola bars.

The bear then nosed the backpack hanging from my other hand. I opened it and let him poke his head inside.

"There's not anything else to eat, you poor starving fellow." I glanced at Yuri. "We need to find him some food. What does he eat? Meat?"

Yuri shook his head. "Grain. Grass. Hay." He brightened. "Greets!"

I smiled. "We have several bags in the cabin. Let's go back and fix him up."

As we made our way back to the cabin, the bear followed like a trained dog. Occasionally he would nuzzle Yuri's hand. Once or twice he nuzzled mine. It startled me the first time, but from then on I stroked his nose like I'd seen Yuri do.

"He's starved for affection, isn't he?"

"Yah. Iz good bear. Not hurt, I tink, by people."

"Not abused."

"Yah. He love people, so I tink not abused. Cage open and he smelled voman bear, maybe. No circus I work for abuse bear. I do not understand this. Bear iz partner in act. Why hurt partner?"

I finally had to voice to my astonishment. "How did you know? I mean, approaching that bear was either incredibly brave or incredibly stupid. How could you possibly know that it wouldn't hurt you?"

"Yuri not stupid, my friend, and only little beet brave. Is knowing. I know bears. I first start in Moscow Circus with bears. First I feed them, then later I train and perform with bear. When Iron Curtain fell and the Moscow Circus began touring beyond, I see that bear dancing iz not considered good thing outside Mother Russia. I see writing on wall, so I learn new trade. I still young man, and foot juggling take strength, which I had much. I still strong."

"Yes, no doubt about that," I murmured. This was the most Yuri had said in the last two days, and I was extremely curious to hear his story. "But what if the bear had attacked?"

"I knew he vould not," Yuri replied. "As I said to you, is knowing. I could hear in his cry. This bear iz old. Starving. But not abused, I tink. Bear has long memory. Like elephant. He remembers that man iz friend. Man feeds bear. Bear misses good food when he iz not vith the humans."

"That makes sense."

We made it to the cabin, then. Yuri stayed outside with the bear while I went inside and put on the grits. It didn't take long to rekindle the fire that had so recently been put out in the cast iron stove. I brought out the largest pot I had and cooked half a pound of grits. Yuri and I watched as the bear slurped them up, licking the bucket that I'd served them in until it was clean. The bear nuzzled Yuri one more time, then ambled underneath the steps and went to sleep.

"Bear love greets like Yuri," the Russian said.

I sat beside him on the top step and consulted my watch. "It's almost three o'clock. It gets dark up here by five. We need to head on back, if we're going."

Yuri frowned. "I tink if ve leave, may not see bear tomorrow."

I nodded. "That's true enough. I've never seen him, and I've been working up here several years. You are welcome to stay here in my cabin tonight, if you like. I need to get back, though. Tomorrow is Valentine's Day. Do they celebrate Valentine's Day in Russia?"

He shrugged. "I never knew Valentine's vhen I live in Russia, but I know it now. Tatiana, she love Valentine presents."

"Well, if I spend the night before Valentine's several miles up the mountain—with a bear and a Russian—Josie will not be a happy wife."

"I understand, my friend. I yam most happy to be here myself alone. Bear good company."

"Chances are he'll sleep under there for days, if not weeks."

"Yah. He could. But I tink he vill vant to eat again soon."

"Well, there's plenty of food to last you—and the bear—for a week at least."

"Greets?"

I smiled. "Yes, there are four pounds of grits in there. I'll be back up tomorrow. I'll bring what we have at the house. Knowing Josie, we have several more pounds. At four cups of water to every cup of grits, a pound goes a long way. What I fixed earlier was just half a pound."

"I tank you." He kissed the tips of his fingers and threw the kiss into the air. "I love the greets. Breeng cheese, too? So Yuri make like Josie?"

"Okay, I'll bring cheese. Josie will come, too, I'm sure. She won't want to miss seeing a dancing bear. Probably has *feng shui* possibilities we're not even considering."

"Fung—vhat you say?"

"Don't ask. I couldn't even begin to explain Chinese decorating philosophy to a Russian." My smile faded as I stared into the woods for a moment. Finally, I said, "They were expecting the *Cirque d'Europa* bus to be fixed tomorrow. When it is, they'll be on their way."

"Yah." He nodded slowly. "I know this."

I hesitated, but the question had to be asked. "Are you planning to go with them? Have you thought that far ahead?"

Yuri stared across the vista that the cabin enjoyed. If you knew what you were looking for, you could see seven mountain ranges from the front porch. I'd built it there deliberately when I'd come to Colchik Mountain to establish my research. The view had given me the illusion of being on top of the world, instead of miles away from it.

"I do not know," he said at last. "I vas already tinking about leaving *Cirque d'Europa*. I have no partner. I am useless to them now."

"Can't you find a new partner?"

The Russian sighed. "I am feefty-and-two. I do not vant to keep tossing young weemen in air. My feet hurt."

I snorted. "I can imagine."

"But circus is all I know."

I contemplated Yuri's dilemma. As I did, the wooden steps shifted as the bear beneath grunted and settled into a more comfortable position.

"What about the bear?" I asked. "Could you take him with you and have a bear act instead of a foot juggling act?"

The Russian shook his head. "*Cirque d'Europa* has no animals. Not even trained dog. Peeple act only."

"Ah." I didn't ask if the business-like Miss Quinn would make an exception. If they weren't already set up for it, there were too many hurdles to clear—facilities, transportation, insurance, just to name a few. "What about joining another circus?"

"Yah, I must. But I don't know if possible soon." Yuri drew a large hand down his dark face.

"You're tired," I said, stating the obvious. "There's no need to decide anything now. We can discuss it more tomorrow."

I stood. "I'll get a fire started, then let you get some rest."

After getting Yuri settled, I headed down the mountain. Josie was going to love this story.

Saturday Afternoon

The Circus Fun Continues
Chapter 4

Ida

"It is *Monsieur* Rhett Butler in the flesh, again!"

Philippe's starry-eyed teenager, Camille, squealed that greeting as June ushered Amos into the leather-and-lace comfort of my den that afternoon. Philippe, his sons, his daughter-in-law, and I looked up from a spirited game of Texas Hold 'Em at a card table in front of a crackling fireplace. I forgot the straight flush in my hand.

"Rhett," Camille crooned once more, grinning at Amos with her delicate, muscular hands clasped to the front of a *Cirque d'Europa* sweatshirt. She didn't seem to notice that Amos had no mustache, looked more like George Clooney than Clark Gable, and was dressed in a decidedly non-Rhettish khaki uniform under a quilted, dark-blue jacket bearing the insignia of the Mossy Creek police department on one shoulder. But okay, yes, Rhett Butler. Absolutely. Amos has the style, the smile, the worldly wiles. He was that deadly combination known as a "man's man" and a "woman's downfall." Mine.

Camille's effusive and embarrassing welcome might have flummoxed lesser men, but Amos merely arched a dark brow and nodded to her. His shrewd gaze remained where it had been from the moment he entered the room—on me and Philippe.

Trouble.

I stood quickly. So did Philippe, who was seated close, probably too close, beside me. The confident way he brushed against me was such a simple gesture, yet how territorial. *Men.* It's a wonder they don't crane their heads and charge each other like mad bulls.

"Chief Royden," I said gracefully. "I'm glad you dropped by. Just checking to see if I'm mistreating our guests? Other than luring them into a poker game, I'd say I've kept them all in good stead."

Amos studied Philippe and offered a warning. "If you're going to play games with Ida you'd better know that the mayor likes to bluff."

"Only when the stakes are high," I countered.

"Aren't they always?" Philippe countered, smiling.

Camille continued to gaze at Amos dreamily. "Oh, Monsieur Police Chief, you're so . . . so suave and enigmatic, yes, just like Rhett Butler. Are you terribly overwhelmed with girlfriends? I suppose so. A pity. I would gladly stay here for your sake."

I wouldn't say Amos was flummoxed but he did open and close his mouth as if uncertain what to say to that declaration. If we'd been on friendlier terms I'm sure he would have looked to me for help, but he's not stupid. He opened and closed his mouth one more time and was finally saved from having to respond by Philippe's quick intervention. "My daughter is a fan of *Gone With The Wind.* She sees romantic ideals everywhere."

"I see. Well, I'm honored then," Amos said to Camille, who blushed deep pink.

"Good for her," I added, though my heart was on the floor. Give Camille ten years and she'd be a perfectly mature age to marry Amos on his forty-sixth birthday. I, on the other hand, would be testing my latest bifocals and smearing extra sunscreen on my liver spots. "No harm in romantic ideals. As I always say to cynics: *Fiddle dee dee.*"

Camille gaped at me then applauded. "Scarlett O'Hara! You are Scarlett!"

Oh, no. I'd been sucked into her fantasy world and paired with Amos in literary romance. *Quick. Bluff.*

"Hardly. But thank you." I smiled as I strode to Amos, hooking one hand around his elbow like a steel claw. "Chief, I appreciate you checking in on us, but I'm sure you have lots of other folks to visit. So let me fix you some coffee and a bag of homemade cheese straws. *To go.*"

Amos gave me a slit-eyed smile, didn't budge an inch, then looked at Philippe. "One more thing. The mayor's left eyebrow twitches when she gets a good hand."

"I noticed," Philippe replied.

Amos kept smiling. Except for his eyes. The man was no longer pleased. Time to go. I hauled on his arm to get him moving.

"He noticed? He already *noticed*? As if he needs no advice about you? As if he has everything under control?" Amos whispered as I tugged him down a back hall into the kitchen. "*Pepe Le Pew* is making himself right at home."

I hissed. "That's low, Amos. A French cartoon skunk? You're better than that."

"I'm out of dignified approaches where you're concerned. Besides he's a juggler for God's sake. How dignified is that?"

As we stepped into the kitchen his gaze fell to my hand. I was massaging his arm through his jacket, soothing him. I let go quickly. "If you're making insinuations, take a ticket and get in line. Del's already dropped a couple of insulting comments about Philippe."

"Good for Del. For once, we agree."

"I won't have a guest in my home treated rudely."

"Except for me apparently. I doubt Philippe Chu cares what Del and I think about him. He's too busy softening *you* up."

"I've already got two bull-headed men causing me grief. Why would I add a third?"

"Good point. Don't forget it."

"Just for the record, Philippe Chu's almost a grandfather. His daughter-in-law, Lien, just found out she's pregnant. Believe it or not, he's sixty-one years old."

"You say that as if it means something. You label yourself by age, you label him, you label me. As if age defines us. You know what I see? I see you with a man his age and I think: That's my competition. That's the kind of man Ida thinks she should be with."

"I'm practical. And realistic."

"You're blind. Chu could put you in his juggling act and you wouldn't even need a rehearsal." He nodded to himself. "Yep, you could give him lessons in juggling. You've been doing that for so long I'm not sure you know how to stop and hold on to anything."

I grabbed a bowl of cheese straws and fiercely shoved handfuls into a paper lunch bag. "Time for you to go, Chief. You're on duty. Here." I tucked the bag in his jacket's deep side pocket because he made no move to take them from me and I couldn't win a staring contest with him. Not at the moment. So I made the moment about the cheese straws. That seemed safe.

"Yes, I know. It's not ethical for you to take even the smallest, most innocent gifts from your Creekite citizenry; your father carried off a few too many homemade cakes from attentive local women and so you automatically want to turn down even a bag of well-intentioned cheese straws. But you're not Battle and I'm not trying to get you to fix a traffic ticket for me. So take the damned cheese straws and go. Have a nice day."

He didn't.

"Ida, it's nice to see you value me so highly. I get cheese straws and a cold shoulder to leave. Cheese straws wouldn't have bought you squat with Battle. What'd he get to put you in the Mayor's chair?"

"Nothing." This time I stared him down for all I was worth. "Your father made his own decision to support my first run for mayor at a time when a lot of people said no woman—let alone one as young as I was then—could lead Mossy Creek. After I won that first election he stood up at my swearing-in ceremony and told everyone he was proud to be my police chief. I felt like the only cowgirl at the rodeo and here was John Wayne, telling everybody the little lady could punch cows as well as any man. Because of Battle's endorsement, all the grumbling old-timers gave me a chance. He might not have been perfect, but he was fair and honorable where it counted most."

"You didn't grow up with a mother who cried every time Battle brought home some other woman's pound cake because sometimes a pound cake wasn't just a pound cake."

"I know he wasn't a perfect husband or father. But you're not him, Amos, so you've got nothing to prove. Not to me. Why are we having this discussion?"

"Because you won't have the one we need to have."

"There isn't anything to discuss. And even if there

were, arguing ethics isn't helping your case. As mayor, I'm your boss. I have my code of ethics, just as you do. I'm thinking of your reputation as well as mine. Why aren't you concerned about the conflict of interest issue?"

"Because I'll always do my job by the book, no matter what our relationship is. People know they can count on me. I've arrested you enough times to prove myself to them. Are you worried I'll sue you for sexual harassment?" He leaned forward as if he had a secret, never took his gaze from mine. He lowered his voice. "Tell you what. I'll make the first move. Then you're safe. You can't harass a man who's ready . . . willing . . . and able." He slid a hand to the nape of my neck. "Come on, Ida. Go for it."

The universe swallowed every sound in that moment. Every sound except the loud click of a French clock on the wall. It was time passing, passing me by, reminding me that this was such a bad idea. All of that and more in every tick. The deep breath I took almost hurt because it was like breathing in the earth when Amos was this close. So solid. So real. So risky. "Please, Amos. Just *go*."

He started to say something else, frowned deeply, then shook his head and walked out. After I heard the heavy click of my double front doors shut behind him, I followed wearily up the front hall. *Oh, Amos. You always leave me feeling weak-kneed and deprived. I want to be with you so much.*

Just as I expected, I found the bag of cheese straws on a small marble table in the foyer, where he'd left them.

Peggy

Marcel and I spent Saturday ambling around town. He bought me lunch at Mama's, we browsed the bookstore, then spent the afternoon sipping lattes at The Naked Bean. He flirted innocently with Bean owner Jayne Reynolds, who was close to his age. Jayne is a solemn, pretty young widow with a small child to raise, but Marcel had her blushing and tossing her hair wantonly. Word spread by osmosis, and soon at least half the women in Mossy Creek found some excuse to drop by the coffee shop.

By the time Marcel and I strolled back to my house I was exhausted just from watching other women fall all over themselves. "You're a wonder," I told him.

He smiled. "I like women. I respect them. I adore them. They respond." He grabbed my hand and tugged me into the back yard. "Plenty of time to swing before dark!"

Having a professional circus performer put up a swing is rather like having I.M. Pei design and build a tree house. Marcel leapt atop the swing, spreading his feet wide and gracefully rocking in a high arc. I felt certain the sturdily orchestrated project qualified for an F. H. A. loan. I was also certain it would not break or splinter the limb and dump Josie on her head. As a matter of fact, it would probably not dump Hulk Hogan on his head should he swing in it.

"So, Madame." Marcel bounded to earth then graciously pointed toward the seat of the swing. "Your turn."

"No way. You do it some more."

So he did.

All the remembered joy of childhood came back to me as I watched him haul back on the chains—neatly covered by non-slip rubber, by the way, to avoid burning Josie's tender hands or breaking her grip. He pumped higher and higher, flying way over my head. If he were to fall from that height, he'd break his neck.

Finally, he reached the apex of the swing. For a nanosecond the chains lifted past taut so that he soared free before the arc caught him again and he swung back to earth.

"Marcel, please be careful!"

He grinned over his shoulder on the way by.

"Marcel, let the cat die!"

"What?"

"Let the cat die, dammit!"

"Why do you wish to kill a cat?" he asked as he caught his feet on the ground and stopped.

"Haven't you ever heard that? It means let the swing slow down and stop. I didn't know I even remembered that."

"I am happy that you intend no harm to your cats. Now, please, you try."

I sat gingerly down on the wooden seat. It was broad enough to support a four-year-old's rump, but barely broad enough for mine.

I began to swing carefully, holding on for dear life. How long since I had done this? When Marilee was a baby, probably. When I was still young enough not to worry so much about danger or breaking things or making a fool of myself.

"It's lovely," I said after a few tentative passes.

Louise

Saturday afternoon, Lisa joined Charlie and me in a tonic water when he came home from a chilly game of golf. The man will play in a blizzard. Our cool, clear winter day didn't give him the slightest pause. I offered Lisa some gin in her drink but she politely refused. She and a few of her fellow performers would be demonstrating their talents in the brand-new gym at Mossy Creek High School that evening.

Governor Ham Bigelow, who is Mayor Ida's nephew,

had finally come through with the funds for the school, thanks to some creative arm-twisting and even, it was rumored, outright blackmail. The gym was a jewel, but somehow there wasn't enough money in Ham's budget to restore the football field, a legendary relic from the old high school, which burned down decades ago. A lot of Creekites, including yours truly, suspect the governor's stalling on the football field funds because his hometown team, in Bigelow, doesn't want to lose several powerhouse players who live in Mossy Creek. But that's another story.

At any rate, after a long procrastination on the part of Governor Bigelow, the school was scheduled to open in the fall. The gym hadn't yet been painted inside, and its parking lot was a pot-holed construction site, but nothing could keep eager Creekites away. A recently formed booster club was already raising money for clubs and sports teams. The owner of *Cirque d'Europa*, Mr. Polaski, had volunteered the demonstration and was also making a donation to the school.

"Fine people, you theatrical folks," Charlie said, beaming at Lisa. Charlie was enchanted. Smitten. She was charming to him, but I could see that yesterday's talk about his dependence on me had colored her view. She kept assessing him even while she was listening raptly to a play-by-play of his last nine holes.

"Would you like to watch us perform tonight?" she asked Charlie. "We won't have costumes, but have a CD with our music."

"Of course!" I said. I didn't even give Charlie a chance to respond. I didn't have to. He was already grabbing his coat and car keys.

Hannah

Saturday afternoon, which happened to be my day off, Dave Crogan dangled something in front of me that smelled like anchovies and had spookily staring eyes. "Trust me," he said with a smirk.

We were sitting on a blanket at the town park, with his camera tripod anchoring one end and a picnic basket anchoring the other. He'd spent half the morning shooting while we'd all watched, but Rachel and Monique had disappeared through the woods in search of the fish pond, so it was just he and I right now.

Despite a sweater and a heavy wool coat, I was freezing my behind off on this admittedly sunny February day, but Scotsman that Dave was, he didn't seem to notice the cold. He'd even removed his leather jacket, leaving him in a heather-gray sweater that made his eyes sparkle like sleet on slate.

He waved the kipper at me again, and I winced.

"Chickening out already?" he quipped.

Oh, he had no idea. Last night at my house, we'd spent hours talking, but the more fun he and I had together, the more worried I got. This was happening sort of fast. After the steady, safe life I'd grown used to, I felt like sharp objects were flying past me right and left, and one false move would get me skewered. Especially since Dave was probably leaving town in a few weeks or even days. He'd spent only a month in Provence, after all.

"Come on," he coaxed, "just a bite."

"Where did you get that thing anyway?" I asked, stalling for time as I looked the kipper over, suddenly queasy.

"Your mayor was kind enough to stock some at the Hamilton Inn." He grinned. "She said she wanted to make me feel at home."

"You knew that when you laid down this challenge, didn't you?"

"Of course." He waved the fish under my nose again. "Remember, I did eat your pizza."

"Hey, you said you *liked* my pizza!"

"I did. Smoked turkey breast, Vidalia onion, and asiago cheese—how could I not? And you'll like this, too, I swear. They taste much like sardines, and as I recall, you said that you liked sardines."

"I do, but they don't have eyes when I eat them."

He laughed. "Americans are such hypocrites. You eat steak and chicken, but God forbid you should be reminded that they come from living creatures. At least we Scots aren't afraid to stare a fish in the eye as we devour him."

He had a point. "You still haven't tried the peanut butter and ketchup," I said peevishly, picking up one of the wrapped sandwiches Rachel had insisted on including in our picnic basket.

"All right, we'll do it together. I'll even hide the kipper eyes if you like." Separating a piece of kipper from the head, he held the portion up to my mouth as I broke off a quarter of a sandwich. "On the count of three," he said. "One, two . . ."

He put the kipper in my mouth, and I put the sandwich in his. We chewed. For several seconds.

"Well?" he asked.

"Tastes like chicken," I joked, though he was right—it *was* much like sardines. "What do you think of the pb and k?"

"Not bad." When I started to smile, he said, "Not great, but it's more edible than I expected."

"I like the kippers," I broke down and admitted. "They're salty, and I'm a sucker for salty."

I licked my lips, and his eyes followed the motion like a

compass needle swinging north. Suddenly it wasn't about the food anymore. He'd scooted closer to feed me the kipper, and now his crossed legs pressed against mine, reminding me that we were alone. That we were touching. That this was a date. Sort of.

Apparently he realized all of that, too, because he reached up to brush a fleck of kipper from my chin before letting his fingers stray along my jaw. "More?" he rasped.

"More what?" I managed to choke out.

"Kippers."

Did I imagine it or was his breath coming faster? Lord knows I was having plenty of trouble breathing myself. "No."

"Something else, then," he murmured, before sliding his hand to the back of my neck. "Something like this."

Then he kissed me. Right there in the park under the trees in the middle of town.

Like any good first kiss, it started small and soft and warm. But it rapidly turned bigger and harder and way hotter, until it made me remember exactly why I'd avoided dating. Because being this intimate with a man again was almost too much to stand. Especially when I didn't know where it was going, and how long it would last.

Neither did he, apparently, judging from how he jerked back, then cast me a remorseful glance, his eyes the smoky gray of ashes. "Hannah, there's something I should tell you before this goes any further."

"You're married."

He looked startled. "No, of course not."

"*Of course not?*" Then I groaned. "Ohhh, you mean you're too young to be married."

Now he was smiling. "Not that either. I meant . . . I wouldn't be kissing you if I were married."

My world steadied. "Oh."

"I'm divorced." A strand of hair blew into my eyes, and he brushed it aside with a tenderness that made my throat ache. "And I'm thirty-six, probably older than you."

I cast him a rueful smile. "Actually, I'm the one who's older, but only by a year." Then what he'd said registered. "You're divorced?"

"Five years now. My wife and I married very young. Too young."

"No children?"

"No. We were only together for a couple of years. She rapidly tired of the traveling I did in the early days of my career."

"As a stock photographer," I prodded.

"Right. I mean . . . that's what I should tell—"

"Mom!" cried Rachel as she came bounding up. Monique followed behind, beaming broadly.

"Yes, Rachel," I answered, though my heart was pounding and I wanted to scream at having my conversation with Dave interrupted.

There's something I should tell you. That was *never* good.

"Mom, watch this!" Rachel positioned herself in front of me and Dave, demanding our attention. Then she pulled out knives. Three of them. Which she threw at a nearby oak, one after another, where they quivered in the air but miraculously stayed stuck.

I gaped at her. My daughter, who couldn't even brush her teeth without dropping the toothpaste, had thrown three knives at an oak. And had hit it dead on.

"I don't believe it," I said, then winced when Rachel's face fell. "Sorry, sweetie, I only meant . . . well, knife-throwing isn't a skill I would expect you . . . er . . . anyone in our family to have."

A smug look passed over Rachel's face. "I know." She went over to the tree and plucked out the knives.

Dave said something to Monique, and she answered with a spate of French. He shot me a smile. "Monique says that sometimes people who are routinely unaware of their physical surroundings just need a focus for their awareness."

I stared at him blankly.

He leaned close and whispered, "Clumsy people sometimes make good knife-throwers. Depends on why they're clumsy."

"I see," I responded, though I didn't really see at all.

But it was hard not to notice the self-satisfied expression on Rachel's face. Or the almost parental pride that Monique—and Dave—showed her, as if they'd both had some part in bringing out her hidden talent. Which I supposed they had.

"Thank you," I said to Monique, though I meant it for Dave, too.

Dave translated. Monique smiled, then answered in French.

"She says it was easy," Dave told me. "That you raised a very stubborn daughter who was determined to learn."

"Can you take a picture of me throwing a knife, Mr. Crogan?" Rachel asked as she aimed at the oak and let fly. She missed that time, but the second one hit its mark.

"I'd be honored." He rose and went to the camera. "But only if you'll do *me* a favor."

"Sure," she said with the blithe generosity of the young. "Whatever."

"Let me steal your mother tonight. I'd like to take her to dinner."

As I caught my breath, Rachel swung around to stare at Dave. "Like on a date, you mean?"

194

"If you approve."

"I do, I do! I've been trying to get Mom to go on a date for-*ever*!"

As I glowered at my daughter, Dave glanced at me. "Doesn't she date much?"

"Never. She keeps saying she's too busy at the library."

"That's the absolute truth, Rachel Marie," I protested, "and you know it."

"It's practically *your* library, Mom. You're in charge. And it's not like you don't have other people who can work." She planted her hands on her hips in a blatantly rebellious stance. "Besides, tonight's your night off."

I glanced nervously at Monique. "But we have a guest—"

"Monique and me will go over to the Blackshears'." I'd never seen my daughter look so determined. "And you can go out with Mr. Crogan."

"But only if she really wants to," Dave said in a quiet voice, and it occurred to me how my protests must sound. "Perhaps your mother has things to do."

"No," I said, so hastily it was embarrassing. When his eyes turned sultry, I added, "I . . . well, it *is* my night off."

And just like that, I had a real date with Dave.

We spent the rest of the afternoon "helping" him take pictures of Rachel throwing knives, of Monique throwing knives, of me *not* throwing knives. He would reposition the camera for a shot, and we would fetch or move things. He told Rachel teasingly that she made an excellent photographer's assistant and offered her a job, but she informed him with the lofty assurance of adolescence that she planned to be a knife-thrower.

What she *ought* to be was a spy. In the course of one afternoon she managed to glean more about Dave's past than the rest of us had done in three weeks. I didn't know if it was because he couldn't say no to a child or if he was just finally ready to talk, but thanks to my daughter's eager questions I found out that he'd been born in Edinburgh to a Scottish photo-journalist father and an African reporter mother. They'd met during their work on a project in Burundi. He'd been educated at George Washington University and had taken his first job at the New York Museum of Modern Art. He had an obsession with American baseball.

It was a wealth of info. I'd be spending half the night on Google. If I wasn't too tired after our date. The thought made me nervous and giddy all at the same time.

After a while the light waned, and Dave started packing up his camera equipment. "Why don't you ladies head home while I haul these back to the inn?"

I folded up the blanket. "I can help you carry the equipment to your room—"

"No," he said, so quickly it gave me pause. He managed a smile that didn't stretch beyond the curve of his mouth. "I'm used to handling it on my own. And I must change clothes for dinner. I'll stop by your place when I'm done at the hotel."

"Sure," I said, though my curiosity was raging. He didn't even want me near his room? Why?

"See you in a bit." Seconds later, he disappeared through the woods, hauling the tripod's huge silver case, the massive camera, and a canvas bag that held his film and other photographer stuff.

I tried not to dwell on his behavior as we busied ourselves with cleaning up the remains of our picnic, but I couldn't help it. Something wasn't right about our Mr. Crogan, and that unnerved me.

Monique suddenly exclaimed in French, and I looked

over to see her holding up Dave's jacket. He'd been in such an all-fired hurry that he'd left it behind.

"You can give it to him tonight, Mom," Rachel said.

"Or . . ." I paused. The reason he didn't want any of us near his room probably had to do with his evasiveness about why he was in Mossy Creek. "Maybe I'll just run up and give it to him now. He might want it later."

Ignoring my daughter's grin, I took the jacket from Monique, then hurried across the park in the direction he'd gone. When I got to the inn, I took the side door that led right to his hall. But when I reached Room 101, I was shocked to find that his door wasn't closed, just pulled to. I knocked, but there was no answer.

The sensible part of me said to go home and give him the jacket later. The nervous part insisted on pushing open the door. "Dave?" I called out when I saw that the inner door to the other room of his suite was ajar. Still no answer.

Then I spotted the contact sheets spread out on the desk. Curiosity got the better of me, and I stepped inside.

It took me a second to assimilate the images in the black-and-white photos because I couldn't at first recognize the subjects. Who were these downtrodden people?

I stared hard at the tired elderly man driving a smoking tractor, the gray-haired black woman with a wild-eyed gaze struggling with a walker, and the boy with the dirt-streaked face sitting cross-legged beneath the town sign that proclaimed our town motto, "Ain't goin' nowhere and don't want to."

Then I saw. I *saw*. These were Creekites—Ed Brady, Sr., Eula Mae Whit, and Clay Campbell. Only I'd never seen them portrayed like this—as sad and demented and dirty denizens of a seemingly dying Southern town. The pictures had the bleak feel of Ansel Adams photos of the Japanese interment camps and migrant workers. They were accurate pictures. And they were utterly untrue. They had no heart. Mossy Creek was vibrant, prosperous and progressive. Our people weren't miserable or destitute.

No wonder Dave hadn't let any of us see his work.

I'd never felt so betrayed in all my life, not even when Bobby Jackson from ninth grade had turned out to be a dog-kicking, foul-mouthed creep who liked to feel up girls behind the bleachers whether they wanted him to or not.

And it only got worse from there. Just as I tossed down Dave's leather jacket and turned to flee, I saw the name printed at the top of one contact sheet. Dave Brodie. *Not* Dave Crogan. That's why I hadn't found him on the web.

Oh Lord, he was probably famous, with a big New York studio and a reputation for photographic artistry. Not that it mattered. Talk about sharp objects hurtling toward me—Dave Brodie was one giant sharp object. And I must have been insane not to realize it before now.

"Hannah?" came a voice from the doorway.

I looked up to see him standing with a bucket of ice in his hand. His gaze flicked to the pictures, and the sudden flare of guilt on his face only got my dander up even more.

I stabbed a finger at the contact sheet. "Is this how we look to you? Like some stereotype with nothing to offer but rust and dirt and good ole Southern craziness?"

He looked as stricken as I felt. "No, I swear."

"You sure could have fooled me, Mr. *Brodie.*" When the name made him pale, I stalked toward the door, all but daring him to let me pass or be run down.

"I was going to tell you my real name," he said as I

pushed past him into the hall.

"I'll just bet you were." I'd worked up a good head of steam, and I was afraid I'd blow if I didn't get out of there. Especially when I realized that I'd spent the entire afternoon letting him photograph me and Rachel.

Oh God.

I whirled around. "Do me a favor, will you? Use all the pictures of me that you want, but if you so much as attempt to use a picture of my daughter, I swear I'll find you in your fancy studio, wherever it is, and I'll stake that tripod right through your weaselly heart."

That set off his temper. "If I'd meant to use the photos I took today, I'd first have had you sign releases, as I did with everyone else. But I didn't, because—"

"—you can't make us look pathetic enough?" I glared at him. "No, wait—if you could turn sweet little Clay Campbell into a hopeless urchin, it ought to be easy to transform my clumsy Rachel into a c-clown."

Cursing the tears coursing down my cheeks, I started to turn away, but he caught my arm. "You have to let me explain, Hannah . . ."

"I don't have to let you do anything." I jerked my arm free, then added peevishly, "And it's Mrs. Longstreet to *you*, mister."

"Yes, it's been Mrs. Longstreet from the beginning, hasn't it?" he shot back. Fury carved lines in his features. "That's how you stay safe, by keeping that circulation desk between you and the rest of us. Hell, we chatted for three weeks before I even learned that you weren't married, because you refuse to let any of us close enough to prove ourselves worthy of you."

The fact that there was a grain of truth to his words only irritated me more. "What? You accuse *me* of not letting people close, Mr. *Brodie*?"

He winced. "All right, that's fair. But the thing is—"

"Mr. Crogan!" called a voice from down the hall.

Muttering a curse, he turned.

"I thought I heard you down here." Mrs. Sikes, the manager of Hamilton's Inn, bustled toward us with a package in her hand. "That Fed-Ex delivery you been waiting for just came in. Tom said he got held up by an accident, or he would've been here sooner."

She handed Dave the package, and relief showed in his face. "Great, thank you," he told her, while I debated how to make my escape without rousing any gossip.

Although it was probably too late for that, since Mrs. Sikes was already eyeing me with a knowing look. "Tom says he's swinging by the newspaper, but he'll be back in a few minutes if you got anything you want to send."

Dave stared at her, then me, then her. "I do, thanks. I'll bring it down in just a second if you can tell him to wait."

"Sure thing." She flashed him a coquettish smile. "Anything for you, Mr. Crogan."

I scowled. Apparently I wasn't the only one to be taken in by "Mr. Crogan."

As she waddled off, he ripped the tear strip off with his teeth and then thrust the package at me. When I just glared at him, he said, "Please take it. Look at *these* pictures, all right? And wait here for me. I'm going to grab my film. I'll be right back."

I took the package numbly as he went through his room into the adjoining one, leaving the front door open. For a minute, I just stood there staring at the package, not sure what to do.

One thing I did know—I couldn't stand to see any more of his awful photos.

I started to toss them through the door. Then it occurred to me that if people had signed photo releases, it had to have been without knowing what they were agreeing to. But if I showed them what he'd done, then maybe they could prevail upon Ida or Amos or *somebody* to get them their releases back—

I made a split-second decision. Then I stepped inside his room, scooped up the other contact sheets, stuffed them into the package with the new ones, and fled. Mr. Brodie would never get a chance to print these if I had anything to say about it.

Saturday Night

The Show Must Go On

Chapter 5

Eula Mae

I'm sitting in my room reading my Bible Saturday night when Estelle comes in late.

"How are our guests getting along?" I ask.

"They're bickering like they've been all day. But, Great Nan, can we expect anything else?"

"Yes, 'cause I'm planning their wedding. This afternoon I called the mayor and the radio station. They agreed to have everyone assembled at two sharp tomorrow."

"Great Nan, there isn't going to be a wedding. Now I'm going to have to insist you call Mayor Ida back and tell her you've made a terrible mistake."

"No, I won't. There's going to be a wedding. Cowboy came in a while ago and asked for a dictionary of English words. That means he wants to spell something."

Estelle still doesn't believe me.

I'm suddenly very tired. "Estelle, I'd like nothing better than to visit with you all night long, but I've got to get up in the morning and bake four dozen buttermilk biscuits."

"Great Nan, you have four funerals tomorrow?"

"No. These are to announce my engagement to Mr. Wiley and the marriage of Cowboy and Roxie. I need my rest. Tomorrow I've got to look like a fresh sprig of mint."

Estelle goes to my door. "I'll leave after you call Mayor Ida."

I'm doing no such thing. "Good night, Clara's granddaughter," I say.

"Great Nan, that really hurts."

"Then think positive, Estelle. The best is yet to come."

Ida

Bubba Rice's Diner was a romantic Valentine's Eve world of candlelight, clinking crystal, and out-of-control mimes. What must have seemed like a good idea at the time—letting Win's mime guests help out as waiters on one of the busiest nights of the year—had clearly backfired. The mimes—in whiteface—refused to break character. Thus Del and I, like other vaguely annoyed and impatient customers, were reduced to not only pointing silently at menu listings but trying to mime back.

Halfway through dinner our preciously coy waiter fluttered his hands over his heart at us one time too many—signaling what a darling couple we made or, possibly, that he was suffering from mitral valve prolapse. Del stood with slow, sinister grace. He had finally had enough. Del crooked a finger at the mime, and when the mime leaned close, Del mimed slashing a throat.

After that, the mime kept his distance.

Dinner was a lost cause, regardless. The tension frosted our champagne glasses. Everyone in the place kept glancing our way. Twenty years in a small-town spotlight as mayor had taught me to keep a smile on my face even when I wanted to scream. I prodded a piece of chicken and roasted red pepper with Alfredo sauce, one of Win's signature entrees, with my fork. Del made a good show of looking casual, though the fierce way he sawed his sixteen-ounce prime rib made our waiter-mime turn a shade whiter.

"Everyone in the place is gawking at us," Del muttered.

"I'm sorry. I really am. I hoped we'd have a romantic dinner. That we might find some way to be friends, again."

"There's nothing 'romantic' about a dinner that will end with you going home to another man."

I stabbed my fork into a roll and left it there. Our waiter whisked it away. He must have glimpsed my dangerous stare. "Colonel Jackson, you might like to rephrase that," I said between gritted teeth. "Before I signal Orlon the mime to bring me an extra-sharp steak knife." Going home to another man? Del knew I'd left Jayne Reynolds in charge of a small party at my farm in honor of Philippe and his family.

Del lifted his grim eyes to mine. "I apologize. That was stupid. Ida, I know I'm acting like a bastard." His throat worked. He cleared it roughly. "But I feel as though I'm losing you, and it hurts."

I melted inside and quickly put a hand over his. "You don't need to worry about Philippe Chu. I swear to you."

He twined his fingers through mine tightly. "He's not the man I worry about."

"Del. *Del.* I don't know what to say. Except that I *miss* you. I miss your friendship. I miss your trust."

"I miss you, too," he said gruffly.

We leaned toward each other, sorrow and affection rising like a poignant shadow between us. Nothing was settled, but at least we had gotten past my betrayal—for now. I managed a teary, sincere smile. Del lifted his other hand and tenderly stroked the back of his fingers along my cheek. For a minute we forgot that our fellow Creekites were gaping at us in the candlelight.

Pitty pat pitty pat. Pitty pitty pat. The sound of mime fingers fluttering over the starched heartland of a waiter's coat.

We looked up. The mime stood there, smiling as he fluttered. He mimed a huge, happy sigh of admiration. The restaurant erupted in applause.

"I'm going to hurt you *bad*," Del told him.

The mime froze. He looked at me for some hint Del was joking.

"They'll never even find the body," I said.

Peggy

As Marcel and I walked to my house under streetlights that cast a chilly glow, I thanked him profusely for a lovely day. "How about some dinner? I am not the world's greatest cook, Marcel. Nothing like your wife, I'm sure."

"I am a circus performer, my dear Peggy." At some point I had gone from *Madame* to Peggy, which I preferred. "Anything that is not a cold cheeseburger between shows is haute cuisine."

I broke out a lovely white Bordeaux that would probably be past its prime in another year, anyway. Marcel approved, or said he did. I baked hunter's chicken with wild rice, salad and as close to real French bread as you can get at Ingrid Beechum's bakery on the town square. For a man who looked as if he lived on health-food shakes and tofu, Marcel ate as though he were going to the guillotine come morning.

"Is your wife having a baby a boy or girl?" I asked. "If you don't want to say, please don't feel you have to."

"She is a girl. We are still arguing about names, I'm afraid."

"I'm so glad! I mean, that she's a girl."

He raised his eyebrows.

"Oh, I know how men feel about sons, but having had only a daughter, I like them. And so do daddies. My husband spoiled Marilee rotten."

"I, too, like the idea of having a daughter."

"And she'll be a performer?"

"She can take up medicine or be an astronaut, so long as she is happy. The circus is actually a good place to raise children. If, as they say, it takes a village to raise a child, the circus is very much a village. All the children have many parents, excellent tutors, and they see the world."

The telephone rang. When I picked it up, it was Carlyle. I must have blushed, because Marcel raised his eyebrows and started to get up to leave me alone with the call. I waved for him to remain. "Tomorrow night? Yes, I'm still coming . . . "

I caught Marcel's eye. He was grinning and nodding. "A romantic dinner for Valentine's?" he mouthed.

"Well, I suppose," I whispered. Then, to Carlyle, "What? Oh, that's Marcel. I have a houseguest—one of the *Cirque d'Europa* performers. He's young enough to be my grandson—well, my son." We chatted a bit longer then I hung up.

Marcel smiled. "Your son? Nonsense. So he was jealous?"

"Now *you're* being silly. He's just a friend. A colleague from the university before I retired."

Marcel made that *pouf* sound only the French can manage. "If he is a man, he wishes to be more than a colleague to a beautiful woman like you."

"Knock it off, Marcel. Your charm worked with Marilee, but I'm a much older her."

I started to take the dirty dishes to the kitchen. He picked up his dishes and followed me. "I prefer women of a certain age."

"Are you hitting on me?"

He raised his hands in front of his chest. I could see the calluses. His hands were ugly. Good to see he wasn't perfect. "I am very much married and completely faithful to my wife. Before Jeanne I must admit I took advantage of a number of opportunities presented to me."

"I'll bet you had to beat women away with a stick."

He shrugged. "I didn't carry a stick." Then he grinned and winked and took my hand. "Come sit on your deck with me. I am not hitting on you, I promise, but the night is beautiful, and I don't get outside all that often."

So we put on our coats then sat companionably side-by-side in the swing.

"Your lover, he was jealous?" he persisted.

"He's not my lover!"

"He wants to be?"

"Yeah."

"And you?"

"I don't know. I mean, the whole logistics thing . . . "

He began to laugh. I joined him, and we sat there hooting like owls. Finally, he sputtered into silence. "For an intelligent and charming woman, Peggy, you are nuts."

"Not very romantic."

"I'm French. We are the least romantic people in the world."

"You're kidding."

"We're practical about sex and love."

"I'm worried I'll disappoint Carlyle. I haven't a clue whether I'm sexy, or whether I'm good in bed, or even what being good in bed means."

"It means he pleases *you*. Sex is supposed to be fun, not a test one either passes or fails. Take a chance."

He stood and pulled me to my feet. "I am going to bed. Alone. Think about what I said. Maybe it's time you swung free, pretty Peggy."

Louise

When Charlie, Lisa and I reached the gym that night, Lisa introduced us to the three other members of her group—all male and all about half my size, not to mention Charlie's.

We sat on the bleachers among an excited crowd of Creekites, while the performers put out tumbling mats and other things I couldn't identify. Everybody was wearing sweats. The gym was freezing cold and bare. The basketball goals hadn't been installed yet, and the wooden floor hadn't even been sanded. The scene was far from festive.

We watched Lisa and her guys finish warming up. "And now, we invite you to enter the magical world of *Cirque d'Europa*," Lisa announced to the crowd. "Where circus and theater meet in the realm of fantasy."

Ethereal music poured from the CD player. Lisa had already told me the bones of the story, so I did know what I was watching. It was a kind of Chinese *Cinderella*. A Tang Dynasty prince is searching for a concubine. He has princesses to dance for him and play for him, but he is not interested. The other girls weren't there, so we had to imagine that part.

Then the prince spots a slave girl in the market. He has her brought to entertain him with gymnastics and spinning poles.

He is enchanted and demands that she become his concubine, so that she will spin only for him. Instead of being delighted, she is annoyed with his arrogance. She tosses the plates and the poles to the prince. He keeps the first three aloft with ease, but when she tosses the fourth, he throws it and all the others to his two counselors, who scramble for them, but wind up dropping everything. In the process, they do a very involved tumbling routine. Even Charlie clapped in amazement. He never does that.

The counselors are furious and embarrassed. They demand that the prince have her beheaded. Instead, he vaults over her head, lands on one knee, and offers her his hand humbly. When she takes it, he tosses her up so that she's standing on his shoulders, and they walk off in triumph.

As she's leaving, she waves at the audience and gives them a big thumbs-up. It's obvious she doesn't plan to do much spinning in the future. He may carry her off in triumph, but it's obvious that she's the winner. In the future, he'll be the one performing for *her*.

The Creekite audience, including me and Charlie, gave the troupe a standing ovation. I had tears in my eyes. For a few minutes I'd forgotten my fear of the future, and I smiled.

Magic.

Harry

Josie and I got very little sleep that Valentine's Eve.

Dinner was ready by the time I made it home an hour after dark. After explaining why I'd arrived short one guest, I told Josie the whole story as we ate. As I'd known she would be, Josie was enthralled by the bear's tale.

We spent the next several hours discussing possibilities for Yuri's future. Everything from Yuri living in the cabin and helping me expand my research, to finding a new circus troupe for him to join with the bear, to me writing a grant and helping him establish the first Appalachian Home for Aging Dancing Bears.

When Josie came up with that one, I knew she was exhausted. She'd spent most of the day tending to her sick parents. I was tired, too. I didn't exactly wrestle a bear, but I felt as if I were wrestling a bear of a problem.

Josie, however, noticed that it was past midnight and declared it officially Valentine's Day. She slipped into the bedroom and donned her present to me, a nightgown she'd ordered from Victoria's Secret.

I forgot all about being tired.

Sunday Morning

The Grand Finale
Chapter 6

Eula Mae

I awaken Valentine's Day morning to someone shaking my bed. Cowboy is in my room and he looks frantic.

I get frantic also. It's been fifty years since a man's been in my room. I call for Estelle and she comes running.

"What's wrong?"

Cowboy speaks in broken languages, gestures and looks.

"Roxie's gone," I tell Estelle.

"Great Nan, I'll go check." She runs to their room and hurries back. "Her bag is gone. She left you, Cowboy."

He sinks onto the corner of my bed and starts crying, big gulping sobs that make my skin get bumpy.

Now this is three new things for me in a short period of time. A man asks me to marry him. Another man comes into my room. That man sits on my bed and cries. Normally this would bring me a great deal of joy, but most people that know me know I have a desire to meet Jesus at the soonest opportunity.

Now that fun and interesting things are happening, I'm a little torn. It's not as if I can compare the activity list from Heaven to Mossy Creek, so I'm not sure which is more fun.

"Cowboy, how about we sit in the kitchen and talk this thing over? I'm sure after we have breakfast, we'll have it all figured out."

He starts talking his gibberish and I can't wait for him to leave. I have to hurry to the powder room or there's going to be a great flood in Mossy Creek. I hurry as fast as an old woman can and finally meet Cowboy and Estelle in the kitchen.

We get the biscuits going and I'm real surprised at how good Estelle is at mixing the ingredients without measuring. She was watching and that's a good thing.

"Cowboy, you can find another Roxie," I say. "The circus must have a way to hire another girl that wants to climb trees with you."

Cowboy pulls out a tattered notepad from his pocket. "He. . .want. . .her."

Me and Estelle look at each other like somebody in the room is crazy and it ain't us.

"What?" I say.

"He—"

"No," Estelle cuts him off. "*I* want her. Repeat, Cowboy, I want—"

"I want her. Roxie," he says and tears up. "Her here," he says, holding his chest.

"You had her," I tell him, putting a plate of smoking biscuits in front of him. "You had your chance. Maybe another circus man will want her. Or maybe she'll settle down in Mossy Creek and start a business. I think that's what she was saying last night when we were talking."

Estelle stares at me. "You talked to her, Great Nan?"

"Yes, I did. She said she might leave and apparently she did."

Cowboy has a mouth full of biscuits and he starts to cry again. He sho' look like my nephew Junior used to look before he died in the forties. He was a crier, too. That wasn't a good thing on the chain gang. Oh well.

"Cowboy," Estelle snaps, "Great Nana and I have about had it with your crying. We're about to float out of here if you keep it up. Roxie is moving on because of you. All you men want the same thing. Well she's tired of giving it away. So pack up, Bucko. Your bus is moving on tomorrow and you're going to have to face the facts that it's moving on without Roxie."

By now the man is sobbing and bits of chewed biscuits is flying all over the table. I feel like going to get my badminton racquet to protect myself from the spray.

I've never seen my great-great-granddaughter take charge like this.

Frankly, I'm stunned.

"Estelle," I say real quiet, trying to talk her off the prison guard ledge.

"Yes," she says, baring her fangs at Cowboy, who has quieted considerably.

"I think we don't want to tear him down to nothin'. That's how you get four generation of kinfolk livin' in one house. It ain't pretty. It's usually cigarettes and guns involved, and probably some cussin'."

"Great Nan, you're lucky. You got Mr. Wiley. And Roxie, she's got him, but he didn't want her. But guess what? She probably doesn't know that he's probably the last good man she's going to get. I've been sitting here rotting away for almost a year and if it weren't for my job at the coffee shop, I'd be applying for a room at the rest home waiting to die, too.

"But men like Cowboy, well, in this world, he's got choices. But I'll make him a promise. If he lets Roxie go, I'll make it my personal goal to make sure she gets herself a real good man. *Real* good."

Cowboy shoots out of his chair and runs to his room.

Estelle grabs my hand. "Come on, Great Nan! We've got to keep up if we're goin' to get the wedding organized on time."

"What in tarnation just happened?" I start throwing biscuits in traveling bowls not even caring that they're on top of each other.

"It's called *a set up*," she says as she slaps one of Harriet's best wigs on my head.

I shrug. I know I'm lookin' my best. I'm going to a wedding. And I'm going to be in the circus.

Louise

Valentine's Day. Charlie stuck a card on the bathroom mirror. At least it was a nice card.

I came downstairs to find Lisa doing *Tai Chi* in the den. She continued while I fixed her French toast with fresh strawberries.

"Did you enjoy the performance last night?" she asked.

"Marvelous! I just wish I could have seen the entire thing complete with the costumes and the rest of the troupe."

"Did you learn something?"

"What was I supposed to learn?"

"I think of you as a kind friend, even though we have known one another such a short time. Louise, my friend, toss your Charlie the plates. If he drops them, what does it matter? Eventually, he will learn to pick them up."

"But your prince dropped them."

"No, he tossed them to others who dropped them. To have her love was more important to him than her ability to spin. Your Charlie loves you. I see it in his eyes, in the way he looks at you when you do not see him."

"He loves *this* Louise. When the going gets rough, men generally get going the other way."

"That is arrogant, Louise. Let the plates go. Give him the chance to pick them up." She shrugged. "Probably most of them don't even need to be picked up anyway."

Was I really being arrogant?

"Do you think your good Charlie is so shallow that he sees you only as a slave, the way the prince saw me at first? If he must nurse you, he will not like it. He will feel guilty, and angry with you, but perhaps you can both find that love is more important than deeds."

At that moment Charlie came into the kitchen dressed for golf. He kissed me on the cheek, spoke to Lisa, and reached out for the glass of orange juice I had already poured for him.

Then I caught Lisa's eye. She shook her head. I drank the juice myself, although I hate the stuff. "The pitcher's in the refrigerator," I said.

"Okay," said my Charlie, and poured himself a glass. "I'll pick up a couple of sausage biscuits on the way to the club. Happy Valentine's Day." He kissed me on the cheek again, waved to Lisa, and left.

Sagan

Valentine's Day dawned chilly but clear and sunny, dropping needlepoint shadows among the evergreens and gray hardwoods that covered the mountains outside my cabin. I heard the distant peel of Sunday church bells.

Nikoli paced uneasily. I took him by the sleeve and pointed him toward the bathroom. "Take a shower," I ordered loudly and slowly, hoping it made my English easier to understand. "We're going to town."

He seemed to catch my drift. His shoulders slumped but he didn't argue. I guess he figured that we'd survived a journey of sorts so he might as well take a chance. After he got cleaned up I handed him an old jacket of mine and my spare motorcycle helmet. "Let's go."

When he caught site of the Harley he grinned. "Okey dokey," he said.

I took him to Mama's All You Can Eat Café for a big breakfast. If the kid had to be turned over to immigration at least he'd get one last taste of freedom. We grabbed a booth, or rather, I grabbed one just as he was about to bolt. Then he saw a waitress walk by carrying a plate of hot cakes. That's when I found out that Nikoli spoke more English than anybody seemed to know.

"Hot cakes?" he asked as he tried to lose himself in the corner of the booth.

I nodded. "You want bacon?"

He nodded, and asked, "Vodka?"

He had a sense of humor, too. "No vodka. How about some orange juice?"

The waitress took our order, giving Nikoli a disapproving look. After she brought heaping platters of food he dug in voraciously. I toyed with a piece of toast and tried to think of the best way to discuss his situation. There was the matter of his being on the run, the ransacking of my kitchen and the missing exotic bird. I started to ask about the bird then decided instead to talk about me.

"I ran away more than once. In fact, you might say I've been on the move since I was fifteen. That's when my parents died. So, I know how it feels not to belong."

He peered at me and nodded. "Sucks. Mother and father die."

"You know the police are looking for you. Because of the bird, the necklace you stole—and the fact that you shouldn't be out in the world on your own."

He forked another mouthful of hot cakes into his mouth grimly. "No police. You stop. I give you necklace I took."

"What about the bird?"

"Bird?"

"Yes. The bird you stole from the pet shop. The bird that was in my house Friday night. The bird that led me to you in the mountains."

Nikoli stood. "No. Spirit bird is free." Before I knew what he was doing he headed for the door. But his luck had run out. He plowed straight into Amos, who clamped a hand on his arm. Amos gave me a somber glance. "How'd you find him, Sagan?"

"I didn't. He found me."

"And you were bringing him in by way of Mama's?"

"A condemned man deserves a last meal."

The café had gone silent. Everyone was staring at the drama. Nikoli looked as if he might cry with frustration. Amos looked unhappy to be there, which was exactly how I felt, too. I stood. "Let's go, Nikoli," I said, stepping around Amos and out the door, where I waited for Nikoli to make up his mind. "I won't let anyone hurt you."

To my surprise, he came along.

"Not run away again," he said in a pleading tone. "I stay here. I work."

He could have been me as a boy. Lost. Alone. Not sure of who he was or where he belonged. I didn't have anybody after my parents died, either. I understood his fear and his need, even if he didn't. I never conjured up spirit birds to lead me, but I searched for visions and guidance.

I turned to Amos and spoke in a low voice. "Let him stay with me while you talk to immigration. I'll see that he doesn't run away again."

Amos studied Nikoli. "What makes you think he's in the mood to cooperate?"

Nikoli must have understood. He slid his hand in his pocket then pulled it out holding the necklace. "Not mean to take. In candy box."

Amos took the necklace and nodded. "Okay, Nikoli. I'm leaving you with Mr. Salter for a few days. Don't do anything foolish. Sagan, I hope you know the responsibility you're taking on."

Responsibility. That thing I'd always avoided. I'd walked my own path, searching for a place to belong. Now I was committed, temporarily at least, to being a father figure for Nikoli. "I'll manage," I grunted.

"Party? Vodka?" Nikoli said eagerly.

I only knew one word in Russian. "Nyet."

Quinn

Sunday morning, dim winter sunlight peeked through the shades of my room at the Finch house. I blinked lazily. Someone was practicing scales on the violin. Must be one of the Finch kids. Wait a minute, I could hear!

I sat up in bed, and the room didn't tilt near as bad as yesterday. My bout with vertigo was almost over—just like my friendship with Erik. I'd spent most of Saturday avoiding him, which wasn't that hard considering I couldn't hear all that well and I was on the phone with Mr. Polaski most of the time, anyway. The good news was that Peavey's Garage called to say the *Cirque d'Europa* bus would be ready this afternoon; the bad news was that I'd be trapped on it with Erik and Magdalene and wouldn't be able to avoid the conversation I didn't want to have.

The sweet-batter smell of pancakes or waffles tempted me to risk seeing Erik at breakfast. It wasn't like he'd speak to me about ending our friendship in front of the Finches. Still wearing my flying monkey pajamas, I got out of bed with only minor dizziness and snuck down the stairs. I paused on the second to last step, listening to what was being said, hoping to determine my strategy before anyone noticed me. I heard the Finches and Erik talking of church and grumbling about Sunday school. Maybe Erik would go with them. If not, I could. Unless I was too late.

"You shouldn't spy on the ladies like that," I heard Erik say, undoubtedly scolding *randy* Randy.

Yet more evidence of Erik's affection for Magdalene. I turned to go back upstairs, but Mr. Finch, dapper in a charcoal suit and blue silk tie, was coming down. "Good morning, Quinn," he boomed. "And how are you? Full of vim, vigor, and vitality?"

"I'm good," I said, having no choice but to slink downstairs to the living room.

Randy had his binoculars at the table. "Dad! Can I look next door *without* using the binoculars?"

"No," Mr. Finch said and took the binoculars from his son. "Quinn, we're heading to church. Quinn? Erik? Y'all feel like accompanying us?"

A glance passed among the Finch family and Erik, whose outfit was casual yet nice enough for church. I smelled conspiracy in the air along with breakfast. Then everyone looked at me.

I feigned a smile. "I'm definitely on the mend, but not sure I'm up to church yet. You all go." I made a point of looking at Erik, who grabbed his coffee mug as if in defense.

The scent of chocolate wafted from the kitchen. But Mrs. Finch was emerging from the powder room with Charles in tow. Who was cooking? "Did you brush your teeth?" she asked.

"Yes."

"Charles Albert Finch?"

"I wasn't lying. I brushed them last night."

Mr. Finch looked at his watch, the Rolex Charles tried to give Erik on my behalf. "He can brush them when we get back. Let's go, family. If we're late, we won't be able to sit together."

"Yes!" Charles grinned, as Mrs. Finch helped him into his coat.

Mary Alice shook her head and followed her mother and Charles out of the house. Randy and Mr. Finch followed, which left me alone with Erik.

"Aren't you going with them?" I asked.

"No."

I took a deep breath and crossed my arms over my chest. "Well, I guess now is as good a time as any. Go ahead. Tell me what you want to say about our friendship. I'll listen."

He tried not to smile, but I could tell it was an effort on his part. How could he find the end of our friendship so damned amusing?

I plopped down on the sofa with only a flutter of dizziness. He sat right next to me so that I could smell that sandalwood aftershave I liked. I wondered if he'd wear something else if I asked him to.

"Quinn, as I was trying to say yesterday, I think friendships either fade out or they deepen."

I couldn't let him see the stupid tears filling my eyes, so I looked down at the monkeys cavorting across the flannel fabric on my thighs. Several strands of my long hair swung over my face, hiding it. I bit my lip. "I understand."

"I can't be your friend any longer," he said.

I couldn't breathe. I'd sob, and I wouldn't cry in front of him. I wouldn't. "Why not?" I squeaked out.

"Because I want more," he said, only the *want* sounded like *vant*, which was so cute and made his rejection somehow hurt more. More?

He tucked the hair hanging in my face behind my ear, warming my neck and face with his touch. "More," he said, "as in a romantic relationship with you."

My heart sped in my chest like I was running. "But Magdalene's sexy and Belgian. You speak the same language, grew up with waffles and *frites*, bicycles and canals and the musty smell of centuries-old buildings. I can barely manage to walk upright some days, I—"

He placed an index finger against my lips, stopping me from saying more. "I want you, Quinn. And I asked for a little help from our Creekite cupids this morning to show you what I feel, since my attempts to talk to you only seem to end in confusion."

"What about Magdalene?"

He winced. "I went out with her twice and that was all it took for me to know she wasn't right, to see that I'd been looking at the world with my own kind of vertigo."

"But she's always touching you."

"She chooses to think there's something there that

isn't. While *you've* chosen to believe there isn't something here that is. It's been quite a . . . problem."

He stood and held his hand out to me. I rose and allowed him to escort me to the Finch's formal dining room, where two places were set at the end of the table in a cozy arrangement of fine silver and crystal.

How could I have misinterpreted everything he said and did? And when had he planned this breakfast?

In one corner was a violin stand, a dulcimer and a steel guitar with *Joe Biddly's String Quartet* stenciled on its side. I noted the colorful flowers Mrs. Finch had sent Erik on my behalf displayed on the table. "Where are Magdalene's roses?"

"I offered them to Randy to replace the candy Charles stole."

"Won't she be mad?"

"I can find a new partner."

Bakery owner Ingrid Beechum, who'd taken one of the Bulgarians, poked her head out of the kitchen as Erik seated me. "Y'all about ready to eat?" she asked.

"Absolutely," I said, too stunned to question anything that was happening.

A little yip sounded at her feet. Bob the Chihuahua seemed pleased as well. I wondered where the Finch's cat was.

Erik poured us both a mimosa and raised his glass in a toast. "Happy Valentine's Day," he said gently.

Ingrid entered with a steaming plate of Belgian waffles drizzled with melted chocolate.

A serenade began in some strange, Southern-accented language, thanks to Joe Biddly's String Quartet, who walked in from the study, sporting sweaters with the band's logo and website address knitted in. Erik leaned over to whisper against my ear, and I felt like doing a triple twist. "Belgian folk music."

"I love it," I said, when I really wanted to say *I love you*. It was probably too early for declarations of love. My head was spinning from the revelation rather than vertigo. I could get used to this sort of breathless feeling. "How did you know I wasn't going to church?"

"I knew if I dressed like I was going with the Finches, you would choose to stay home," Erik said. "Between Mrs. Finch's words of wisdom and your own admission that you felt something more than friendship . . . how could I lose?"

He pulled a card from his pocket and handed it to me. I opened it and read, *One kiss bridges the distance between friendship and love*.

I tilted my head to the side. "Only you haven't kissed me."

Locking his gaze with mine, he leaned in even closer. I could feel his warm breath on my face. His thumb grazed my cheekbone, sending a shiver down my spine. My heart pounded as eyelids lowered. This was it. The kiss I could build a dream on.

His lips pressed against mine, gentle yet firm, and thorough in their exploration of mine.

I'd allowed my vertigo to color everything I saw. I wasn't going to do that anymore. Erik wanted me, even with my problem, even though we'd grown up in different worlds, even though we couldn't partner anymore on the stage. I looked forward to that afternoon's bus ride to Dollywood; I looked forward to life.

By the time the Finches returned from church, my stomach was full of sweet waffles and my heart with the love that shone in Erik's hazel eyes. Mr. and Mrs. Finch hugged each other. "See? The flowers worked," she said.

Charles squinched up his nose. "Na-uh. It was me."

Mary Alice sniffed. "I hardly think so. Quinn followed my advice and was honest about her feelings."

"Sorry folks," Ingrid yelled from the kitchen. "It was the waffles!" Bob added a yip for emphasis. The cat hissed and chased him. Bob stopped long enough to pee on the carpet.

Randy scratched his head. "So, like, Erik, the hottie with the red hair next door. You don't want her?"

"No," Erik said, smiling at me. "I don't."

Harry

I awoke on Valentine's Day well before sunrise and lay with Josie's warmth curled against my side as I went back over the possibilities for Yuri. It was frustrating. We didn't even know if he had a green card, although that wasn't an insurmountable hurdle. If our local lawyer, Mac Campbell, could arrange the adoption of three Mexican children for Opal Suggs, one little green card would be nothing for him to secure.

The more I wrapped my mind around Yuri's predicament, though, the more Josie's suggestion made sense. Not establishing a home for aging bears, necessarily, but finding a bear sanctuary that already existed. With all the animal rights groups out there, surely someone had come up with the funds to establish a sanctuary for circus animals to be put out to pasture, as it were.

My first thought was doing an internet search. That would net me information, but I wasn't just looking for a bear sanctuary. I was looking for a well-established organization that had a good reputation.

This was one of those times when having connections within the educational community came in handy. I knew a number of professors at the University of Georgia College of Veterinary Medicine. One of them was bound to have come across a first-rate sanctuary while conducting some research project. At least they could get me on the right track.

I checked the clock. Six a.m. A tad early to be disturbing anyone on a Sunday morning, much less Valentine's Day.

Still, I couldn't sleep. I slipped out of bed, took a shower, fixed ham and eggs and biscuits, and took a tray into the bedroom to surprise my wife with breakfast in bed. Breakfast led to other bedroom activities where Josie had still another surprise for me. I knew my wife was creative, but I never dreamed she had so many uses for muscadine jelly.

By nine o'clock I was on the phone. My third call netted the name of a well-known rescued-animal sanctuary in California that took in abused and abandoned wild animals. They had a special section for bears.

Bingo.

"Thanks, Dave." I checked my watch. "California is three hours behind us, which means it's 6:30 there. A little early to—"

"Are you kidding me? They've been up for an hour at least, feeding the animals. I'll give Pat a call. What's your number there?"

An hour later, I sauntered into the kitchen where Josie was stuffing supplies into our backpacks. "My wife is a genius."

She straightened from her task at the kitchen table. "You found a home for aging dancing bears?"

I grinned. "Dave came through. He put me in touch with a rescued animal sanctuary in California. I just got off the phone with the head honcho out there. They not only have room for the bear, but they're so excited about having an experienced bear handler, I swear I could hear the director doing a happy dance. Especially since they'll get Yuri and some cash, as well."

"Cash? Oh. You mean, you'll write them a grant."

"Yes. I have no doubt I can secure funds for a place like that. And after all, grants are what researchers do best. Well, maybe not best, but second-best."

"Second-best?" Josie wriggled her eyebrows.

I laughed. I adored her playfulness. "Okay, third-best."

She regarded me, her face shining with love. "Harry Rutherford, you are the most giving man I know. Who else would go to so much trouble for a Russian you barely know and a beat-up old bear?"

Pleased with herself and me, Josie returned her attention to packing.

I walked up behind her, pulled her back against my chest, and dropped a kiss on her neck. "Don't ever change, my love."

She melted into me. "One thing that will never change is how much I love you. Now, help me pack. I want to see that bear!"

Right before we left our house, Ida called about the *Cirque d'Europa* bus. The bus would be fixed by late afternoon. The troupe expected to leave town around five that evening. Ida mentioned that the Methodist church was offering a special circus blessing for our guests, but I made our regrets. Josie and I weren't even making it to our own church this morning, since we had to get up the mountain.

I didn't tell Ida that Yuri would not be rejoining the troupe. Anything could've happened during the night to change his mind.

Josie and I reached the cabin around noon. Yuri and

the bear weren't there. We left our backpacks on the porch and quickly found the unlikely pair fishing in the stream that tumbled down the mountain about fifty yards away from the cabin. They were only a hundred yards above "Josie Falls," where Josie and I had first met. I'd been following her on her mountain walks for several months, not wanting to show myself because of my scars. That day, however, I had to make myself known in order to rescue her when she came close to killing herself with a freezing dive into the pool below the falls. Josie had come up the mountain to escape her mother's disdainful disappointment in her after she lost the Miss Bigelow County Pageant. We'd been inseparable ever since.

Josie and I both stopped dead when the bear roared and took several lunging steps toward us.

Yuri barked a command in Russian, and the bear turned to him instead, ambling over to tamely take the fish Yuri offered him.

"Bear good fisherman," Yuri said with a grin. "But he still hungry. So he guard fish."

"Goodness, Yuri," Josie exclaimed. "This is all so amazing. Is it okay if we come closer?"

Yuri regarded the bear that was tearing the brook trout apart. "Maybe iz better that ve meet you back at cabin. Bears do not like to share food and if you come closer. . ."

"We'll see you there," I said. Taking Josie's arm, I turned her back toward the cabin.

We'd just finished putting up the supplies we'd brought when I spied the pair walking back.

Josie and I met them on the porch.

"Iz vonderful here." Yuri waved his arms around the clearing. "Vhy you not live on mountain?"

"I work in downtown Mossy Creek," Josie explained.

"While I do love this place, hiking up and down every day would get old."

A shadow passed over Yuri's face at the same time that he threw me a crooked smile. "Ah, the tings ve do for our vemen."

Since I could tell Josie was dying to pet the bear, I took her hand and we descended the steps.

The bear sniffed the hand I extended briefly, then snuffled as he sniffed hers.

Josie pulled a large milk bone from her pocket and offered it to the bear. He was not shy about taking it.

"Where did you get that?" I asked.

"While you were on the phone, I went to check on Mama and Daddy. I raided their dog treats."

"Iz circus bus leaving today?" Yuri asked.

I nodded. "Got the call just before we left the house. They're leaving around five o'clock."

"Ah."

"Are you sure you don't want to go with them?" Josie asked.

"If okay to stay here until I find another circus that vill take bear. . ."

"You don't need to do that," I said, then explained about the California sanctuary. When I mentioned how delighted the director was to add Yuri to his staff, the shadows from Yuri's face cleared.

His relief was so irrepressible, he began to dance around the clearing with joyful laughter.

The bear immediately roared and reared, joining the dance.

Josie clapped her hands.

Seeing Josie's delight, Yuri sang the Russian folk song and gave the bear more dancing cues. Josie watched for a minute, then joined them, laughing and dancing and singing words she didn't understand.

Their happiness was so palpable, I couldn't budge.

When the song ended and the bear dropped to all fours, Josie gave it a hug and another milk bone. "What's his name?"

Yuri shrugged. "I do not know bear's name."

"He has to have a name! You can't just call him *Bear*."

"My beautiful friend, you give bear name."

Josie's eyes widened in excitement. "Me? Okay." She thought a minute, then shook her head. "I need time to think about this. I'll let you know in a day or two."

"Yah. Iz good."

"If you want to say goodbyes to your circus friends, we need to head on down the mountain," I said.

Yuri scratched his head. "I tink maybe if I leave, bear follow."

"As much as this fellow seems to love you," Josie said, "I think you can pretty much count on that."

Yuri obviously had no pressing desire to see his friends before they left. Tatiana's hold had gone deep, her desertion ripping part of Yuri away.

"I think it's a pretty good idea for you to stay here until we can arrange transport to California. Josie and I can say your goodbyes."

"I tank you both," Yuri said. "So very kind to me."

"Do we need to pick up anything for you?" Josie asked. "Did you leave anything on the bus or in one of the trucks that you might want?"

Yuri shook his head. "Foot jugglers have not much equipment but muscles. I bring bag with me to your house. I can tink of nothing to bring away with you."

Josie and I hiked back down the mountain, then drove into town. We met the troupe gathering around their repaired bus.

Hannah

After spending my Saturday night avoiding David Brodie—refusing his calls and closeting myself in my bedroom with the claim that I had gotten indigestion from his stupid kippers—I awoke on Valentine's Day to a pounding headache.

That wasn't surprising, since I'd spent half the night on Google. Google was no stranger to Dave Brodie. The man darned near *owned* the search engine. Typing in "Dave Brodie" and "photographer" on my laptop got me 52,081 hits, everything from galleries to newspaper bios to his photo essay in *Vanity Fair*. The man was amazing, darn him.

I hated him for that. So much talent, so many photos. Not the photos he'd taken in Mossy Creek—I still couldn't bring myself to look at *those*. They sat on my dresser exactly where I'd left them when I'd arrived home last night from the park.

But the other ones? Let's just say that the man knew how to capture a subject. And looking at the eloquent images tore my heart in two. Because for whatever reason, he'd decided that *my* town, the town that I loved, wasn't worthy of the care he seemed to show his other subjects.

"You're not going to church with me and the Blackshears?" Rachel asked plaintively from the doorway of my bedroom.

"Sorry, sweetie. My headache is really bad." That was the God's honest truth, although it was only part of it. I wasn't going anywhere until I figured out what to do about Dave's pictures. I was liable to erupt into tears if I ran into anybody he'd featured so cruelly.

"Monique's not going, either," Rachel grumbled. "She says she's an atheist."

"Does she?" I murmured absently, then started as her words registered. "Since when did you learn to speak French?"

Rachel dropped her gaze to the carpet. "Um . . . well . . . she's leaving today, so I wanted to talk to her before she left so . . . well . . . I called and asked Mr. Crogan if he'd come over and translate. H-He's downstairs."

I gaped at my daughter. "You *asked* him here without my permission?"

She thrust out her lower lip. "He's *my* friend, too, you know. And you were supposed to have a date with him until you got sick last night and made me call Mrs. Sikes and give him a message not to come."

"Darn it, Rachel, how do you know I didn't have a perfectly good reason for not wanting to see him? How do you know I hadn't found out he was a murderer or a thief or—" *A famous photographer who wants to make fools of us all.*

"Mr. Crogan? Puh-lease." She rolled her eyes. "He's, like, the nicest man I ever met. And you didn't say he did anything wrong—you just said to tell him you were sick." A canny look crossed her face. "Are you saying you *weren't* sick? That you made me lie to him and Mrs. Sikes?"

Busted. And by my daughter, no less. She got smarter by the minute, the little imp. And that, along with the discovery that she actually had good hand-eye coordination, was disconcerting. Everything was disconcerting these days.

Sharp objects again.

I sighed. "It doesn't matter."

"You want me to tell him to go away?"

"Yes." As her face fell, I said, "No." The truth was, I'd

have to deal with him sooner or later. And it wasn't fair to use Rachel as a go-between, even if she *was* eleven-going-on-twenty. "Tell him I'll be down in a minute."

"He . . . um . . . asked me if you'd looked at the pictures yet. I didn't know what he meant, so I didn't know what to tell him."

I sucked in a breath. "Tell him . . . I'm looking at them now." And just so she'd know I wasn't lying, I got up and grabbed his package, then carried it to the bed.

Time to rip off the bandage. Find out just how bad it was. Then at least I could make an informed decision. And if the photos riled me up, that was all the better—it would make it easy for me to kick his famous behind out of my house.

As soon as Rachel left, I took out the contact sheets. The initial ones I'd seen were on top, and I looked at them again to help me brace myself for the new ones. I still hated them, but now I could see the artistry behind them. That almost made it worse, because it was the artistry that shaped the vision.

Of Mossy Creek as some sort of broken-down hell full of pathetic people.

Blinking back tears, I pulled out the rest of the sheets. The first half of the initial sheet looked like more of the same. And then . . .

The vision changed. There was no other way to describe it.

I knew it the minute I saw the shot of Jayne Reynolds making a *latte* at The Naked Bean. The camera had caught her in the midst of a smile at a customer. The soft and subtly shadowed lighting gave it a feel of homey comfort, while the focus still crisply captured the modern espresso machine in the background.

My breath catching, I looked at the next and the next

and the next. The Sitting Tree awash with morning light—you could practically hear the holy hush of the clearing. How many Creekite romances had begun under that tree including, it was rumored, our mayor's and police chief's, years ago? And here was Marle and Hope Settles kissing, with the covered bridge of Bailey Branch glistening behind them on a wintry afternoon. It went on and on until I came to a set of photos that caught me up short.

"Hannah?" said a tentative female voice from the doorway.

I looked up to see Monique watching me with concern. Only then did I realize that tears were streaming down my cheeks. "Yes?"

She glanced down at the pictures, and her face cleared. Coming over to the bed, she took the contact sheet from me, her gaze fixing immediately on the set of photos I'd just been looking at. I'd forgotten about the afternoon Dave had taken them.

A week ago, I'd hurried out of the library to run an errand, only to be met by a sudden downpour. Pausing to wait under the overhang, I'd glanced over to see Dave standing in the parking lot to the left of the entrance with a tarp half-slung over his camera, his sweater plastered to his skin and his hair lying in ruins about his face. I'd smiled and waved, and he'd just kept his eye to the camera, snapping pictures madly as rain beat down on his back.

Monique laid the sheet in front of me. "*L'amour,*" she said, tapping her finger on one particular photo.

More tears escaped. I might not speak French, but I sure as heck knew what *that* meant.

I stared at the picture she'd indicated. In most of the others I was backlit by the fluorescent lights of the library so you could see only a silhouette. But in this photo, I'd turned my head toward the window, and Dave had caught me half in shadow, half in light, on the cusp of a smile, looking as alluring and mysterious as any Parisian model.

L'amour.

"Excuse me," came a familiar male voice from the doorway, "but I thought you might need a translator."

I lifted my gaze to find Dave wearing blue jeans and a Yankees t-shirt, his hands shoved into his pockets and his chin thrust out as if he braced himself for a final judgment. Mine.

Monique smiled, said something in French, then eased herself from the room. But I could only stare at him, completely at a loss for words. Finally I said, "I have to take Monique to the bus. But afterwards, you and I will talk, all right?"

He nodded.

Eula Mae

A bunch of the circus people and a mess of Creekites are lolling in the yard at WMOS radio station and they don't look happy to be outdoors in the cold weather. But it's Valentine's Day and that's always in February, so it ain't my fault. I'm having a good time with my guests. We have to take them to the bus in a few minutes.

Mayor Ida walks up and she gives me a big hug and that always sets me in a good mood. Since I'm already in a good mood, I feel like a firecracker. "I hear there's going to be a wedding and then you're going to be in the circus?" she says.

"That's exactly right."

The mayor's granddaughter, Little Ida, gives me a hug and kisses my forehead. "You're my idol, Miz Whit," she says. This little girl is a politician like her grandma. She's going to be president of the big ol' U S of A one day. I wonder if I can cast my vote for her now?

I nod to Mayor Ida. "Is the preacher here?"

"Yes, Miz Eula Mae, but I don't know if the ceremony will be legally binding. Roxie and Cowboy aren't U.S. citizens."

"I see where that might cause a problem. However, we made exceptions before, so I figure there's a law somewhere they can get married under. We'll figure it out. There's Cowboy. I hope he ain't still crying."

Mayor Ida raises a brow but she don't ask any questions.

All the rest of the circus performers are buzzin' around like flies. They seem to all know about the rift between Cowboy and Roxie. Did our ruse work? Has she been lured back? We wait and wait, then we spot her, long off in the field behind the radio station, where wisteria blooms in April but there's just empty vines in February, taking her time as all women should, finally calm.

Cowboy goes to meet her and for the first time since I arrive, everyone is quiet. This is a big deal for Mossy Creekites. We have big hearts and we use them liberally, although it don't mean we won't talk about you later.

Mr. Wiley comes by my side and two chairs are brought over so we can rest our old bones. We sit together and talk about what kind of future we can have. I'm a hundred and one, he's seventy-eight, and we're realistic.

Getting married and blending houses isn't a good idea. The move might just kill one or both of us. But we will stay engaged and be sweethearts forever.

Suddenly Cowboy falls to one knee before Roxie and then she lets out a whoop and does some back flips before ending up in his arms.

The preacher steps forward and within minutes Cowboy and Roxie are declared man and wife.

The circus people and Creekites cheer them on. Then the circus folk come for me.

I hear Estelle hollerin', but I tell her I'm fine.

They form a human swing and I sit on the arms of some of the men who have linked their hands together. Ever so gently I am rocked. I'm thrilled because another of my wishes has come true. I am in the circus.

I think about that fine lady, Oprah, and I just betcha I got her beat again, 'cause I'm pretty sure she ain't never rocked on a human swing.

This is a dandy day to be alive.

Sunday Afternoon

The Circus Moves On
Chapter 7

Sandy

As Sunday afternoon rolled around, Mutt got word to me that the bus had been repaired. Our circus guests were to meet back in the parking lot at Mount Gilead Methodist. So I drove the feuding foreigners back to the bus where the other circus folk were gathering from all the places where they'd been farmed out the last couple of nights. Sergei and Mariska sat in stony silence the whole way.

I parked and helped them get their things together. Sergei announced, "Come, Mariska, ve must practice," and headed back to the target board. Standing beside it was a small, husky man smoking a long cigar. Sergei laid his knife case on the grass and opened it. Meanwhile, a petite Asian lady handed Mariska what looked like a telegram. She read it quickly as Sergei selected a knife for each hand.

"I still am not standink in front of target," Mariska declared. This pronouncement unleashed a torrent of guttural statements from her cigar-chomping coach, who evidently spoke enough English to understand that Mariska, the *throw-ee*, still balked. You didn't have to understand the language he was speaking in order to hear the threat in his voice. Sergei held out his hands to her.

"Mariska, you heard heem. He will fire us both if you do not work with me."

"Nyet," Mariska stated firmly. "I steel do not trust you."

Sergei flipped several knives in the air and caught them by their blades. He held them out to a startled Mariska by their handles. "Then *you* throw knives at *me*." Sergei stepped in front of the bus and stretched out his arms. "Because if I have lost your trust, I have lost your love, so you might as well pierce me in my broken heart." He looked imploringly at Mariska, and then gave me quick, sidelong glance and a barely perceptible wink.

Well, now, this was a fine howdy do. When I suggested he prove his love with actions, I was more in mind of him taking out the garbage. But I had to admit that offering to make like a pin cushion for your lady love is a tad more dramatic. For my part, I thought about the heirloom quilt incident with Miss Addie Lou and Miss Inez, back in January, and wondered why all my conflict resolutions had to do with knife play.

The coach muttered something out of the edge of his mouth. "What'd he say?" I asked Sergei.

Despite the chilly air, a bead of sweat had popped out on Sergei's forehead. "He said that somebody needs to start throwing knives at somebody or he vill be throwing dem at *both* of us."

Mariska suddenly burst into tears. "Here is real reason I refuse to stand in front of knives. I am going to be aerialist again." She thrust the telegram into Sergei's hand.

Sergei read the telegram while the coach peeked over his arm and read along. "You were goink to leef me all along," Sergei said. "How long have you been planning this escape?"

"Since you keesed LuLu-san!" Tears ran down Mariska's alabaster cheeks.

"LuLu-san keeses everyone. Even me," said the coach. He took the telegram from Sergei's hand. "I know this troupe. They have opening for business manager, Sergei. I would hate to lose you, but it would be good position for man of your skeels."

Sergei looked interested. "What happened to business manager they had?"

"He ran away to dental school," said the coach.

"Wait a minute," I said. "He ran away from the circus to join dental school?"

The coach shrugged. "It happens."

"So, Sergei, what are these skills that qualify you for the business manager job?"

"I have MBA."

"You're kidding."

Mariska put her arms around her husband's waist. "From ULCA."

"UCLA," Sergei corrected. "Where do you tink I learn to speak English so well?"

Mariska took the telegram from the boss. "My babushka always said it is nice to have sometink to—how you say?—fall back on. Sergei, I must call this number to confirm the acceptink of aerialist position. Inquire about manager job as well."

"Lemme help," I said. I whipped out my cell phone like a quick-draw artist. In minutes the deal was done. The other circus was thrilled to have someone who had an MBA and experience under the big top. Sergei and Mariska kissed passionately before breaking off their embrace so Sergei could speak to his coach about terminating their employment.

Before Mariska went skipping off to give her friends the good news, she paused to give me a hug. "Tank you for your hospitality, Officer Crane."

"You're welcome. I'm glad you and Sergei have a chance to make a new start."

"Yes!" Mariska said, clearly delighted. "I cannot vait to go and tell that beetch, LuLu-san!"

Sergei and his boss shook hands and the older man walked away. "Tank you for everyting, Officer Sandy Crane," Sergei said.

"That was quite a sacrifice you made for your wife," I said. "Being a business manager can't be half as exciting as being a lion tamer or knife thrower."

Sergei sighed. "It vill be worth eet," he said. "I really scored some points today. She owes me—how do you American say?—beeg time."

Some things are the same in any language.

Harry

When we told the manager, Quinn James, about Yuri's new plans, she threw up her hands and laughed. "That's just great. Sergei and Mariska are leaving to join another troupe. Cowboy and Roxie got married. The mimes want to stay here and work for Win Allen, and even though he says *No* they may throw themselves on his doorstep and pretend to cry until he gives in."

She gestured at the performers and Creekites hugging each other goodbye outside the newly fixed bus. There were tears and smiles, photos were being snapped, video cameras and cell phones were recording the action, and penpal information was being exchanged. It was a love fest. "My circus is never going to be the same."

"Mossy Creek has an amazing effect on people. We like to say it's something in the water."

"You're right. But I have to say, Yuri's decision to stay is the least shocking. I like Yuri and all, but he isn't much good to us without a partner."

"He's got one now," Josie told her.

Quinn smiled wryly. "One better for him than Tatiana. I knew she was trouble the first time I laid eyes on her. Too bad we're not equipped to handle circus animals."

"I think both Yuri and the bear are going to be happier where they're going," I said.

"No doubt. Thanks for letting me know. Give Yuri my regards, and tell him that we all wish him the best of luck."

"We'll do that."

Quinn James smiled past us, and after a second we realized she was smiling at a performer named Erik, who was smiling back at her. Her vertigo had cleared up, and so, apparently, had her love life.

"Something in the water," I repeated to Josie.

She grinned and nodded.

Louise

I drove Lisa to the troupe's bus, wishing she could stay a little longer and keep me company. Most of the town was there at the church to see the performers on their way. There were lots of hugs and even a few sentimental tears. I admit to my fair share. Lisa wiped her eyes and we shared a smile at our mawkish goodbye. As Lisa climbed onto the bus, she leaned back and waved at me. Then she said, one last time, "Let the plates go."

I took a deep breath and nodded.

Sagan

The weather was cooperating, turning surprisingly warm for a February where snow had fallen in the mountains the night before. The parking lot at Mount Gilead Methodist was alive with activity. Nikoli, dressed in new American jeans and cowboy boots, was as excited as if the celebration was in his honor. I tried to explain that staying with me was only temporary, but he didn't understand. Or, maybe he didn't want to understand.

Mayor Walker gave a short speech thanking the performers for being such good guests and also thanking the Creekites who'd hosted them. I was surprised when she walked over to me. Nikolai was busy learning a "high-five" from Willie Bigelow, Sue Ora's son.

"I've got some connections through the governor's office," the mayor whispered. "If I can find a way for Nikolai to stay permanently, are you serious about being responsible for him?"

"Yes." It was as simple as that. I didn't have to think about it.

"Good." She went back to her official hosting duties. I stood there watching Nikolai trying to teach Willie a few words in Russian. A soft hand touched my shoulder. It was Emily.

"Looks like you may have found what you were looking for."

"Emily. I thought you'd gone."

"I heard about you taking care of Nikolai. I wanted to

see for myself."

I got caught up in watching her face. Why hadn't I noticed before how lovely she was, how melodious her voice was? How come I'd let her go before I realized how much I missed her?

"I feel like I've been on a long flight," I told her. "And now I've come back to earth. I traveled back to my childhood, and I visited my forebearers on the reservation. Through the sweat lodges and vision quests, I searched for a vision, but I never saw one—until I came back here. I'm home, in a place where people genuinely care about each other." I studied her intensely, looking for signs of forgiveness. "Or at least they tolerate the imperfections of others. My imperfections. My mistakes."

"What did you learn from your long trip home?" she asked gently.

"I'm not sure yet. I . . . only know this much. I was meant to find Nikolai, to help him. And . . . I'm glad you haven't left town."

She smiled and linked an arm through mine.

Emily and I were okay.

It was as simple as that.

Peggy

I kissed Marcel chastely on the cheek and put him on the *Cirque d'Europa* bus. Mossy Creek gave the troupe a nice send-off. There was a crowd, and I got quite a few curious looks and wink-wink smiles from Marcel's many admirers. I went home, walked into the back yard and sat down in the swing. In a few hours I'd go to Carlyle's place for dinner—and more.

I began very slowly and gently, barely moving my

feet off the ground. It's like riding a bicycle. You don't forget how to pump a swing. The higher I rose, the more I pumped my arms and legs, the freer I felt. I wanted to hit that apex Marcel had touched, and when I did, when I lifted past gravity for a nano-second, I shouted.

I was going to Valentine's Day dinner with a man who wanted to make love to me. I intended to let him. I darned near fell off the swing. I gripped harder and started to kill the cat. Then I laughed and pumped for that nano-second one more time.

It felt great.

Ida

As I went through the crowd at the church, wishing each performer a fond farewell, I mentally checked off the weekend's astonishing results. Found: one dancing bear and a Russian to care for him. Married: one bizarre pair of acrobats. Informally adopted: One runaway boy. Reunited: A matched set of knife throwers. Named an honorary circus performer: Eula Mae Whit. Newly minted or happily restored romances? Too many to name, both among the performers and the Creekites.

What a weekend. I craned my head at the sight of Hannah Longstreet hugging her guest, Monique, goodbye. Hmmm. Hannah looked a little pale and worried. My guess was that Dave Brodie hadn't explained himself to her, yet. When he did, Hannah would be fine.

Dave's reasons for coming to Mossy Creek were complicated, and when he first arrived and spoke to me about his intentions, I considered strangling him then using his own camera to photograph the crime scene. But my intuition told me Dave was a good man, so I stood back and let him learn a few lessons about Mossy Creek on his own. I had a feeling I was right about his integrity.

I also had a feeling I could use his circumstances for a nice little bit of blackmail against my dear nephew, the governor. But more about that, later.

"Bye!" I heard loudly. "No. You're not staying. You're going. Bye!" I pivoted and watched Win Allen looking up at his two mimes. They were wearing their white-face performance make-up, black sweaters, slacks and Bubba Rice aprons Win had given them. They stood on the bus steps, miming goodbye and rubbing tears from their eyes. Clearly, they weren't leaving until Win mimed goodbye in return.

Win raised a hand. For just a second I feared he was about to mime a message involving his middle finger, but he got himself under control and merely waved. The mimes sighed, made an elaborate show of dejection, then disappeared inside the bus.

My mayoral duties were nearly done. Now, for the hard part. Now, it got personal. I walked into the crowd, my eyes going to Philippe and his family. Among them, standing out like a red-headed poppy in a field of Asiatic lilies, was June.

June, my proper Scottish housekeeper, thirty-two years old and never yet married, quoter of poetry, a couch potato barely able to leap tall dust bunnies in a single bound, June was running away with the circus. More precisely, with Philippe's son, Jean. Who was ten years her junior, two inches shorter than she, and able to leap entire stages while twirling a pair of hoops.

"Please say you forgive me," June begged as I helped her carry her luggage to the bus.

Philippe and his family walked discreetly ahead of us, allowing me one last chance to examine June's head for holes. "I can find another housekeeper. It's just that I think you're being impulsive."

"I've waited all my life to be carried away by passion."

"Passion, yes. But a tour bus headed for Dollywood? I don't . . ."

"The joy is in the journey, not just the occasional strange destination."

We reached the bus. As Philippe and his sons loaded June's things, I gave up all pretense of disapproval. She and I hugged. "You'll write and call, won't you?" I ordered. "Send text messages and emails? And update your coordinates so I can find you on a Google map?"

She smiled, cried and nodded. "Yes to all of the above. I'm so going to miss you! When I came to Mossy Creek I assumed my only adventures would be escaping into fantasy at the library, but working for you has given me a whole universe of bizarre and unsettling experiences I shall never, ever regret."

I made a motherly fuss with the collar of her tweed overcoat. "I'll take that as a compliment."

"It is, it is." She bent her head close to mine. "The one thing I'll miss most is seeing you *get it on* with Chief Royden. I had so hoped to see that."

Get it on? "I should never have given you a Marvin Gaye CD for your birthday."

"Please, ma'am, be serious." She grasped me by the arms. "The chief loves you so. Don't miss your own chance to run away with the circus."

"Time to go, *ma petite*," Jean said, bounding up beside us. His face glowed as he looked at June. She hugged me one more time. "I'll text message you when we reach Dollywood!"

"Take care of yourself. And whatever you do, don't

sit near the mimes. They're upset and they might start another fire."

She laughed and waved goodbye. I stood there in for-lorn farewell as she and Jean climbed into the bus. A cold finger of breeze made me shiver despite a long leather coat. I felt lonely.

Philippe finished loading the luggage and slipped through the crowd. "I won't say goodbye, I'll say *A plus*. I'll see you later."

I smiled. "And I'll say '*Adieu.*' Goodbye."

He laughed. "Ida, you are a cool-hearted heartbreak-er."

"I'm actually quite fond of you. Under different cir-cumstances—"

He kissed me. Just lightly, on the mouth, cupping my chilled chin with one hand as he did. He packed a lot of know-how in that quick kiss. "Why, sir!" I said with a dra-matic chagrin, "how dare you, right out here in front of God and a passel of acrobats!"

"*Mademoiselle* Scarlett, I simply want you to remember me, should your circumstances ever change."

"I'll never forget you," I said sincerely, then added, to keep things light, "because your son has seduced my housekeeper, and tomorrow is vacuuming day."

"Your June will be well cared for, I promise you." He raised my hand to his lips. "Take care of *yourself*, Ida. And don't forget what I told you about love."

I said nothing, just smiled gamely. He boarded the bus, blowing me another kiss right before he disappeared from sight.

A minute later, the bus rumbled out of the parking lot. I waved and applauded alongside my fellow Creekites. It was a sunny, cold, Valentine's Sunday, the kind of winter day when the air seems blue with clarity and the world can feel both fresh and lonely.

It was bittersweet to watch the reckless magic of *Cirque d'Europa* roll out of Mossy Creek. The experience seemed to leave the slightest swirl of glitter in the air. Around me, dozens of Creekites waved until the tour bus could be seen no more. They lowered their hands slowly. We all heaved a collective sigh of sorrow but also relief. A dose of hot-blooded theatrics goes a long way.

Now that the bus was gone, people suddenly turned their attention to me. "Why, I haven't seen this many wide eyes and arched brows since I stumbled into a meeting of the Mossy Creek Facelift Club," I said dryly.

"We saw the kiss," my cousin Ingrid retorted. "We're just wondering what *else* you did to entertain Philippe over the weekend."

"It was just a kiss. He couldn't help himself. He's French."

Old Ed Brady, never one to mince words, asked solemnly, "Was it a French kiss, mayor?"

That brought a flurry of snorts and snickers. I rolled my eyes and strode up the street to town hall. Del was picking me up there. He and I had a Valentine's Day date. We'd go to a movie down in Bigelow, have dinner afterward at Bigelow's new (and, so far, only) sushi restaurant, and then come back to my house for champagne, cheesecake, and a little privacy, if you know what I mean.

And my life would get back to normal.

The instant I walked into my office and saw Del's haggard face I knew "normal" was a lost hope. "What's wrong?" I rushed to him, thinking something had happened to his son or grandson.

He planted his hands firmly but gently on my shoulders and held me at arm's length. "I've been doing a lot of thinking since yesterday. It comes down to a simple question.

Just answer me honestly, Ida. *Do you love me?*"

I froze. I wanted to say yes, I wanted it to be so, but the words and the emotion refused to cooperate. Finally, defeated, I looked at him and shook my head.

Del held his breath a few seconds, composing himself, then exhaled. "I just needed to know before I made a decision," he said in a low, hoarse voice. "I'm going back to my ex-wife."

Sunday Evening

Curtain Up—Life Goes On
Chapter 8

Sagan

I didn't know what would happen or where my path would lead, at least not until Nikoli and I started home. We rode my Harley up the mountain, followed by Emily in her car. There was a mystical shimmer in the late-afternoon air. "Interested in dinner?" I asked Emily. "I have grits."

She smiled. "I'll raid my pantry and bring some food over. See you in a minute. Nikolai, want to help me carry things?"

"Carry, yes. Grits, no."

I watched him follow Emily, his head up, his walk jaunty. They made a good picture, together. I turned to watch the sunset. And then it came, the flutter of wings and a shadow of movement. The bird soared, hung for a moment in the gold-and-red sky, then disappeared. It's fine to follow dreams and seek visions, but a person needs more than wings to be happy. A person needs both feet on the ground, too. I was walking a new path, now. And I wasn't alone, anymore. I didn't know what would happen next between Emily and me, or how Nikolai's new life would turn out, but now we all had a chance at happiness. I knew I'd truly come home.

Harry

After the circus bus left I took Josie's hand and pulled her toward our truck. I still had one more Valentine's surprise for her, and I wanted to get there before dark.

Josie was thoughtful as we headed back toward Bailey Mill. Suddenly she said, "Colchik."

"Pardon me?"

"The bear's name. Why not call him Colchik? Name him after the mountain. That's where he was born, in a way. At least, for the life that he's about to live."

I ran it around on my tongue. "Colchik. It even sounds Russian."

"A little bit, doesn't it?"

"I think it's the perfect name, and I think Yuri will, too."

She settled back against the seat. "Well, that's settled, then. Just in time for—wait a minute. You passed our driveway."

I couldn't contain my smile. "I've got something to show you."

"What?"

"It's a surprise."

"What kind of surprise?"

"A Valentine surprise, my impatient wife."

"But you already gave me the *Martha Stewart Baking Cookbook* and apron."

"As if those qualify for Valentine gifts," I scoffed.

"Yes, well, that's pretty much what I was thinking, but hey, I figured this is your first Valentine's Day with a wife. I have years to train you."

I chuckled and put on my right turn signal.

"Why are you—" She turned to watch the unchained gate I passed. "This is Nate Hankin's property. It's always locked."

I didn't reply, just gunned the engine up the pot-holed gravel drive.

"Harry. . ."

"Patience, my love."

The drive loosely ran alongside a tributary of Mossy Creek. Like most Appalachian streams, it ran too fast to freeze in all but the coldest weather. It was just a brook now, but in the spring the rains would engorge it into a full-fledged roaring stream.

A quarter-mile past the road, we reached a break in forest. The brook had formed a natural waterfall here, falling in three tiers from a combined height of ten feet. The pebble-lined pool formed at the bottom was six feet deep in the middle and twenty feet wide.

Right on cue, Josie caught her breath.

I'd hiked here Friday to tie red velvet bows around every tree surrounding the pond.

I couldn't keep my eyes off Josie's face as I turned off the engine. She looked around in wonder, her eyes wide, her mouth open.

Without tearing her gaze from the pool, she grabbed for my hand.

I locked my fingers through hers.

"Oh, Harry. Is this what I think it is?"

I brought her hand up to my lips. "It's ours, if you approve."

"If I approve. . .? Geez, Louise." She finally turned to me, her face shining. "Where will we put the house? Not too far from the stream, okay?"

"You're the *feng shui* expert," I said. "You tell me."

She shoved open the car door and spent ten minutes darting around the pool and clearing, chattering the whole time. I leaned against the Explorer and watched, my heart so full of love I feared it might come apart at the seams.

Finally she stilled, staring down into the pool. Brookies were visible swimming in the crystal clear water. I came up beside her, and she melted against me.

"Thank you, Harry," she said softly. "It's perfect."

"I'm glad you're not put out that I did this on my own."

"You *found* it on your own," she clarified, "but we've been looking together for six months."

"I haven't actually bought it yet. I wanted it to be in both our names, and that will require your signature."

"How much land?"

"It's about seventy-five acres, all told. Enough so that we'll never catch sight of any neighbors who might build on our mountain."

"Let's go to the bank tomorrow."

I kissed the top of her head. "We have an appointment at one-thirty."

She nodded against my chest. "I'll take a late lunch."

I pointed across the stream. "Colchik is in that direction. Our cabin is three-quarters of a mile closer to this spot than from the house we live in now. Your parents are five miles further."

She giggled. "They'll survive."

"Have you decided where to put the house?"

"Not yet. It's going to require more thought, and detailed measurements. It'll have to face the pool, of course.

Water should always be in the front of a house, with a mountain in the rear. But I don't know which direction is which, so I don't know if it should be on this side of the pool or the other."

"North is—"

"Not tonight, Harry. It's cold and it's getting dark. And we have plenty of time."

"Yes, we do."

"Can we come back tomorrow after we sign the papers? I'll tell Swee I'm taking the rest of the afternoon off."

"Of course."

She sighed and settled against me. We watched the water tumble down the falls until the darkness was almost complete.

I lifted her chin so I could peer down into her face. "So you approve? We're going to live here?"

"Yes, my sweet Harry, we are." She pulled my head down to kiss me, whispering just before, "Happily ever after."

Sandy

When I got home, Jess was there, but he wasn't dressed for our Valentine's Day dinner out. In fact, he still had on his hiking boots, jeans, and camo jacket. "Let's go fishing," he suggested.

"What about our 'special date?'"

"I canceled the reservation. What I have in mind is way cooler than that. I've packed your backpack. Put on your hiking clothes and boots and let's get started. We've got a ways to go before dark."

I walked to the bedroom as fast as I could go to get myself out of his sight before I said something that would not be becoming to an officer of the law. What was this man thinking? I thought about my conversation with Sergei and decided that I would not become a high-maintenance woman. So I changed into my loosest-fitting jeans—dang that Bubba Rice and his high-fat burritos—hiking boots with wool socks, a flannel shirt and a quilted, down coat.

It was almost dark when we reached Jess's camp site in a little hollow in one of the foothills of Colchik Mountain north of town. The northern tributary of Mossy Creek ran right beside where Jess had pitched the two-man tent and set up his Coleman stove and other niceties. Our his-and-her rods and reels were leaning against a loblolly pine nearby.

Jess went to the side of the creek and turned to face me, spreading his arms wide. "How do you like your Valentine's present?"

I stared at him blankly and could feel the feelings of resentment I'd tamped down so long start to bubble to the surface. Choosing my words carefully I said, "A fishing trip. For my Valentine's present. It's sure an interesting choice, I have to say. I wonder how many other lucky women across America have longed for a romantic fishing trip so they can scrape and gut fish for their men?"

"Sandy," Jess began, but I was just getting revved up so I cut him off.

"I have spent all stinking weekend trying to keep two knife-happy foreigners who can barely speak English from slicing and dicing each other all the way up and down Main Street."

"Wait, you don't—" Jess tried to butt in.

I felt my voice rising a half-octave or so. "This is the second weekend you've left me alone while you went off by yourself. It's not like I get any of your time on weeknights anymore what with you sitting down at the computer as soon as you get off from work and barely saying two words to me for the rest of the night."

"But, I—"

Praise the Lord and pass the ammunition. "And now, now you cancel our dinner reservation at Bubba's for a nice night out and instead you take me on a forced march up a mountain to the middle of nowhere and *that's* my Valentine's present? You must have found a moonshine still or some of those funny mushrooms up here somewhere or else you have lost every bit of sense you ever had."

The corner's of Jess's mouth twitched, and he looked like he was about to break out into a giggle. I wanted to smack him one, but it wouldn't do for an officer of the law to commit spousal abuse, much less an officer bucking for chief crisis negotiator, so I just took a deep breath.

"Are you finished?" he asked.

"For now."

"While you're taking a breather, let me explain." Jess gestured behind himself again. "This. This place, a ten-acre chunk of it centered right here where we're standing, it's yours. This is where we're going to build our dream house—the one we've always talked about."

I felt my mouth working like a guppy, but nothing came out. As vocal as I'd been a minute ago, that's how speechless I was now. "But how? How is that possible?"

Jess reached into the pocket of his jeans and unfolded what looked like a check. "Remember that manuscript I sent off six months ago? Well, the editor made an offer—for three books! So I hired an agent who got them to up the offer to this. I signed the contract and here's the first of the advance money."

"And this is the first you're telling me?"

"I couldn't tell you until now because I was so afraid

something would fall through. I wasn't going to relax until the check was in my hand. And then when I realized that the check was going to get here around Valentine's Day, it all seemed too perfect.

"I know how much you love the mountains so I scoured the hills all around to find the perfect spot. Then I worked with Julie Honeycutt—who, you know, *is* a real estate agent—to do the deal. So, how do you like it?"

I took the check from him and nearly choked on my own spit when I saw the amount. "I like it. I like it right fine."

Jess laughed. "I know you like the money. I mean the spot. How do you like our new place?"

I looked around at the little clearing, really seeing it for the first time. Mossy Creek was named for places like this, where the moss-covered river stones lined the gently babbling creek and tall ferns and clover grew lush and green. Even in winter it looked lush. The scent of evergreen lightly perfumed the air. The way the waning sunlight played among the pines put me in mind of the magical woodland glades filed with elves, wood nymphs, and fairies like in the fantasy books Jess had introduced me to in books.

I half expected to see a unicorn step out from behind a tree, stamp its foot and rear its sleek head. In the spring the wildflowers would sprout and the dogwoods that dotted the hillside would bloom in pink and white. This enchanted place would be my home, thanks to Jess.

I put my arms around him and laid my head against his chest. Somewhere under his thick camo coat was the hair I loved. "It's perfect," I said. "And you're going to be a famous novelist, just like Stephen King. You've worked so hard. You deserve all the success in the world. I'm sorry for complaining." And for being such a *beech*, I thought.

Jess gave me a big hug and a kiss and took me by the hand toward the center of the campsite. "Now it's time for our special date," he said. He got our big picnic basket out of the tent and spread out a table cloth. Then he set our places with some fancy Lucite dishes he said he'd picked up at Hamilton's Department Store in town. "Rob and Teresa helped me pick 'em out," he bragged. Rob Walker was Mayor Ida's son. He had turned Hamilton's, a dusty has-been of a dry-goods store, into a sleek modern retail heaven. His wife, Teresa, was a fancy lawyer. "Rob's got style," Jess added, nodding. "He reads men's magazines and whatever. And Teresa says Lucite plates are the new plastic."

I was so choked up I could only nod and smile.

"I've got your favorite," Jess went on as he fired up the camp stove. He reached into the cooler and removed two takeout boxes from Bubba Rice's diner. He shoveled the burritos and rice into the skillet sitting on the stovetop.

"Wow, you really went all-out," I said. "This is the best Valentine's Day of my life! The only thing missing is the champagne to toast our new home."

Jess chuckled. "You can't drink champagne, silly."

"Whyever not?" I dearly love champagne, how the bubbles tickle my lips as I tip the glass.

He turned away from the camp stove and looked at me for several seconds. "Don't play coy. Do you think I don't know? When were you going to tell me, anyway? I gave you a nice surprise just now. Don't you think it's about time you returned the favor?" He gave me a sly wink and one of those grins that made me fall in love with him.

"Jess Crane, what in the Sam Hill are you talking about?" Had the boy done gone and lost his mind?

His expression turned from teasing to wonder. "You really don't know, do you?"

I shook my head dumbly.

"Babe, think about it—the burrito cravings, the five pounds you keep trying to lose, the house-cleaning spells, irritability that's not like you—it all adds up. Sandy, sweetheart, I'm bettin' you're going to have a baby."

"I—I—I am?" My hands went to my belly and I thought about what day it was on the calendar. After some quick calculations my jaw went slack. He was right. So it wasn't just burritos after all. "I'm going to have a baby! A Baby Crane!"

Jess laughed. "The stork is coming to the Crane house. There's got to be a joke in there somewhere."

My husband put down his spatula and came to sit beside me. He put his arms around me and covered me with kisses. How's that for a sensitive, twenty-first century man? He knew I was pregnant before I did. My man was definitely a keeper.

After we ate our burritos and toasted our home, our baby, and each other with spring water, we snuggled deep into a sleeping bag and made love under the stars. Jess went into a deep sleep as I lay in his arms, letting his chest hair tickle my cheek. Even though it was wintertime, I'd never felt warmer or cozier than I did snuggled up to my tall bear of a man.

I thought about the little girl in my dreams the night before. The one with blond ringlets like mine and fireflies in her hair and Tinkerbell wings on her tiny back. Now I knew who she was. Not me. Our baby.

I hoped I'd give Jess a baby as smart and as talented and as sweet and sensitive as her daddy. I had a lot of points to score to catch up with Jess. I owed him big-time.

Hannah

"I shouldn't have lied to you," Dave said softly. He'd walked me to the library after I dropped Monique at the circus bus. Now we sat in my office in the quiet, empty building, a private place where I steeled myself to deal with the truth about his motives.

"I'm listening," I said.

"But I didn't see it like that, at first," Dave went on. "I routinely take a false name these days, because I'm so well-known that once people go on the web and find out about my work, it changes how they behave toward me."

The web. Busted again. As I hurriedly closed my laptop, he added, "It makes it hard to get a real photo."

Thinking of those initial images, I raised my eyebrow. "And by 'real photo,' you mean . . ."

He grimaced. "All right, yes, I admit it. When I first came here, I was predisposed to . . . shoot a certain sort of image." He stepped further into the room. "After I'd seen the coverage about Hurricane Katrina, I'd proposed a series to the Museum of Modern Art that I was calling "Beneath the Mask of the South." They were damned eager for it. Since I'd already met Ardaleen Bigelow at an exhibition and she's the First Mother of Georgia, I'd thought she'd be the perfect source for information about a town to photograph, one that fit my admittedly biased opinion."

I blinked. "*Ardaleen* was behind this?" Mayor Ida Hamilton Walker's much-older sister, mother of Governor Ham Bigelow, was notoriously anti-Creekite, the result not only of a long sibling feud between her and Ida but a rivalry between small-town Mossy Creek and big-city Bigelow that went back over 150 years. "The *governor's mother* was willing to help you make Mossy Creek look bad to the world? And by extension to slander the entire state of Georgia—and not just the state, but the whole Southern region?"

"I know, I know," he said ruefully. "It only took me a week here to realize that asking Ardaleen Bigelow where to shoot photos was like asking a wolf to help me deliver mail to Red Riding Hood's house. But I rationalized that it was all right because your mayor knew everything."

"What?!!" I said, outraged. I would have to have a talk with Ida.

"I contacted her the minute I came to town. I told her what I wanted to do, and after she calmed down—I thought, for moment, she might kill me—she agreed to let me shoot wherever I wanted. She even promised to keep my identity secret."

When I shook my head in disbelief, he added dryly, "I suspect that Mayor Walker knew I couldn't spend more than a week in Mossy Creek without abandoning my original vision." He looked suddenly embarrassed. "I also suspect that I . . . er . . . raised her hackles when I pomp-ously explained how I wanted to capture the inequities that I *knew* ran rampant in small Southern towns. She practically gave me the keys to the city." His eyes gleamed. "She even suggested places I should shoot. Canny woman, your mayor."

My admiration of Ida went up another notch. Sud-denly her true intentions dawned on me. "She's going to blackmail the governor with this scheme of his mother's." I clapped my hands and laughed. "We're going to get a football stadium at the new high school! You watch! Sud-denly the governor will find plenty of funding for it."

Dave leaned over my desk. "But just so you won't think I'm a complete arse, there's something else. It's no excuse, but . . ." His face flushed. "Though I *was* born in Edinburgh, I was raised in a remote Scottish village in the

Highlands. That's where my father chose to bury himself after my mother died. I think he was trying to gain comfort by returning to his roots, but for me—"

He broke off, and suddenly I understood. "I don't guess there were many half-Burundians in the Highlands."

"None. No one of color at all. While I fell in love with the mountains and lochs and burns, school was hell. And my father was oblivious." He cast me a self-deprecating smile. "So I caught the brunt of the bullying, not only because of my mixed blood but because I was a science-fiction-loving geek. I wasn't a bluff and braw Scot. I didn't fit in. So I came to Mossy Creek with a chip the size of all Scotland on my shoulder." His voice softened. "Until you knocked it off."

I was having trouble holding back my happy tears. "Mossy Creek knocked it off."

He shook his head. "You did it first. From the day I entered that library, you treated me like any of your other patrons, fussing over me, ordering in books to suit my reading tastes, recommending places to eat and sights to photograph . . . And you did it without knowing I was the famous Dave Brodie."

My cheeks got hot. "I didn't think you noticed."

"Oh, I noticed." His gaze held an unnerving intensity. "Just like I noticed the brilliant green of your eyes and the sweet curve of your hip and the innocent way you had of rousing a man's guilt with one gentle word." He dragged in a heavy breath. "I'm sorry for what I said about you and the library yesterday. It was a knee-jerk reaction to watching you close me out again."

"No, you were right. This library *has* been my haven, maybe the same way your Scottish village was for your dad." I'd used it like a vampire's coffin, a place where I could avoid seeing that my daughter was growing up.

From acknowledging that I *did* want more in my life than comfort and safety. "But for better or worse, you dragged me from behind the desk, so don't you go apologizing for it now."

"All right."

I fumbled with his contact sheets. "So . . . um . . . what are you going to do about the pictures?"

He gave a strained laugh. "If the museum will agree to a new exhibit entitled 'Revisiting the South,' then I'll use the later ones."

"And if the museum refuses?"

"I'll take the exhibit elsewhere. I might do that anyway."

"Why?"

He flashed the heart-dissolving smile I was rapidly growing to love. "Because I don't intend to stay around in New York to oversee it." Nervously, he thrust his hands in his pockets again. "I've been considering leaving the city for some time now to settle in an area more like the Highland countryside where I grew up. And while the mountains around here aren't quite the same, I begin to think they just might do."

My throat felt so tight with joy that I wasn't sure I could trust myself to speak.

After a moment passed, he rasped, "For God's sake, say something, Hannah."

I gave him the most brilliant smile I could muster. "Looks like I'll be ordering a lot of new books for the library's science fiction collection."

His face lit up. "Damned right you will." Then he stared at me. "I almost forgot—wait here." He turned toward the door, then paused to scowl at me. "And I mean it this time. Don't you *dare* go running off."

"I won't," I said, feeling suddenly giddy. Never again.

He was back in a second with a disposable digital camera tied up in a bright red ribbon. He set the camera on the desk in front of me. "Happy Valentine's Day."

I actually blushed. And I hadn't done that in close to ten years. "What's this for?"

"Now you can take mortifying pictures of *me* to even the score."

"Yes, I noticed that there were few photos of you on the web. Why is that?"

It was his turn to blush. "Well . . . you see . . . I'm afraid I have an embarrassing confession to make."

"Oh?"

A rueful smile touched his lips. "I'm camera-shy."

I blinked at him. Then I burst into laughter. And as he laughed, too, I realized that you couldn't always avoid sharp objects in life—none of us could, not even the famous Dave Brodie. Besides, sometimes it took sharp objects to cut away the old habits, the old comfortable ways of life we fall into because we're afraid of the next step.

But I was finally ready for any sharp object life threw at me. What the hey, I might even join my daughter in her new hobby and throw a few sharp objects myself. Just for fun. Just to see if I could.

I picked up the digital camera. "Happy Valentine's Day, Dave Brodie," I said and aimed.

Then I let fly.

Amos

Circuses will come and go but Mossy Creek will always be the same. I had only to look at the flyer in my hand to know that for true. I'd pulled it off one of the light poles in the square on my way from the church to check on Tweedle and set him up for the night. As police station mascots go, parakeets are pretty low-maintenance.

Lost Kitten
Name: Maple May Murray
Size: 1-3/4' feet; skinny, 13 inches.5
Color: Calaco
Tip: If you hear a meow look outside.
She eats people food so give her a
chereo and if she eats it call
555-6783
Owener: Sissy Murray

Below the words was a hand-drawn picture of a cat's face. A very happy and well-loved kitten judging by all the evidence. Worth crawling under a house or two. I left it centered on my desk. I'd call the family tomorrow. That done, I browsed my growing collection of Irish folk and whistle music. Tweedle wasn't originally my parakeet but entrusted to me by a woman who made him a CD of Irish whistle tunes before she died. For a long time I pretended I bought the music for him, but I'd pretty much given up on that personal lie. Celtic music was part of my play list these days. Not that I didn't appreciate Ida's rabid attachment to Fleetwood Mac.

I looked across to the credenza behind my desk, to the near-mint piece of Fleetwood vinyl I'd found on eBay. The day would come I'd be needing that album as proof

I paid attention. I didn't want to be scrambling when the time came. Too bad it couldn't have been a Valentine's gift this year. Tweedle chirped at me.

"Okay, bird brain. What's it going to be tonight? "

He chirped again and tapped the cage with his beak.

"Mary Bergen it is then. Excellent choice." I popped in the CD and offered him one of the special mail-order seeds Sandy'd bought him for treats. Who knew seeds could cost an arm and a leg.

As I covered him I heard Mutt come in the door. "Mutt, I told you not to come down. I was closing up tonight, tucking Tweedle in. The bird brain near took my finger off grabbing for his treat. We need a Bird Whisperer."

"It's Del."

Great. Nothing says "I'm your big hunk of scary rival," like putting your parakeet to bed with treats and music. No help for it now. I turned out the light in my office and closed the door. Del waited by the dispatch counter. The look on his face brought me up short. Not sad exactly. Resigned. Not a mood I ever expected to settle over Del.

"What can I do for you, Del?"

"All things considered I'm a lucky man. I shouldn't complain or regret, but I've never liked to lose. The thing is, it took me a long time to realize I wasn't even in the game. You must have had a good laugh at that."

I tilted my head. Not certain what he was trying to say. "Come again?"

"You. You got in the game." He put his hands on his hips and shook his head, radiating disbelief. "God knows I've wracked my brain trying to figure out how and I can't. Ida's not talking. And I'm tired. I can't fight the both of you."

"You won't have to. The Frenchman's gone. Like the wind." I shook my head at his puzzled expression. "Never mind. Bad joke. But he's gone."

Del put his hand on the doorknob. "He'll be back."

I laughed out loud. "He's a juggler, not the Terminator. He won't be back."

"He'll. Be. Back. Trust me. I don't know when and I don't know why but that Frenchman is going to turn up like a bad penny. What started as a little something to irritate me is going to backfire on you. I'm an expert on the other men in Ida's life." He pulled open the door. February's cold greedily rushed in to the steal all warmth.

"Whoa. I've had a long weekend. I'm not as sharp as usual. What did you come here to tell me, Del? You not making much sense."

"I'm finally making more sense than I have in a long time. You get some perspective when you realize you're out numbered. I'm fighting you . . . and a ghost. You're just fighting the ghost. I can't win, and I think you can. That's what scares her." Just before he shut the door, he said, "I'm going back to my wife."

Ida

I didn't cry. I curled up on a deep couch in the front living room of my big, elegant, empty Victorian at Hamilton Farm, and I drank. Two fingers of bourbon in a short tumbler with just enough ice to smooth the edges. I listened to the silence of the house, the quiet solitude of my life. Clocks ticked loudly—heirloom clocks on two fireplace mantels, a cuckoo clock in the kitchen. A massive Grandfather clock in the front foyer chimed five times. Afternoon fading. Shadows creeping. Time passing. Getting older. All alone. Tick. Tock. Alone.

I finished the bourbon and didn't even feel a buzz. Time for another round. As I pushed myself off the couch my eyes caught a flash of movement in the front yard. I frowned as a Mossy Creek patrol car pulled to a stop.

When Amos stepped out, I carefully sat my bourbon glass down on a coffee table, took several deep breaths, and walked out on the veranda to confront the unknown.

He walked through the slanting light of the winter day, stopped at the base of the broad steps, and looked up at me somberly. A trickle of breeze shifted a lock of dark hair off his forehead, such a gentling effect. I glimpsed the teenager who'd consoled me beneath The Sitting Tree. The air quieted and that boy was absorbed inside the man Amos had become.

"How do you know?" I asked.

"Del stopped by the station. He told me."

I exhaled wearily. "All right. It's over."

"Forgive me for being blunt, Ida, but . . . *good*. And it's about damn time."

"I'm not in a mood to celebrate."

"I'm not asking you to. All you have to do is stand there and listen."

"I'm listening."

"Admit it. What you're really afraid of is that you might love me as much as you loved Jeb. That I'm the only man you've ever known who might just possibly be able to take his place."

I said nothing, agonized.

"But here's the thing, Ida. I don't want to take Jeb's place. I want to make my *own* place in your life. He's a memory, I'm not. Give me a chance and I'll give you some good memories, too."

"And what if you suddenly decide, in a few years, that you want to be a father? Don't tell me it couldn't happen. Then what do we do?"

"I'll make you a deal. You live to be, oh, ninety or so. You die, and I'll bury you. I'll just be in my late seventies then, and I promise to marry a thirty-year-old immediately and have five or six kids. Okay?"

"You can show them my picture. Tell them I was your grandmother."

"You don't get it. I don't see age. I see *you*."

"A day will come when I won't be this . . . perky."

"Neither will I. What if I promise to gain fifty pounds, go bald, and wear my pants buckled below my beer gut? People will say, 'What's that attractive older woman doing with Homer Simpson?'"

"I have a different vision: You get silver gray at the temples, develop some great laugh lines, look sexy in hiking shorts, and people say, 'What's that hunky older man doing with Granny Clampett?'"

"As a kid, I had a thing for Granny. I never told anyone before. When she put that little flowered hat on her hair and tilted it just so—"

"Amos, quit dodging. We can't have children. Not without a Petri dish. I'm not interested in raising a fungus. Even if it looks like you."

"Is there some reason we can't adopt?"

"So you *do* want children."

"I don't know. Maybe the Battle Royden line should end with me."

"Amos, you shouldn't feel that way about—"

"I'm just not worried about it."

"I am. Amos. I am."

"All I need from you today is the promise that there might be a tomorrow. That's all you have to say, and I'll leave. 'I promise you, Amos. I promise you we've got a chance for tomorrow.'"

I struggled, tried to speak, couldn't. A thousand battles raged inside me. I don't know long I stood there silently, but Amos's expression fell. "Sorry. My timing's lousy. Forget it. We'll talk again sometime." He chuckled darkly. "My mistake. I thought if I lit a fire under you, you'd break your silence. Like Win's mimes."

He turned and started down my front walk, toward his cruiser.

He's walking away. He's walking away. If you don't give him an answer right now you'll go back in this empty house with nothing but those clocks for company.

I forced one foot forward. Then the other. The next thing I knew I was running down the steps. Amos pivoted. I halted a few yards from him. That was as close as I could allow myself to come, at the moment. I had to say something, anything. "Mr. Butler?" I said crisply. "Rhett?"

His mouth quirked. "Okay. Yes?"

"*Rhett.* Don't make me promise you too much tonight. But . . . tomorrow *is* another day."

Slowly, he began to smile. A magnificent, happy smile. I've never seen Amos smile that freely, before. After a moment he remembered his boundaries and tempered it with a rakish tilt of his head. Clark Gable would have been proud. He gave a slight bow. He had gotten the answer he'd come for, what he, and I, had been waiting twenty years to give each other. A chance.

"That works for me because, frankly my dear," he said, "I *do* give a damn."

Now it was my turn to smile. "See you tomorrow, then."

He nodded. As he walked to his car his broad shoulders seemed comfortable for the first time, square and even with the weight off them. One hand chucked the air just a little, giving a thumbs-up to the future. I laughed at his exuberance. What was this feeling, this youthful emotion we shared? Reckless hope. Carefree joy.

A chance for happiness. Imperfect, unpredictable happiness.

Somewhere beyond a distant horizon, St. Valentine's surely approved.

Monday Morning

The Magic Still Lingers

Chapter 9

Louise

Monday morning I went to the doctor's office to get my biopsy results. Lisa wanted me to call her with the news, either way. When I got the information, I called her on my cell. "I'm okay," I said. "False alarm. I want a drink."

She laughed. "Keep your balance and keep taking risks, no matter what."

I drove home and started my new life, post-circus. Charlie may be confused by the new "me," but he'll come around. He'll learn to stack the dishwasher. I'll learn to drive the riding lawnmower.

I feel oddly deprived. I hadn't realized how much my own sense of self depended on being the only one that could do things right. This week I'm signing up for Tai Chi at the church, and a watercolor class at the junior college down in Bigelow.

Someday we won't dodge the bullet. But in the meantime, I've let the plates go.

Recipes from
Bubba Rice

Bubba's Artichoke Dip

I tweaked a recipe from an old friend to come up with this one.
It goes well with just about any kind of chip or snack cracker.

Ingredients:

> 4 cups fresh Parmesan cheese, finely grated
> 1 cup mayonnaise (or, if you really want to impress
> someone, how about some homemade aioli
> mayonnaise???)
> 1/3 cup chopped mild green chili peppers
> 1 can artichoke hearts, quartered, drained well

Preparation:

Blend the mayonnaise, chopped chili peppers, artichoke hearts
and half the cheese in a large bowl. Pour into an 8" x 8" Pyrex
baking dish. Top off with the remaining cheese and bake for
30 minutes at 325 degrees.

Serves 8
Prep time: 5 minutes
Cooking time: 30 minutes

Bubba's Broccoli Cheese Soup

This is a great meal for a cold winter night. It started off as a foiled attempt at broccoli with cheese sauce. After 3 unsuccessful attempts to fix the consistency of the sauce, presto, it's SOUP!

Ingredients:

>   16 ounces sharp cheddar cheese, grated
>   2 (two) 14 ounce packages frozen broccoli florettes
>   16 ounces sour cream
>   16 ounces heavy cream
>   4 ounces butter
>   1 tbsp flour
>   1 tsp kosher salt

Preparation:

In a large stock pot, bring the broccoli to a boil in about 6 quarts of water, then lower the heat to a simmer, cover and cook for 5 minutes (it should still be a little bit crisp and have a bright green color). Immediately remove from heat and drain. Using the same pot, melt the butter over low heat. Add the flour and salt and stir until the mixture comes to a boil. Add the sour cream and blend well. Add the cheese and stir until all the cheese has melted. Add the cream and the drained broccoli and stir. Cover and cook on low heat (do not boil) for 20 minutes, stir occasionally.

Serve with hot French or Italian bread.

Serves 4

Prep time: 5 minutes

Cooking time: 45 minutes

Chicken & Roasted Red Pepper Pasta with Alfredo Sauce

Another one of those dishes that just "came to me" one night when I was looking in the pantry to see what was for dinner. Simple, elegant and just plain good.

Ingredients:

1 pound chicken breast meat, diced

1 medium sweet yellow onion, diced

1 red pepper, roasted, peeled and diced

2 cups Parmesan cheese, finely grated

1/4 cup unsalted butter

1 pint heavy cream

3 tbsp extra virgin olive oil

1/2 pound pasta (I do this one with capellini, but you can use any kind of pasta)

Salt and pepper to taste

Preparation:

Coat the red pepper with 1 tbsp of the extra virgin olive oil and roast for 30 minutes at 350 degrees. Remove from the oven and allow to cool for 15 minutes. Remove the skin, core and seeds, then dice. Sautee the chicken and onion in the remaining olive oil until the onion begins to caramelize. Add the red pepper and stir until well blended. Remove from heat. While the chicken and onion are sautéing, cook the pasta and prepare the Alfredo sauce.

Alfredo Sauce

Basic Alfredo sauce:

Heat the heavy cream over low heat. Add the butter and melt. Then add the cheese a little at a time and stir until melted. Salt and pepper to taste. When the cheese has melted and the sauce has a smooth consistency (coats the back of a metal spoon), it is done.

To serve:

Serve in a bowl (or wear the sauce, it's up to you). Add some pasta to the bowl, top with some of the chicken/onion/red pepper mixture and cover with the Alfredo sauce.

Serves 6

Prep time: 20 minutes

Cooking time: 45 minutes

Bubba's Creamy Tomato Soup

Here's a great winter meal that you can make from things that are probably already in your pantry and refrigerator. It's pretty easy and oh, so much better than that stuff in the red and white can that you had with your grilled cheese sandwich when you were a kid.

Ingredients:

1 (one) 28 ounce can peeled whole tomatoes
32 ounces chicken stock
1 cup heavy cream
2 slices bacon, diced
1 small onion, diced
2 stalks celery, chopped
2 carrots, chopped
1 tbsp flour
1 bay leaf
2 tsp kosher salt

Preparation:

In a large stock pot, cook the bacon over medium low heat until crisp. Add the onion, celery, carrots, flour and salt. Sautee until the onions start to caramelize. Add the flour and stir until well blended. Add the tomatoes and the chicken stock and bring to a low boil, then reduce the heat to low and cover. Cook for 30 minutes, stirring occasionally. Remove from heat and remove the bay leaf. Puree in small batches in a blender or food processor. Return the pureed soup to the stock pot over low heat (do not boil). Stir in the cream.

Serve with garlic bread, or how about a grown up version of a grilled cheese sandwich?

Serves 4
Prep time: 10 minutes
Cooking time: 45 minutes

Excerpt from
On Grandma's Porch

GRANDMA'S CUPBOARDS

by Susan Sipal

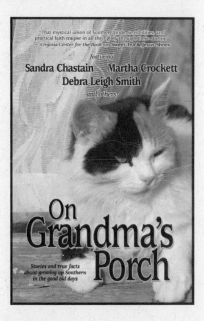

High on the ridge above the farm
I think of my people that
have gone on
Like a tree that grows in the
mountain ground
The storms of life have cut
them down
But the new wood springs from the roots underground
Gone, gonna rise again
—*Si Kahn, North Carolina songwriter*

Along about the time I was a senior in college, and knew all there was to know about *Life*, and was so much smarter than my upbringing, my granddaddy was hospitalized with a bleeding ulcer for several weeks, leaving Grandma to stay at their ancient farmhouse alone.

Now, don't get me wrong, Grandma was as feisty as any ornery farmwife could get. In fact she'd won blue ribbons at the state fair for her mulish ways. At least that's what Granddaddy muttered, in his age-raspy voice, when she nagged him for tracking red Warren County mud into the house once again. Point being, I'm sure Grandma could probably have managed fine on her own, even with diabetes.

But most of Granddaddy's illness fell over winter break and I wanted to be there, with them, with Grandma. I preferred being at Grandma's farm with the turmoil in my life above anywhere else at the time. Even with Granddaddy sick, still, there was a sort of welcome . . . of peace, less stress, less activity, more simple.

I needed time to sort things out in my life. Where was I going after graduation? More school? A job? Plus there was this guy I liked, and I didn't know how he felt about me. It was confusing. And he was going to be out of state over Christmas, so I wouldn't see him anyhow. May as well hide out, I mean help out, at Grandma's and be of some use. Especially as she didn't drive and would have to depend on neighbors to carry her to the hospital every day.

See, Grandma ran over a piglet as a teenager, and ever since refused to get behind the wheel. In a small community like Arcola, however, this was never a big deal. She walked many places she wanted to go, like nearby neighbors, or off to Harvey's—the small country grocery and gas-stop down the road—and church. Usually, however, Granddaddy, one of her children or neighbors (half of them kin as well), were willing and able to carry her whenever she needed to venture further away from what we grandkids called Plumb-Nelly—plumb in the country and nelly out of this world. Like her weekly go-to-town Fridays to the "big" town of Warrenton—to the bank, hairdresser, and Piggly Wiggly.

But I'm venturing off the story, way too easy to do when you get into that Plumb-Nelly mind-frame. Anyhow, as I mentioned, the hospital was thirty-five miles away, in the next county, as Warrenton had been too poor for too long to currently have a hospital. Grandma, of course, needed to go every day to be with Granddaddy. So I acted as chauffeur and did whatever I could to take care of her, especially as Granddaddy's condition weakened, and she became more upset and sickened with worry.

Then, Grandma started doing something she'd never

done in her whole life, at least not that Mama or I could remember. She slept late. Late for her being around 7:30. For a working farmer, though, that was sinful. For some reason, I seemed to reverse time sense with Grandma and awoke with the crowing of the rooster. This left me a good hour of free time in which I devised a special project.

Cleaning out Grandma's cupboards.

If you've ever known anyone who lived through the Great Depression, you'll nod your head and mutter, "Yep, yeah, yes-sirree," under your breath at what I'm about to say. Grandma's cupboards were crammed full of every single piece of aluminum foil, bread bag, twist tie, paper bag, plastic wrap, broken mugs, chipped glassware, and other miscellaneous debris hoarded amid her sixty-plus years of marriage. Aside from the pure junk, her cabinets cached a collection of mismatched china, that ugly jade Fire King (which Martha Stewart somehow thought pretty enough to reissue), green and pink Depression glass pieces in various patterns, and every collectible glass piece ever pulled out of an old box of oatmeal or soapsuds.

She'd never thrown nothing away. Never knew when it might come in handy again. Especially when she'd been a dirt farmer all her life and knew what it meant to go without.

But I was going to clean it up. I knew better. Those cupboards hid cockroaches and disease, as well as the trash. Surely Grandma would feel a lot better with clean, organized cabinets, and would never miss all that junk.

One morning I awoke to the sound of little mice feet pattering overhead in the attic, the pinkish light of dawn peeking through the shades, and Grandma snoring on the other side of the bedroom. I slept in the combination bedroom/family room with Grandma as it was the only one we heated at night. With Granddaddy in the hospital it had become my job to toss another log in the stove when it got low, and keep the cast-iron kettle on top filled with water.

Trying my hardest not to wake Grandma, I eased myself up by the nearby stairwell, the sofa-bed protesting with a give-away creak. Grandma snuffled lightly in her blackened iron-post bed, but kept on sleeping. I grabbed my bedroom shoes and crept across the freezing wood plank floor, cracking the door to the dining room.

Which squeaked loudly in the silent house.

I'd have to remember to oil it.

Crossing my arms against the cold, I hurried to the kitchen, less afraid of noise with the bedroom door now shut behind me.

But where to start?

Heat, obviously.

Watching my breath float in front of my face, I searched for matches to light the knee-high gas furnace, which as a child Grandma'd let me use as a stove to cook oatmeal. It would take awhile for the furnace to heat up, even in this small a kitchen, so I pulled back the faded-pink pantry curtain, pushed aside a hanging country ham, and snatched one of Grandma's threadbare cardigans off a nail-hook, buttoning it to my throat.

Knowing movement would generate heat as well, I opened one of the smaller cupboards and gazed with amazement at the chaos within. A deep breath of pent-up air escaped my pursed lips. I could handle this. I could.

On Grandma's Porch

is available from BelleBooks at <u>www.BelleBooks.com</u>

The Mossy Creek
Storytelling Club

(In order of appearance)

Amos ....Debra Dixon

Sandy.. Susan Goggins

Sagan ....Sandra Chastain

Hannah..Sabrina Jeffries

Harry ....Martha Crockett

Eula Mae .... Carmen Green

Peggy..Carolyn McSparren

Louise...Carolyn McSparren

Ida .... Debra Leigh Smith

Quinn.......................................Maureen Hardegree

Win/Bubba...Wayne Dixon